STEPHEN EARLY

ETERNALS OF SHALISTAR

THE ENEMY OF MAGIC

Eternals of Shalistar: The Enemy of Magic

Copyright © 2021 by Stephen Early

All rights reserved

This is a self-publication
created through blood, sweat and tears.

Published in Fort Worth, TX

Library of Congress Control Number: 2021921414

ISBN: 978-1-7379411-0-1 (pbk)

0 0 0 0 0 0 2

Cover art, map design and graphics by Adam Potter

Visit us at EternalsofShalistar.com

For Esther

PRONUNCIATION
OF NAMES

Aleph | awe-lef

Daeric | day-ric

Anlace | an-luss

Jeru | jay-roo

Esgar | ez-gar

Iska | ees-ka

Baelor | bay-lore

Agus Tull | agg-us, tull

Lucien | loosh-un

Remus | ree-muss

Artour | are-tore

Balafas | bal-ah-fas

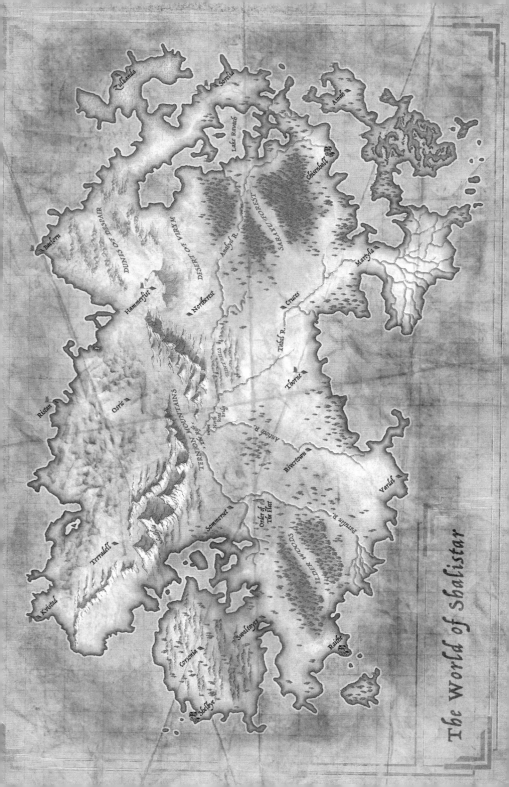

The World of Shalistar

PART I

ETERNALS OF SHALISTAR

⊂ 2 ⊃

CHAPTER
1

The rays of a magnificent sunset began to disappear behind the peaks of the Ternion Mountains as the cart rolled to an abrupt stop in front of the sanctuary's front gate. It had been a long day of toil for me, and my arms were happy to set the axe down upon the ground. Stretched out before me was a battalion of warriors that stood in tight ranks up and down the horizon, past the crossroads, to the Parulin River. I couldn't guess as to how many there were. Every soldier was draped in black. I could barely see the faces of these men because the cowl of their cloaks overshadowed them. As I investigated the crowd, a cold shudder passed completely through me.

The soldiers were hard and muscled men of all ages, adorned under the cloak with shining bright golden armor. Each soldier had a sword sheathed to his side as well as a shield slung on his back. Upon a horse in armor and a cape of crimson, sat a captain of the battalion. I heard a soldier call a halt to the march. Out of a slung pouch from his shoulder came a map of the land. I watched in wonder as the captain jumped from his horse and sidled up to the tracker.

"Why are we stopped, soldier? We must make it to Raithe

by tomorrow evening. It is imperative. We cannot be late."
They continued to speak in whispered voices. My attention
was drawn to the cart. The people on the cart had sackcloth
over their heads so the world could not see their faces. "What
had they done?" I wondered. "Was it murder, thievery?"

Suddenly a cry came from the cart. A young boy of only
several years had wriggled out of the ropes that had bound
him and ripped off the sack from his head. He was running
towards the back of the cart. I immediately dropped my axe
and ran to the front gate of the sanctuary's lawn. I saw the
cloaked soldiers turn their heads in surprise. The captain's
head had turned in the direction of the cart as well. The boy
was running along the center of the cart between the legs
of the prisoners. Without any hesitation, I threw open the
gate and ran into the road. The boy had reached the end of
the cart, and a look of surprise came over his face as his next
step found only air. He screamed as he fell off the cart and
landed with a thud onto the road, his face pointed to the
sky. I arrived only seconds later and bent down, gathering
the child into my arms. I started to stand when I felt a blow
upon my head from behind.

"Let the heathen go! Don't touch the unclean wretch!" I
turned around in fright and wonder to look into the eyes of
the burly, full-muscled captain with shiny white teeth and
cheeks full of blonde hair. "Touch him again, and I throw
you onto the cart as well. It has been spoken."

Suddenly, out of nowhere, recognition of the boy in my arms
flooded me. I seemed to know this boy from somewhere. It
was hard to say exactly where, maybe it was a long-forgotten
dream? I had never left the sanctuary, so I could not have
ever met him. Because his face was covered in mud and dirt,

it was hard to tell. But I just knew I had seen him before.

I looked over at the rest of the people in the cart. I couldn't see their faces, but I could tell it was a man, a woman, two older boys, a girl, and the young boy in my arms. I heard them grunting but couldn't recall any words because they had probably been gagged. They were huddled together in fear, unable to do anything because of the bonds that tied them. The young one had somehow wriggled loose. The captain was standing over me, staring at me.

"Sir if I may," I spoke haltingly.

"If you do, then I'll beat you till you bleed."

Gathering all the courage I could muster, I continued my interrogation of the menacing captain. "What could this boy possibly have done wrong to deserve such a permanent fate?" Without any further hesitation, the officer struck me a blow to the head with his mailed fist. An explosion of pain erupted in my skull as I felt gravity taking hold of my body. Then I felt the hard rock of the road under me. The world spun in multiple colors. I heard garbled voices above me that I could no longer decipher. Then the whole world went black.

Consciousness returned, slowly accompanied by the sound of Fathers' voice. "That is my boy! You had no right." The next thing I heard was the raspy sound of the captain's voice.

"You had better teach him the order of authority in Shalistar. I don't have to explain myself to him." My head was pounding and ringing. I also felt a sticky wet liquid along the side of my face, which I assumed to be my blood. I slowly righted myself to a fetal position to see the scene before me. Father stood before the officer with anger in his eyes.

"You had no right to harm my son. You are a man who represents the king," shouted Father.

"How dare you speak to me about the king. You are a minister of a dead God, and you presume to talk down to an officer of the royal court. I ought to run you through this instant."

Father quickly changed his tone. "I am not looking to usurp your power, sir. But I would like to know why my son's head is lying in a pool of his blood?"

"He was interfering with official business." I could stay silent no longer.

"I helped a child after he fell off the cart." The officer looked at me in rage. I thought he was going to strike me again. Father quickly jumped in.

"That is enough Daeric, silence!" Father then turned to the officer. "You hit my boy because he was helping a lad who was in need?"

"This lad is marked for execution."

Father looked hard at the boy in the cart and then turned his gaze to the brute. "What was his crime?" Father asked.

"I will not discuss the King's business with you, or anyone else except the King or magistrate himself. It has been spoken." Father was taken aback by that final word.

"This is not right. The king does not condemn children to die! I demand to have an audience with him." The officer looked hard at Father and stepped up until his face was merely inches away. He spoke menacingly, just above a whisper.

"Maybe you ought to take that demand to the one you worship. Because all I am going to say is for you to go to hell. Nobody demands anything from Agus Tull, captain of the magistrate's army. Especially not a minister of the cursed faith! If you so much as mutter another word, Father, I'll use my sword to send you to your God." He then slowly retreated backwards, never letting his eyes leave those of my Father.

"I'm not finished with him," he said, pointing at me. As quick as a snake, his boot flew into my gut. I wrenched into a pathetic heap as all the breath left my body. Father started forward. Agus Tull quickly reached to his scabbard and drew. The sword gleamed brilliantly as the last rays of the sun shone upon it. I saw a maniacal smile spread across Agus's lips as Father advanced. Father halted and looked at the blade. I saw the color drain from Father's face.

"The King would not approve," Father said pleadingly.

Agus Tull continued to speak softly and menacingly. "He's not here now, is he?" He held Father's gaze for several moments, relishing his moment of victory. He then backed up slowly to the cart. He looked up at the family of prisoners. "If the lad comes off the cart again, I swear by Baelor that he will suffer greatly before his execution."

Agus looked at all those around him. His prisoners on the cart crowded together in their bondage. Father stood frozen, looking at the blade still drawn out in front of him. Agus turned to his soldiers and laughed. "Look at 'em. Pathetic, they are. This is why we are the strength, men. This is why Baelor has chosen us to rule and reign. We rule and control the fear in all, BLESSED BAELOR!" All at once the soldiers shouted in unison, "BLESSED BAELOR!"

I looked at Father from my position on the road and saw a

slight change in his face, from that of anger to sorrow. Agus Tull then sheathed his weapon and commanded his soldiers. "Move along men! We have time to make up. MARCH!" The battalion of soldiers began to move as one along the road, with the cart of desperate prisoners behind them. Agus removed his golden helm and sweat crusted blonde hair fell down the front and sides of his face. He wiped the perspiration from his face and then returned to mount his horse. He stopped and turned around one last time to speak to Father.

"Your God and the faith that kept him alive is dead! You ministers are poison. You cannot match faith for magic! You had best understand that. You might live longer." Agus Tull replaced his helm upon his head and mounted his horse. "Farewell father, for now."

I looked through the lids of my blood-caked eyes as the magistrate's soldiers rode off down the road. I followed the procession to the end of the hill. "I have seen them somewhere before," I thought, and then for the second time that day, I lost all consciousness.

As my world began to come back into existence, I found myself in my soft bed. My head had been bandaged, but the throbbing pain was still there. I looked around my room and immediately felt nausea. The swelling on my forehead had traveled down to my right eye, causing my sight to be squinty from that side. I guess Agus Tull had left his brand on my head for all the world to see. I slowly moved my hands down to the covers and slipped them gently off my body. It was hot this time of year, and I could feel the perspiration of my fever in the sheets. Slowly, I began to bring myself into a sitting position. Pain shot through my body in the direction of my stomach. The recollection of Agus Tull's boot came to mind.

"What a mindless buffoon," I thought. "If I had a sword, I would have cut him down where he stood, right in front of all his cowardly soldiers. He needs to be made an example. The magistrate cannot strike fear into the people anymore. It has gone on too long. The king must know."

"I don't think you would have had a chance against that brute Daeric." Father had quietly entered my room. "His soldiers would have made an example out of you." Father had an uncanny way of guessing my thoughts. Or had I spoken them out loud? "My son, you have a lot to learn about anger. If you do not control your emotions, then you will turn out no different than Agus Tull."

"I was completely defenseless!" I exclaimed. "What kind of a man puts his boot into you when you are down?"

"He is a coward, son, a man driven by fear. He seeks to control the fear in others but has no idea how to control his own. These are the men who have surrendered to the will of the Baelor. They surrender believing their fears will subside by serving our enemy, yet they find themselves in greater danger. Baelor cares nothing for their services. He knows his time has run short, and he is taking as many with him as he can in the process. Fear is the weapon of his war, and his servants are under great delusion that they have control of the fear in people only to find themselves slaves to an unmerciful master. I fear from the words I heard today that the magistrate has made his move on the throne."

"But Father," I interrupted. "We have the ability to wield the sword greater than any of those soldiers. Why must we bridle such incredible strength?" Father looked sternly at me.

"I mean, couldn't we use this to our advantage? Let us ride ahead and meet them."

"That is exactly what they want, son. If we were to go out and cut down all those who offend and humiliate us, then we would be just like them. Aleph has given us a greater strength, yes. But we are His to use as He leads us and as he leads our king. Aleph is great in power and strength and is perfect in timing. We must be sensitive to him. You cannot control these things, Daeric. You must allow Him to rule you. He has been the Most High for much longer than we can imagine. He will call us when we are needed. The message will come to us in his perfect way. Then, and only then, we must be ready to act. In the meantime, we rest. We allow ourselves to learn. For this is the way it has always been done in the past. But come now."

Father gently put his hand on my head and began to pray. Father's words to Aleph penetrated deep into my heart, and I felt warmth that began from my toes spread slowly up my body until I was enveloped in Aleph's holy touch. Then I felt the weight of his peace fall on me, and I drifted off into a peaceful sleep.

CHAPTER
2

The days crept slowly by as I approached my eighteenth birthday. It was the day I officially came of age in the Order of the Elect. Father said this is the time in a lad's life where his patience is tested. I knew that the next couple of days would drag on, and my nights were not blessed with any kind of rest.

As long as the Order of the Elect has been in existence in the land of Shalistar, there has been a moment of recognition in which a boy steps into manhood and receives a white cloak. When a son of Aleph steps into the light and receives his cloak, before men he is given a mantle of authority to do the work of the one who sent him. That boy can now join the ranks of his brothers. I have always wanted to go out into the world and allow Aleph to use me. Now my time has come. At the age of eighteen, a member of the order is allowed outside of the sanctuary of Sommerset to do the will of the Almighty.

It was two days before the ceremony that we received a visitor. The messenger arrived around lunchtime. Father was always eager to receive news from our brothers in Shelbye and Chisenhall. He went out to meet the visitor with great haste. It had been a month since the last time we'd heard from anyone outside of our home, and we were anxious to know what was going on in the world. Father's calm face turned into a picture of shock and awe as the messenger came into view and stopped abruptly in front of us. The next thing I saw was Father dropping everything in his hands and running as fast as he could to the front gate.

"I don't believe it, it's you!" Father cried aloud, as he helped the man off the horse that had carried him. When his feet touched the ground, he turned around quickly and wrapped Father in a grand hug. I saw Father disappear into the brother's massive body and reappear, slightly winded from the strong embrace.

"Blessings to you, Father Anlace, from Aleph, the Most High!" His deep and resonating voice could have shattered the mountains and dried up the seas. I looked at Father and saw his face radiate with pure joy. Father looked into the eyes of the stranger, and tears began to fall. He was swept up in sheer exhilaration. "Yes, my friend. It's been a long time." The stranger continued. "You know why I am here." Father wiped tears from his eyes and slowly looked again into the gentleman's face.

"Is it time? Has he been called?" The big man wrapped his arm around Father and turned him towards the gate of the sanctuary.

"All news will be revealed, but for now allow me to place my eyes upon our young Daeric. He has received favor in the eyes of Aleph."

Father began helping the visitor by taking his belongings

off the horse. When the load was completely removed from the animal's back, the stranger smiled and whispered into the animal's ear. The horse then put all its weight upon its back two legs, stretched its front two hooves above its head, and cried out a salute to his creator. Without any further hesitation, the horse galloped freely down the rolling green hill with a burning fire in his heart that could set the grass ablaze. Father bent down and, taking hold of a bundle the large man had laid on the horse, he lifted it over his shoulder and began walking towards the front gate. The stranger walked beside him. He saw me standing on the other side of the gate and came straight towards me.

The first thing I noticed about him was that he was quite large in build for one of our order. It is normal for us to be lean but tight in the arms and legs, but this man who came calling was well built in the chest and arms. The cloaks that draped our brothers from Shelbye were white with red trim at the bottom. Those in Chisenhall were white with blue trim. This brother's cloak happened to be trimmed with all three colors: red, blue and green.

Their commotion stopped as I opened the gate for them, and for the first time I looked into the eyes of the stranger. I cannot describe in words what I saw. He looked at me and smiled.

"Well, here he is, finally. I cannot tell you how long I have waited to meet you." He put his large hand upon my shoulder. "You are most fortunate. You have found favor with Aleph. He is very pleased with you indeed." I did not know how to respond to this. "Permit me to introduce myself. I have been known by many names, but you may call me, Jeru."

"Thank you, sir...uh Jeru, if you need anything at all let

me know and I'll be happy to serve you." The large stranger cocked his head and looked again into my eyes.

"No, Daeric. It is I who am going to be serving you." He then continued past me. Father walked quickly past him and opened the door to the sanctuary.

The large oak door shut with a hollow sound, and Jeru was greeted in the foyer of the sanctuary by all the members of the order. Jeru smiled and humbly bowed to each of our brothers in turn. He laid hands upon each of their heads and blessed them. There were greetings and many embraces from the members of our order. The sanctuary came alive in the presence of the stranger.

Stewart, the order's watchman, took Jeru to a side room next to the foyer where he removed his cloak and relieved him of his travel accessories. He opened the order's large oaken travel wardrobe and removed a white cloak with green trim, our order's colors, and draped the cloak over Jeru. When a brother from another sanctuary visits our home, he is immediately adorned in our colors. Within our walls, he is one of our family. Stewart took the rest of his belongings and stored them in a separate compartment within the wardrobe. The two of them then rejoined us in the foyer. Jeru was pleased to be in the new garb and looked ready to settle in.

Father explained to Jeru, "The rest of your equipment will be found in your quarters. There you will also find fresh clothing and boots. We will sup tonight in your honor. Feel free to stay with us as long as you like. The battle room courtyard is always available for your use. All you need to do is ask and one of us will help you train. If you need anything, we are at your service."

Jeru smiled broadly. "It is no wonder why you have such favor with Aleph. Has it really been twenty years? You have grown into an incredible leader! I remember the last time I saw you; you were headstrong, confused, and lacking in confidence. But now, a true leader you have become! You possess a servant's heart, Father Anlace. I look forward to the time we will spend together in fellowship. I will go to my room now and join you this evening in the dining hall."

"Daeric will show you to your room." I picked up the bag that was on the ground at the entrance to the sanctuary, gestured to Jeru, and bid him to follow me. Jeru smiled and nodded to the rest of the order and walked beside me. After we had turned the corner into the battle room courtyard, he asked me a question.

"Have you been having dreams that you remember?" That question took me off guard. "I apologize if this seems like abrupt questioning. I mean, we only met several minutes ago."

"No, it's okay. Father obviously trusts you. So, I guess I should do the same.

"I appreciate that, young Daeric. So, your dreams..."

"Yes sir." I responded.

"Tell me about them. What about the dreams of your mother?"

I stopped and looked at him in shock. Jeru had a slight smile and did not look away from me. "How did you know about that? I have never told anyone about that dream, not even Father."

"I know. Don't be afraid, Daeric. Tell me about your dream."

"It's hard for me to even remember all the details. Every time I try to remember it fades from my memory...except for one part of it."

"What part is that?"

"She is panicking, pacing back and forth. I don't remember details about the room or anything like that. Suddenly a door bursts open, and she begins to weep and holds me tighter. Then I see myself, a younger version of myself walking away from her in the company of a younger Father. We walk out the door and I look back one last time. She is weeping and praying to Aleph for my protection. It's really sad, and I am always thankful when I awake."

"What about your father?"

"Anlace is the only Father I have ever known." I replied quickly.

"Has he told you who your birth father is?" Jeru asked.

"Yes. His name was Michael. He was a fellow soldier of his when he served the crown."

"Do you know what happened to Michael?" Jeru urged.

"He died on the same day Father Anlace took me, slain by a rogue soldier who betrayed the King. I have no memory of him except through the stories Father has told me. I wish I had known both of them. But, like I said, Anlace is the only Father I have ever known."

Jeru softly answered. "Daeric. You may be born one way, but Aleph's plans will change everything about you. The person you thought you were...may completely vanish. No matter what happens, you must believe that Aleph is right, and if he wants you to know any of these things, you will know and he will tell you...in a very special way." At the end of that sentence, Jeru continued walking toward his room. I then hefted his luggage and caught up with him.

We entered his room, and I unpacked his belongings. At the bottom of his bag, I saw a package tightly and carefully wrapped in linen and ribbon. I reached my hand out to pull the package from the bag when Jeru quickly took it from me.

"Thank you, lad, for helping me get settled. I can manage the rest of this. I would like a bit of rest before supper this evening." I respected his wishes and left through his chamber door. As the door was closing, I heard Jeru speaking softly under his breath. I was able to decipher one sentence.

"...give them strength."

Before we all gathered that evening in the dining hall, all the brothers were given tasks to complete in preparation. I was assigned to mop the dust from the floors. It was my least favorite task, but I did it regardless. Working beside me that afternoon was my longtime friend Samuel. Being only a few years older than myself, he was easy to talk to, and I enjoyed doing chores with him. Because we could relate to each other, time always passed quickly.

"What do you think about the visitor?" I asked him curiously. Samuel stopped moving his mop and brushed his hands through the mouse brown hair that had fallen over his face.

"I've heard from Halsey that he is not human. He may be a guardian!"

"A guardian!" I shouted. Samuel quickly put a finger to his lips.

"Don't say these things out loud, Daeric! I am not sure it is true. You know Halsey has a gift for the dramatic. He has spun some tales in the past."

"But what if he is?" I whispered into Samuel's ear.

"Well, that would be something then, don't you think? Guardians haven't been seen in a long time."

"He was asking me about my dreams." Samuel stopped the mop for a moment and looked over to me.

"Why would he do that?"

"I don't know."

"Did you tell him?"

"That is what was so strange about it. I don't tell anyone about my dreams, not even Father."

"Well, what did he say about them?"

"He told me I was born one way, but then Aleph's plans may change everything about me."

"He's right, you know?" I stared open-mouthed at Samuel. "Take me for instance. I was a homeless thief in Sommerset, abandoned by my parents and living on the street. That is, until your father caught me while I was trying to pickpocket him. He must have seen something special in me because he brought me here and gave me a home and a family. He taught me who Aleph is. Everything changed for me. I'm no longer who I was."

"I never knew you were a pickpocket," I said, marveling at my friend's story.

"There's a lot about me you don't know," Samuel said to the ground as he continued mopping the floor.

We were both hard workers. Life in the sanctuary was no picnic. Everyone was required to put in a good day's work and keep up with their training. That meant that we gave our all in everything we did, and that included mopping floors.

The evening came, and all the preparations had been made. Merwin had expertly made dinner for all of us. Geoffrey and Mark had laid the table with all the provisions needed for supper. Finally, the bell rang, and we all gathered around the table to dine with our illustrious guest. All twelve of us stood at our places, with Jeru at the place of honor. We bowed our heads and thanked Aleph for this day and the bountiful provision before us. With an agreement from all, we sat down and ate.

Conversation was mild for the most part. Each one of us was talking about our day and what we had learned. Several of the brothers asked me about my confrontation with the magistrate's captain. At the mention of this, I saw Jeru look my way. I did not really care to think about the memory and kept my answers short. Food was passed from member to member until our plates were full and then conversation was sparse as we ate. Merwin knew how to perfectly season and cook a pheasant, and words just got in the way of enjoying the delicious meal.

After the main course had been devoured, we sat back and gave the food a moment to settle in our stomachs. After a moment or two, my brothers turned the topic of conversation to more serious matters.

"Please tell us of the other sanctuaries. Have they been called by the king? Are you here to bring us news of a mission?" My brothers asked of Jeru.

"Brothers, please. I believe our guest could do with some dessert before answering all these pertinent questions," Father exclaimed over the ruckus.

The brothers must not have heard Father and continued asking questions about King Remus and the struggle in Raithe. The uprising of magic and sorcery was mentioned under Merwin's breath to Haywood, the stable master. Lionel, the eldest of our order at 75 years, stood up and looked around the table at us. We could tell he was concerned about the conversation and needed an answer. Unlike the rest of us rattling on, he decided to stand up and demand our attention.

"I have been around the longest of any of you. I fought beside kings before many of you were even a twinkle in your mother's eye." He then looked directly at Jeru. "I have been disturbed in my sleep. Baelor has sent his messengers to strike fear into me. They take human form, sitting on the throne of Raithe." Jeru leaned forward in his chair. "Aleph is warning us to be ready. Do not fall asleep like the rest of the world, and do not take this sanctuary for granted. We will not be spared from the suffering."

"We understand that, brother," snapped Geoffrey. "None of us has the delusion that we are safe. But we have lived in peace for fifteen years! Demons taking human form!? You speak of the end! What comes next? Baelor himself on the soil of our world?"

"You haven't seen what I have! King Remus has no idea what is about to happen. Aleph is warning us, I tell you."

"Your whimsical dreams always seem to contain doom and gloom, brother. We have heard this before." Geoffrey looked directly at Father as he said these words, and I saw a look of sorrow come onto Father's face. It was a quick stab of pain from some past memory. Geoffrey stood up and paced away from the table to the back side of the room. He then turned quickly around. "If what you say is true, then why haven't we been called? King Remus would have sent for us to stand beside him."

"Maybe he is in more danger than he can realize." Samuel quietly stated aloud.

"Who would summon demons to this realm? Who would try to take the throne?" I looked back at Father, and once again I saw the doubt on his face. He knew something, and he was not saying it.

Suddenly, Jeru's booming voice resounded throughout the dining hall. "Don't neglect the advice of your elders. I will confirm that he has been allowed to see these dreams clearly. By Aleph, Lionel is trying to help us. Don't be blinded by fear and complacency." Geoffrey took the rebuke to heart and placed a hand on Lionel's shoulder in a gesture of respect. Lionel acknowledged this with grace and accepted his apology. I looked over to Jeru and noticed our large guest had a pleased look on his face.

All of a sudden, Jeru's smile vanished as quickly as it had come, and I felt a foreboding darkness seep into the great hall around me. Jeru looked at Father and then to the rest of us. "There is not much time." He spoke plainly. "Demons are being summoned. Magic and sorcery are being taught to the young and old alike. Detestable rituals are going on in houses all over Raithe."

I then saw his face bow gently and slowly. His eyes closed, and there followed a silence in the hall as all the brothers looked on inquisitively. The visitor's face clouded over with a look of sorrow, and I stood up to help the larger gentleman. Father's hands grabbed my sleeve to keep me back. My arm jerked loose of Father's grip, and I quickly moved to stand behind Jeru. The silence was terrible. It looked as if he were going to cry...

I leaned forward and placed my arms around his shoulders, and it felt as if I had been struck by a mild form of lightning. My body flew back towards the wall, and I grabbed my arms, which were burning with an intense energy that could only have come from Aleph, himself.

Jeru whipped around and took a walk around the room. We were all struck with an awesome fear as he looked into each one of our eyes. "Now is not a time for fear! We are being prepared for war! Aleph is here in the midst of us right now! He has sent me to you as your guardian. Receive his power now!" Jeru then opened his mouth and blew a stream of air into the atmosphere. Radiance filled the room. Out of the stranger's eyes came tears that looked as if they were glowing. This was no ordinary brother. This was a guardian of Aleph, sent to aid us in this trial. He continued to speak words of courage and strength to each one of our hearts. He confirmed Lionel's warning by telling us to be wary, tread softly, and not to take our lives for granted. He encouraged us not to stop mastering the sword, because the time to wield it was drawing near.

He spoke of times in the past before any of us can remember, and how the Order of the Elect was created by King Rian. He told of how the order would stand beside their King and rout the forces that beset themselves against the will of Aleph. Stories of kings and priests, heroes, and conquerors, those who died in service of the mighty one and the reward they received because of their faithfulness. I was completely taken away by his voice, so soothing and powerful were his words. They lit a fire inside me that fanned the flames of desire. That milestone would keep me as I walked through the flames of hell.

He finished his exhortation and was standing in front of me.

"And you, young one, Aleph has chosen. You will be the one, by your faith and by your courage, who ushers in the End of Times."

As his eyes met mine, my heart became heavy. I also felt a burning in my hands and arms. Upon my back it felt like a cloak of fire and lightning had been draped over me. That feeling went straight to my heart.

Jeru looked into my eyes, and once more a teardrop began to form. Everything vanished in my peripheral vision except the tear that was falling from his face. The tear magnified, and I could see something, a moving picture, within the liquid of the tear. I saw a vision. The scene played out horrifically before me as I viewed the final image. The tear was completely formed and fell from Jeru's face. I followed the tear all the way to the floor where it crashed and splashed. I had to close my eyes. This could not be happening. My feet became like rubber under the power of the vision, and I felt the stone floor of the great hall rushing up to meet me.

Jeru's large hands grabbed me and steadied my body. Father rushed over to me and our guest. "What is going on, Jeru?

What has just happened? Jeru shook his head and gestured to the sky outside through the open window. A look of horror came over each of our faces. Only minutes ago, the sun had shone brightly and the birds were singing in joyous melody. Only now we saw dark oppressive clouds and a moaning wind moving over the land. "Listen brothers!" Exclaimed Samuel. "In the wind, I hear voices crying. I hear weeping."

"The voices you hear are coming from Raithe," said Jeru. Father moved next to Samuel. He looked out into the darkness and then turned his face to Jeru.

"What has happened? What does this mean?" Father asked.

Jeru then turned to look at me. "I will let young Daeric tell you."

I felt the weight of all the burden fall into my heart at that moment. The vision I saw in Jeru's tears was real. There was no doubt about it anymore. I opened my mouth to speak and realized that my mouth had gone completely dry. I could not speak. Father came up to me.

"What did you see, Daeric? What did you see?"

I looked into my father's face and saw the truth emblazoned there. Father was afraid. He had every right to be. I then croaked out my response. "I saw...I mean the prisoners... the cart...Aleph help us!"

Father grabbed me with both hands and shook me where I stood. "What did you see, Daeric? What has happened?!"

"The royal family...they've just been executed."

CHAPTER
3

It took two days for me to be able to look Jeru in the face again, let alone be in the same room with him. I didn't know how to respond to him. What was I supposed to say? Why hadn't any of the other brothers seen the vision? Or better yet, what was going on in the world around me now? It felt like the weight of the whole kingdom was on my brittle shoulders. Why didn't I recognize the young prince in my arms? Am I that blind to not even be able to see evil deeds right in front of me? I could not have stopped the cart from going to Raithe. But I should have tried. I just let them die!

So, for the next couple of days I sat in my room and wrote all my thoughts down in my journal. It was a lot to process, and moving my pen over the pages allowed me to assimilate my thoughts and come to grips with what I had seen. I did not neglect my study of combat either. Being the closest room to the battle courtyard, I arranged my bed so I could watch the sessions from my window.

I was alone, and nobody asked me how I was doing. None of the brothers, Father included, even knocked. They sat my plate outside the door and walked away in silence. Did they even care what was happening inside of me? It was midday on the second day when I finally opened my bedroom door. Without hesitation, I walked down the hall. My fellow brothers resided in the same hall with me, all except Father. His room was across the courtyard in the master's quarters. Although the Master lived separately from the rest of the order, brothers were allowed freely into all parts of the sanctuary.

I walked along the edge of the courtyard watching my brothers practice the sword, one against two as it had always been. Today, there were six brothers in the session. They took turns being the one against the two. Great skill is achieved in the sword when the advantage is always against you. Father always taught me to see two enemies as one, and so on. In this session, Samuel was up against Mark and Gareth. Samuel was only a couple years older than me, and I always paid close attention to his skill. He had taught me many lessons in pain and humility, but I was a better fighter than most because of it.

In silence, they circled each other. Each brother stared at the other with a look of determination and concentration. This was not about rivalry or contest. It was about fellowship and accountability. Each brother was responsible for the other in training for combat. We were here to be each other's teacher. There was no rank or class in combat. We supported and disciplined one another. Bloodshed was just a part of the learning process.

Samuel raised his sword, and the silence was broken as he swung his sword toward Gareth's midsection. Gareth cried out, quickly stepped to the side, and responded with a downward swing of his blade. The sword struck Samuels with a loud clang that rang through the whole courtyard.

Mark fortified their position of attack by moving behind Samuel. He waited. He knew Samuel was ready. Samuel's blade point was almost in the sand of the fighting pit, pinned on top by Gareth's. With incredible strength Samuel lifted his blade as well as Gareth's. Gareth felt the momentum of the sword and countered with his own push back down toward the sand. He needed just a few more moments so that Mark could waylay Samuel with a blow to the head.

Samuel knew he had only seconds to react. As he had guessed, Gareth responded. As his strength was met, there was a clash of forces. He could feel all of Gareth's strength and he released his own, which brought his and Gareth's swords down with great momentum. He quickly pivoted and whirled a kick into Gareth's side as his body was going forward with momentum. As Gareth's body was falling from the power of the kick, Mark attacked from the side.

Samuel was ready. As he came down from the kick, he transferred all the weight to his kicking foot and whirled his body completely out of the way of the slash. Mark's blade bit only air. Samuel's blade was then upon him. Mark barely got his sword back up in time to block. The swords struck. Samuel slashed again toward Mark's right side. Mark parried the blow. Samuel was on him again, this time going for the head, a mistake. Mark met the attempt and lashed out a kick with blazing speed and crushing strength. The kick landed into his wide open, unguarded, chest. Samuel felt all the air leave his body. He crumbled and gasped for air. Mark finished the session with a kick to the back of Samuels head. I saw my brother fall into the sand. Mark had been the teacher today.

The victor of the session turned to see me standing there. I looked back at him, wondering what his reaction would be. A warm smile spread across Mark's face, and he lifted a hand in salute to me. I returned the greeting. Samuel was finding the center of gravity and rising from the sand. He smiled as well when he saw me standing there. Gareth remained laid out in the pit with his hands on the temples of his head, going over his mistakes in the session. Then Samuel spoke to me.

"Happy birthday, Daeric! Your Father wants to see you." It was like sweet music in my ears to hear the voice of another speaking directly to me. I nodded in recognition and continued to walk along the edge of the courtyard. Another session was beginning as I came to the door of the master's quarters. It was slightly open, allowing me to peak into the master's quarters without being seen. Father was at his desk, writing in his journal as he did every day. He seemed to be in the middle of an intense writing session because one of his hands was gripping the tufts of his short, graying brown hair and pulling it as he wrote. He was probably worried about me.

For as long as I could remember, Father had taught me how to read and write and instructed me to journal all my feelings and experiences. He told me that it would allow me to process all that life has to offer, giving me an avenue to vent frustrations and record my deepest desires. At least several times a day, I could see Father writing in one of his journals. He still hadn't seen me and was finishing his final thought. Jeru was across the room from him, sitting with his back to Father.

With his entry completed, Father closed the tome and turned to the wall behind him. It contained a large bookshelf that overflowed with volumes of Father's writing. Each one of his precious journals contained years of thoughts and prayers to Aleph and the history of our order. He shelved the volume he had finished writing in and turned back around towards me.

Father saw me enter and stood up like a fire was under the cushion of his chair. "Daeric, are you okay? I'm sorry nobody has seen you." I glared into his eyes and saw the truth immediately. He was genuinely concerned.

"I'm fine, Father." I responded. "But why was I left alone? I felt such a weight in my heart. I could not bring myself to walk outside the door to my room."

Jeru stood at that moment and walked over to me. He put a large hand on my shoulder. "My young brother, the issues of the heart are always complicated. Aleph is the only one who can deal directly with such things." I saw him pause and think carefully about the next words he was going to say. "The truth, Daeric, is that you have been chosen by Aleph. You are to be a magnificent tool in this holy war."

"Could you help me understand what is going on, Jeru? It has been hell for a week. What is going on? Please tell me."

"Okay, Daeric. I will tell you." He took a deep breath and started. "Since the beginning of this world there has been war between light and darkness, truth against error, life or death, faith and sorcery, heaven or hell, Aleph against Baelor. The people of this world have been given a choice. They freely choose who they will serve. These choices continue in this world upon a course, whether for good or evil.

Baelor has perverted the world through magic and sorcery. He has given men a gift which allows them a chance to experience the power of deity, at the price of their soul. They have chosen this accosted power in hopes to control the fear within them, only to fall prey to such an unruly predator. Baelor cares nothing for them. He only wishes to see them destroyed.

"Aleph has allowed Baelor a moment of time to seduce and enrapture the world in this harlotry. They have gone the way of wickedness and carried out his evil desires. This world will now be ruled by the iron hand of an evil magistrate." I interrupted Jeru at this moment.

"What about him? Did he have the royal family murdered?"

"Yes. Balafas has been ruling this land through a naïve and weak royal family. Under the noses of the monarch, he has built himself an army of unspeakable power. In secret, he has facilitated a school of sorcery to train and discipline an army to carry out all his selfish desires. Any who stand in his way are destroyed. Balafas has been working in secret for many years. He knew that the royal family was a great hindrance to his plans early on.

Through deceit and manipulation, he removed King Remus's father Tark, who was a strong and powerful king, and replaced him with Remus, a weaker version of his father. Balafas promised all things leading to peace and prosperity through the courts. But in secret, he has been facilitating the roll-out of divination and sorcery, holding underground summonings and eliminating anyone who gets in his way. Remus and his family saw only too late what the promises of a follower of Baelor really account for. Now that the king and his legitimate heirs have been removed, there is nothing stopping Balafas from completing his evil deeds and handing over the throne to Baelor himself, except for the will of Aleph."

"What does Aleph want with me?" I asked.

"Just as Balafas has been used to carry out the will of Baelor, you, young Daeric, are to be used to carry out the will of the one who has set you in your place," Jeru concluded.

"Who are you?" I asked incredulously.

"I am a messenger," Jeru answered.

"So why was I in solitude? Why the heavy burden in my heart?" I continued.

Jeru looked directly through me with these next words. "The burden you felt while you were alone... that will be the easiest part of the rest of your life."

CHAPTER

4

"I didn't ask for this," I said as I walked toward the door. Jeru quickly came to stand in front of me.

"No, you didn't." Jeru added. 'But it has been in your heart, a longing to be used by Aleph. He has heard the cry of your spirit and has responded."

"I didn't think it would be like this."

"None of us do, Daeric." Father had finally spoken. "We think of service to Aleph as an opportunity to extend our hands to the poor or to comfort the widow in need, and rightly it is. But we must all remember that these are dark times. We are at war, and we must be ready to sacrifice all for the will of Aleph."

"You didn't see what I saw, Father!" I shouted. "They took their heads, the whole family, even the young one!"

"I didn't see what you saw. But I have seen more bloodshed than you can imagine. I, too, have been in the same position you are in. I have also been called by Aleph to serve him. I know the fear inside you well, son. It is our greatest adversary, and we must learn to conquer it every day. How can we offer hope to a world ravaged by fear if we can't conquer it within ourselves?"

"I have looked into your eyes, Father. You are afraid." Father looked at me with pity. I knew I had gone too far.

"That is why I am strong, son. Because I know that I cannot conquer the fear on my own. Aleph is the source of my courage. He is the one who gives me the strength to win. I surrender fear to him. If I were to battle fear alone, I would lose." Father concluded his remark and walked past me, out the door. I felt small at that moment. The room felt very empty to me, even though Jeru was standing right in front of me. He smiled.

"He will be alright."

"I hurt him."

"No, Daeric, you didn't." Jeru continued. "Your Father is going through what all fathers must go through. He is also Master of the Order, and so the burden is twice as hard."

"What do you mean?" I asked.

"Your father knows in his heart that his boy is becoming a man and he must let go of him. You are now able to decide for yourself. Every father feels the pain of that revelation, because they wonder if what they taught you was enough. Also, as Master of the Order, he knows that you are now in the hands of Aleph and His will. So, your master is now Aleph, and not him. It is a two-sided coin, young Daeric, and your father will have to deal with both fates," Jeru continued. "But you must also realize that your father is overjoyed to see Aleph working so miraculously on your behalf."

"It is true, Daeric." I turned to see Father walking in the doorway with a bundle wrapped in sackcloth. He set it gently upon the table in the center of the room. "Nothing could give me more joy than to see you in the will of Aleph."

"What if I refuse?"

"Then Aleph will choose another. None of us is special. We are simply to be ready when he calls," Father remarked.

"So, what do I do now?" Jeru clapped his hands together excitedly.

"Now, you wait for Aleph to lead you," Father butted in.

"How will I know?"

"When the time comes, you will know," Jeru said, "but it may not always happen the way you expect. Aleph moves in mysterious ways, and we must always remember that we are his tools to build the house."

"You can help me too, son. I am going to town to minister and could always use your help." My eyes got big and bright at this request. "It is your birthday, so you are of age now and may leave the sanctuary. I am going out early this evening and would like your assistance." I could restrain myself no longer. I propelled myself into Father and wrapped my arms around him.

"Thank you, Father," I said through tear-streaked eyes. As he held me, he looked over to Jeru and nodded. I saw the large man move over to the table where Father had sat the bundle down when he entered.

"I hate to interrupt such a moment, but I think it is time the birthday boy receives his present." Jeru walked over to where Father had placed the bundle on the table. I looked at Father, and he silently nodded towards Jeru. My heart began to pound in my chest as I joined the guardian.

"I am sorry this ceremony is not as proper as you would like, but Aleph has seen you and your heart. Your service for many years has been a great joy for him. In recognition of your talents, he has sent me to honor you. Please receive this gift with our appreciation." Jeru finished his statement and handed me the wrapped bundle. I took it, and without any further hesitation, opened the package.

As the brown paper was separated from the gift, I saw what lay underneath and my heart pounded harder than before. The rest of the paper went flying as I completely uncovered my birthday present.

"What do you think?" Father asked with great pleasure.

I looked down at the soft folds of brilliant white cloth in my hands. The stitching of the cloak was perfect in every sense of the word. I let the entire garment fall loose, and at the bottom of the cloak was the dark green trim, just like Father's and the rest of those in my order. I whirled the cloak around me and set it upon my shoulders. The cowl of the cloak rested gently against my neck. I clasped the front and turned towards Father and Jeru. They were both smiling from ear to ear.

"Young Daeric, you are now of the age to be used in any way the Master of the Order sees fit." Jeru continued speaking as he checked the length, just to make sure it was a perfect fit. "This cloak, which was stitched by the hands of the guardians themselves, is a symbol of your bond to Aleph. His power and authority are with you and surround you wherever you go. This cloak will also be a protection to you. If you wear this, the effects of destructive magic will not harm you."

"I now declare you a fully commissioned member of the Order of the Elect!" Father said, looking into my eyes. He then grabbed me and pulled me into him, wrapping me in a powerful embrace, lifting me up from the floor. "I am so proud of you!" He exclaimed loudly.

After several more moments of sentiment, he released me and told me to get ready. I left Father's room quickly and skipped across the courtyard back to my room. All the brothers who were training immediately stopped and erupted in applause as they saw me and the white cloak that was flowing behind me.

"Good job Daeric! We are proud of you! Welcome to the order!" They all shouted as I came into the center of the room. Hearing all their voices warmed my heart. These men I spent so many years with were more than comrades; they were my family. Hearing their roar of applause stopped me completely. Before I knew it, the brothers had laid down their weapons and were surrounding me, extending their hands towards me.

Lionel began speaking out a prayer over me, and one after another, the rest of the brothers followed, adding their own words. Wrapped in the white cloak of my order, I closed my eyes and listened to the love and care each one of them had for me. They prayed over my life and the ministry I would have before Aleph. The feeling and exhilaration I experienced, hearing their power manifest through their voices, was too priceless for words.

After the conclusion of the intimate ceremony, I went to my room and packed whatever I thought I might need for my short journey into town. While I was busy trying to decide the necessities, Father had the cart packed with all types of provender. There was food, soap, baskets, household items, and a pouch that Father kept full of gold pieces. All the members of my order were at the gate to see me off on my first ministry expedition. The brothers wrapped their arms around me and blessed me. Some gave me small gifts to carry. Samuel gave me advice about the streets of Sommerset, who to trust and who to avoid. I gladly took his words to heart. Then they prayed for us and sent us away.

We were drawn by two horses. As the cart lurched forward, I felt a feeling of excitement ripple through me. Who knew what lay ahead for me? As the road began to go downward into the valley, I looked back at the sanctuary. It rested at the top of the hill overlooking the valley of Sommerset. The two stone spires reaching into the sky looked to me as if the building was the guardian of the valley. It had been there watching over the surrounding lands, like a mother hen would her nest. As we passed over the bridge that connected the sanctuary grounds to the rolling hills of the valley, I realized this was the only home I had ever known, and I was leaving it for the first time, if only for a short while.

We traveled to the bottom of the hill and began to head to the North. After several more moments, the sanctuary was lost from our view. Father steered the cart towards the main road and stayed upon it for over an hour. I looked out at the expanse of the world around me and was in absolute awe.

The tri-peaks of the Ternion Mountains loomed high above us in the far distance. I squinted my eyes in the sunlight to see all the way to the top, but every time I tried, the brilliance of the afternoon sun blurred my vision. Nature was on full display in the trees and fields. I heard birds singing all around us. Foxes and smaller animals were out enjoying the beautiful afternoon as well. Part of me wished I could jump off the cart and run through the fields in total abandon, but I knew we were on a mission and that behavior would not be tolerated. I quickly put the thought away and sat back in my seat, enjoying the splendor of creation all around me.

After a good hour of travel, Sommerset was visible to the Northwest. It was an old town, rich in tradition and popular to the traveler. The town boasted some of the finest inns and the softest beds in the land. But these days, it seemed, travel was scarce. I saw chimneys of stone above rooftops of wood. There was a smell in the air of cedar. Sommerset gave me the feeling of a cozy fire on a chilly night. It was very welcome.

The sun began to set as Father and I made our descent into the town. He looked at me with a proud smile. I could tell he was glad I was here. "Daeric, first we are going to unbridle the horses at the Inn of Wayfaring. It is in the center of town, next to the fountain. Then we are going to see Margaret."

"Who's Margaret?"

"She is a widow that the order has provided for since her husband died. She was injured and has a bad back now. It is up to us to help sustain her. Aleph has blessed the order so we may provide for her. Next, we will go to the streets and minister to all in need there. Aleph will use us in many ways at that time. You will see. It is quite extraordinary."

"I can't wait."

"This is why we exist—to extend help to those in need. Help can come in many ways. In battle we will use our skills to protect those who cannot fight for themselves, and in everyday life we provide needs to those in poverty. It is a high calling, my son. The life we live is not easy by any means, but it is the most fulfilling."

Father finished his lecture to me as we stopped at a stable behind the inn. Father jumped off the cart and removed his cloak. "I suggest you do the same, Daeric. Though what we stand for is good, there are many in this world who would like to see us vanish away. It is good not to avert their attention to the deeds we do today. In other words, the cloak is a dead giveaway."

I followed Father's instructions and tucked my cloak under the wooden plank where we sat, out of sight of the eyes. Father handed me a leather vest to wear over my white tunic. He then grabbed a handful of dirt and threw it onto my pants, shirt, and face. I was not going to argue. Father knew what he was doing. He did the same for himself and then turned to me.

"Are you ready?" I felt butterflies in my stomach.

"Yes, sir."

"Let's go." With that, we took all the supplies needed for Margaret, paid the stable boy to watch the cart, and stepped into the streets of Sommerset. I felt a tingle on the back of my neck, and a wave of euphoria rushed through me. So, this is what it was like to be a servant of Aleph. I could get used to this.

Excitement rippled through me as I saw the life of Sommerset all around me. There were people of all shapes and sizes walking and riding horses up and down the streets. I had never felt rough stone streets under my boots. They made them sore to walk upon, but I didn't care. Father kept to himself mostly. Nobody paid us any attention as we made our way along the busy boulevard. We passed stalls and tents of all shapes and sizes. They were overflowing with merchandise and exotic foods from all over Shalistar.

Father told me not to make eye contact with the owners of these carts. He told me they were very aggressive in their technique, and if I were not careful, I would be convinced to buy something I really did not want. I decided to casually glance over the goods from a distance. It was amazing to see such a splendid display of diversity. I saw fruit, meat, carpets of animal fur, honey, beads, jewelry, weapons of all kinds, and much more.

The streets were packed this evening with people running on errands to many different places. I looked upward to the tall stone buildings and saw that the last light was in the sky, which was creating long shadows in between the buildings. It was getting harder to see, so I stayed as close to Father as I could.

We continued down the way until we reached the center of town. The streets opened into a square that was packed with inns, stores, brothels, and all sorts of businesses. I have never seen anything so exciting in all my life. Many aromas, good and bad, filled the streets and entered my nostrils. As we continued walking steadily along the sidewalks among the crowds, I caught myself looking into the eyes of the people all around me.

Suddenly, as if all reality were carried away like a whisper in the wind, the fast industrious environment around me vanished! That is when I saw another vision. I could clearly see a scene within me. It was as if the picture was in both my mind and heart at the same time. I saw a young woman who was huddled in the dark corner of a barn. Around her were barrels and hay. Above her head were different tools for harvesting. She was rocking back and forth, sobbing. She then looked next to her and picked up a dagger. I felt an urgency in my heart to speak this vision, but as quickly as reality vanished, it came back into full view. Father grabbed me and pulled me closer to a building. Seconds later, I saw a pack of horses and their riders fly right past my nose.

"What are you doing?" Father shouted at me. "You must always pay attention, son. Had I not seen them you would have been trampled to death."

"I'm sorry, Father."

"Where did you just go right now? What just happened to you" He responded.

"I have seen something." Father stopped and looked cautiously at me. He looked up the street at the soldiers and then placed his eyes back on me.

"I don't doubt you, especially after the other night. But if it was a vision, I must test it. Not everything you see is necessarily from Aleph." He looked me directly in the eyes. "Do you understand what I'm saying, son?"

"No... but I trust you, Father."

"That is why you can be used so mightily by Aleph, because you are teachable. Never lose the attitude of humility. As for the vision just now, let us discuss it later. We have a lot of work to do."

I quickly looked at the backs of the riders who had nearly ridden over me and saw that they each wore expensive black cloaks. They had stopped briefly at one of the stalls down the way. One of the riders had gotten off his horse and walked up to a vendor. As the black cloak blew in the wind, I could see the gleam of golden armor underneath. A shudder ran through me as memories of that horrific day came to mind. All thoughts were cut short as I saw a peasant run up to one of the magistrate's soldiers, begging for money. All he received was multiple blows to the head. I saw the peasant fall down unconscious into the street.

Then I heard a scream as the vendor fell dead into a cart of jewelry. The soldier stood over him with a bloodied blade in his hands. He looked down at the body of the vendor and spat. Then he turned around and walked back to his horse. The other soldiers on horses were laughing and applauding him as he mounted. A surge of anger began to bubble up inside me. I began to take a step in that direction when I felt hands grab me from behind.

"Stay focused, Daeric. Their time will come." Father spoke softly in my ear. As quickly as the anger came, it left me. I felt peace once again as I turned and followed Father further into Sommerset.

We made many turns into smaller streets. I would have been lost if I were by myself. Father walked as if he had been here many times before. He stopped to look at nothing and was completely focused on what we were here to do. At that moment, I admired Father. Comparing my actions, I could see the impatience in me, and I did not really care too much for it. Father was right; I needed to control my anger and be focused on what I was doing. I decided to drop it. I was not going to let my emotions win. With a sigh, I quickened my step and walked next to Father.

Two more turns brought us to the end of the stone streets. The Parulin River flowed in front of us. The grass of the valley grew all along the riverbank. I looked west and saw a bridge connecting the south-lands to Sommerset. Many people were crossing to go home for the day. To the east, right up against the Parulin, was a small house built of mud and straw, with a short fence along the front. After a few moments, a lady of about fifty years opened the front door. As we stood there, our backs loaded with all sorts of provender, she stopped, her gaze on me. Her mouth opened as she let out a gasp. Her hand came up to cover it. She took several steps towards me and stopped. She looked at Father and then back at me.

I turned my gaze to Father as well and saw he was looking right at me.

Margaret cried and ran into my arms. "I have waited so long to place my eyes upon you!" She tousled my curly brown hair that had fallen over my eyes and put her hands on my cheeks, cupping my face. Her touch was so tender and loving. After several more embraces she released me and took a step back. Her eyes traveled up and down my entire frame, taking all of it in. "You have grown up to be such a handsome young man. You really do look just like your father." As she made that final statement, I noticed she was not looking at Father.

"Did you know my father?" I asked.

"Yes." She was on the edge of tears at this moment. "Yes, I did. I knew him well."

For a good part of an hour, Father allowed me to sit and talk with Margaret. She spoke of my mother Abigail, who was a fellow serving maid in the royal castle during the reign of King Tark. She told me how my mother was young and vibrant, full of life, and loved Aleph with all that was within her. They were best friends after all, having grown up together. Margaret told me of my mother's favorite hobbies and how she used to paint some of the most amazing pictures and decorate her halls with them.

I listened as she continued laying out a beautiful, loving picture of my mother. After she had exhausted all her efforts in describing her to me, I leaned forward, continuing the conversation.

"Where is she now? Is she still alive?" I asked full of hope.

"I hope so," she said, holding her breath, almost reluctant to speak it aloud. "The night of your father's murder was the last time any of us saw her." Margaret placed her hand over her mouth again. "To think what she gave up for you to have a life." I looked over to Father and saw he had gotten up and crossed over to the window, deep in thought as he gazed outside. He was probably wondering the same thing as Margaret.

Our host continued her recounting. "Ever since Balafas's decree sixteen years ago, that had designated the Order from Raithe as outcasts and declared them an enemy to the structure of law and order, the brotherhood was not allowed anywhere near Raithe."

But still, I thought to myself. Maybe one day our paths would cross. Maybe one day I would be able to meet my birth mother. This thought had kept me up many nights in my life, and I decided now was not the best place to dwell on it. However, I did need an answer to another question. Father always avoided discussing any of my past with me for whatever reason. One time he even shouted at me, telling me he was not going to go there! I persisted, but he would not bend. But now, I was in the presence of someone who knew quite a bit about my birth mother...

Although it was painful, I decided I needed to ask another question. "Margaret, how did my father die?"

Margaret looked over at Father, who had moved himself to a small table by the window and was writing in the journal he had brought with him. He looked up at the elderly woman and bowed his head slightly forward, giving Margaret permission to continue. She started by describing him to me, how brave and loyal he was and how he would not bend the knee to sorcery but believed in the will of Aleph up until the day he was betrayed and killed. She spoke about him with such zeal and passion.

I calmly asked her again, "How did he die?" At this question, she got choked up and had a hard time forming the words. I waited patiently as she gathered her thoughts. Then several moments later, she recounted what she knew.

"It was Roderick who killed him. He had been recruited by Balafas and the underground temple of Baelor. After performing many wicked ceremonies in which they had conjured demons through blood sacrifice, the spirits revealed to the higher-ranking members that another one of Aleph's chosen vessels had been born, and Roderick was given the assignment to capture one.

"At that time, Aleph had given the world two. One was your Father, Anlace. Roderick knew that it would be nearly impossible to carry out the task regarding him." She said pointing to Father. "So, he fixed his eyes upon the other vessel.

You." Margaret placed her hand over mine and squeezed it before continuing. "Driven by his lust for power and prestige, Roderick searched and investigated, using unspeakable means until he got what he needed. The other vessel, which was until now shrouded in secret, was finally revealed.

"A short while later, knowing that nothing could stop him, Balafas arranged an assassination for King Tark, and the followers of Baelor took over the palace." Margaret looked pleadingly at Father for a moment, as if asking him silent permission to stop. After several moments and a deep breath, she continued her story.

"We all knew that the vessel needed to disappear, and plans were made to put the child into hiding. As the directive was being put into motion, Balafas, Roderick, and several of his men took over the throne room. Anlace and your father were in the room with this group of traitors. Fear and ambition had completely taken all reasoning away from Roderick, and he fought your birth father to the death on the very steps of the throne room."

I looked over and saw Father had stopped writing. He was just sitting there listening to the story and staring out the window. I could see that his mind was replaying it vividly. I walked over to the table where Father was sitting and placed a hand on his shoulder, letting him know my thanks and appreciation. Margaret looked spent as she stood up and crossed over to the stove to fetch the kettle of tea. She looked back at me several times, and I saw a look of hesitation, like there was something not being said, or better yet, intentionally left out. Margaret kept looking back to Father, and each time she did, her sentences would end abruptly. There was something or someone being left out of this story, but I could see that the memories were bringing pain to both her and Father, so I decided not to press the matter anymore.

"It's getting worse out there, you know?" She said softly as she poured the tea. I noticed this comment was directed toward Father. His eyes only narrowed slightly. He slowly made his way back to the table and sat down. Margaret was patiently waiting for his response.

"These are dark times." Margaret closed her eyes and took a deep breath. "I am so appreciative of all the order has done for me, and you know that I owe you my life. Please do not think me cross to speak out in this way. But it has been on my heart for quite some time now." Father looked gently into Margaret's eyes.

"You know you may speak to me freely in any matter."

"I know," Margaret said humbly. "It's hard for me to believe I would even doubt you. But...well...is the order going to do anything about this? These soldiers are murdering for sport every night, and the streets flow with blood when they drink. Some of the vendors have closed their shops and moved on to Swaltayer. I have heard the western sea front is good for business myself. I could not dream of leaving but...if it got bad enough..." Father cut her off very calmly.

"The order knows. I have spent much time in the presence of Aleph in prayer for the solution to this, and every time I have heard the same thing in my spirit." Father then stood from his chair and set a comforting hand on Margaret's shoulder. "As you very well know, I have my heart constantly bent toward the mouth of Aleph, waiting for him to speak to me. His words to me are constant. Not everything he says is easy to receive. Truth is tied to a weight of responsibility. When you know the truth, you are a steward or an ambassador of the knowledge you receive. I have made a choice to use the wisdom I have gained to serve the interests of others."

"I don't understand," said Margaret.

"Know this," Father continued. "No matter what happens, however bad things get, Aleph knows and is in control. Whatever the enemy is plotting and has meant for evil, Aleph can turn around for the good of all."

After several tight hugs, fond farewells, and promises to return, Father and I set off from Margaret's house.

"Father, she looked at me as if I was her own," I told Father when we were at a safe enough distance that she could no longer hear us.

"She feels responsible for you, and rightly so. Every time I come to her, she asks about you and how you have been. In a way, you are hers. She loved your father and mother. You are what she imagines a son would have been like, had she and her late husband conceived. She sees Michael in you." At that point, I had heard enough about my father and mother for one evening and decided to change the subject.

"You said to Margaret that you've heard from Aleph about these 'Dark Times'." I decided to nudge him a little. "Can you tell me what he said?"

Father immediately stopped and looked directly into my eyes. I saw a burning fire in them. "He said that now is the time to prepare for sacrifice. You have been a faithful servant in the least, and I will now give you a place over many."

CHAPTER
5

About an hour later, after delivering the rest of the goods from the cart to homes around town, we thought it would be a good idea to break for dinner. Father suggested we take a table at the Swarthy Hog, a local tavern in the heart of Sommerset. The Swarthy Hog was renowned for its stew and red potatoes, which Father had spoken of many times before. He thought it was time for me to experience their cooking for myself. My stomach felt as though it was gnawing on my backbone, so I took him up on the offer. As we entered the building, the first thing I noticed was several of the magistrate's soldiers in the far back corner of the tavern. They were being loud and obnoxious, spilling their beer and picking on the barmaid who served them. Father seemed not to even acknowledge their presence and took a table near the front door.

I had never been in a tavern before and felt a tinge of excitement rise within. There were all types of people in this place. I saw businessmen talking about trade over drinks, while masons and builders were celebrating the end of a hard day of work. There was also a group of harlots scurrying around, selling themselves to anyone who would pay. The place was completely crammed full at the peak of the evening.

Father sat down across from me at the large wooden table. He had a sly grin on his face as he looked at me. I slowly met that grin with my own.

"What?" I inquired.

Father leaned forward and spoke almost in a shout. The place was busy, and the only way to talk and be understood was to shout. I kind of found it humorous. "Have you ever had a beer, son?"

"No. Have you?" I shouted back.

"Son, I used to be a soldier. I wasn't always a brother, remember?"

"I suppose so." I saw a younger Father in that moment. It seemed like all the age melted away, and before me was a young, vibrant soldier ready to march into hell itself to rescue the beloved children of Aleph.

"Can I buy you a beer, son?"

I didn't know what to say. Beer was always a topic of the brotherhood that was shunned. Everyone always had his or her own opinion but was not allowed to express it publicly. I remember Samuel and me discussing beer late one night as we sat on the wall looking out over Sommerset. He asked me if I had ever had a beer. I told him no. Then I asked him if he had. He began to tell a tale that lasted an hour and a half. That was the last time I ever brought it up in casual conversation.

"I'll have one if you are," I finally replied. Father got up and made his way to the barkeep. He came back shortly after with two pewter mugs in his hands. He set one of them in front of me. I leaned down and set my lips a couple inches from the tan foam at the top of the mug. It smelled like the barley and wheat I had spent endless hours of my life harvesting in the surrounding fields near the sanctuary. I looked up as Father took a drink. I was shocked to see Father take quite a large gulp. A look of satisfaction came across his face as he set the mug back down on the table.

"Go ahead, Daeric. Have a drink."

I took the mug in my hand and raised the tip to my mouth. The foam tickled my lips. Tipping the mug slightly brought the drink through the foam. It was cold and had a slightly bitter flavor as it went down my throat. I had never tasted anything like it in my life. Father smiled and had another drink. I followed suit. We took turns drinking until nothing was left but an empty mug. I was enthralled by the feeling this drink was giving me. Father left the table and went up to the barkeep for another round. My mind was thinking about all kinds of different things, and all the sounds around me were amplified. The bard in the corner was strumming a musical instrument, to the merriment of all around him. The sound coming from his instrument sounded amazing! I looked around the tavern at all the people and smiled. I realized these people were also drinking beer and having a good time.

"My, what a great end to the day," I thought to myself as Father came back with two more mugs in his hands. "Here, Daeric. Have another," he said as he set it down in front of me.

"Yes, sir." I responded. I did not wait for Father this time. I tipped the mug and let the cold refreshing drink go down my throat. I felt the bubbles in my belly rising to my throat. I let out a belch that shook my whole body. Father laughed as he drank, and foam sprayed out from the top of the mug.

"That's how you know it hit the spot!" Father exclaimed. I began to laugh myself. Father and I drank again until the mug was empty. As we took the last drink and set the mug down, we looked at each other across the table. This was a perfect moment that could never be put into words. I began to feel lightheaded at that moment and my bladder felt like it was about to explode. I excused myself to go to the privy.

As I stood up, my legs felt like a bowl of gelatin under me, and I staggered a bit. The song coming from the lyre of the bard had changed to a song about the rain. The chords came out with precision. The music was ringing clearly in my ears. It sounded so dreamlike. I saw a harlot dancing in front of me to the rhythm. She looked right at me and asked me to come near. I took one step towards her, and deciding that would not be a good idea, I turned around to go the other direction. That was when I ran right into a large man wearing golden-crested armor and a large black cape. The beer he was carrying in his hand flew from his grip. He grunted and looked in horror as his beer fell helplessly to the floor. The mug hit the ground, and the beer spilled out in a puddle. A look of anger flamed across his face. He grabbed me by the collar and pulled me close. He spat in my face as he spoke.

"Why don't you mind where you are going, lad? You just cost me a beer. I ought to skin for that one." I was not prepared for this encounter, and I was afraid. I thought the best thing to do was to make sure I didn't upset him any further. So, I decided to play into this situation.

"How 'bouts I go get you another?" I asked hopefully.

"You better make it two, lad. I sure am thirsty." He loosened his grip on my collar and let me go. I had actually gotten out of this situation without a fight. "I'll be over there with my mates." He pointed to the corner where the rest of the soldiers were. "Bring it quickly." He then pushed me out of the way and went to the back corner where he was greeted by another soldier with a full mug of beer. My bladder was so full it was stinging. I knew I had to be quick about getting him a beer, but I felt like I was about to explode.

I darted quickly into the privy and relieved myself. I used the moment to try and clear my head and assemble my thoughts. The dull roar of the busy tavern continued in the background.

I finished my business and was about to commence buying the soldier two beers when suddenly I heard a commotion and the booming raspy voice that I was not soon to forget. It was the shout of Agus Tull, coming from the direction of the front of the tavern. I quickly poked my head out of the privy entrance to see what was going on. Everyone's attention was towards the front door. I could barely see through the bodies, so I jumped up on a table in the very back. Agus Tull was standing over our table, and Father was sitting in his chair looking up at him.

"So....father. Having a drink? I didn't think brothers were allowed to drink."

"That issue has never been clearly established," Father replied. "Many questions have not been given a full measure of attention in our order."

Agus Tull was not expecting the answer he received, and a look of confusion came across him. It was shortly replaced by a surge of anger. He pounded his un-mailed fist into the wooden table, knocking a shard off in the process. As he did this, he lost his balance and stumbled back. He had obviously had too much to drink.

"Stand up!" Agus snarled. "We have some unfinished business to attend to." At this moment, the soldiers who were drinking in the back of the tavern circled the table where Father was seated. Father looked around him at the soldiers and stopped, his gaze upon Agus.

"What is this?" Father spoke sternly. "A show of strength? Do the people need to see the might of Balafas's army and tremble with fear? I will not submit to you, or your master."

Father then jumped up, and the soldier's hands shot to their scabbards. He looked back at them and continued. "Are you going to run me through in front of all these people?" Father asked the soldier calmly behind him. "Let me share with you this bit of wisdom. Serve those you think are weaker than you, and they will fight beside you." Then he turned back to Agus. "And you...I pity you. You control others through fear, but you are the one who is afraid."

Agus drew his blade and held it an inch from Father's throat. I felt a burning sensation start in my belly and consume my entire body. I felt a rage inside me about to explode.

"I really should finish you now. I would be in my right to do it, too." Agus threatened.

"To do so is to strike down the anointed of Aleph." Father spoke with boldness and conviction. The soldiers looked at Agus. "You may be surrendered to Baelor. But your spirit knows Aleph just as well. Aleph created you spirit, soul, and body."

Agus hesitated. He then looked to his soldiers and nodded

his head to the floor. One soldier dropped his sword at Father's feet. It landed with a loud clang that was heard echoing throughout the entire tavern.

"Pick it up and defend yourself," Agus said menacingly. Father shook his head defiantly.

"No," He replied. Agus again nodded to his soldiers, and two of them came up behind Father, holding his arms behind him. Father did not struggle much at all. I began to move through the crowd, but Father caught my eyes, and I could see the conviction of that gaze. He wanted me to stay still and silent. Agus stepped up to Father and slowly moved the tip of the blade across Father's cheek. Father bit down and took a graze of the blade. A line of blood followed the cut and began to drip down the side of his face.

"Are you ready to fight now?" Agus asked. Father gritted his teeth and stared down to the floor of the tavern. Agus then took his fist and punched Father in the stomach. Father hunched over in pain, gasping for the air that left his body.

I couldn't take it anymore. I screamed and pushed a patron out of my way. As I reached the table where Father was pinned, I executed a strong attack kick right into Agus Tull's sword hand. He never saw it coming. The blade flew from his grip. The next moment was a blur of movements and kicks and ended with Agus Tull on his back on the floor of the tavern, my knee pinning him there by his neck. He gasped for breath under me. I continued to apply subtle pressure as my training had taught me. He knew I was serious. When I had deemed that my opponent was subdued, I snapped a look back at Father's captors.

"Let him go!" I commanded. The soldiers looked shocked

at the scene before them.

"I said, let him go...now!!" I shouted again. The soldiers made no move to release Father. That was when a searing pain shot through my head. Agus had released a blow that knocked me back. I knew better. I should not have taken my eyes off my enemy.

Agus jumped up and kicked me several times the same way he had out in front of the sanctuary the day I'd tried to rescue a captive. I tried to catch my breath, only to have the air knocked out again. As he kicked me, I heard Father crying out for him to stop, as well as muffled curses coming from Agus's mouth. I was spent. There was nothing left in me. That is when I received the final kick, the one that just about blacked me out. I felt a cold piece of steel against my throat. I assumed it was Agus's sword ready to finish me. I couldn't move and just waited for the end. Then I heard Father cry out.

"Enough! I'll fight!" Agus removed the blade and whirled around to face Father.

"Pick up the sword." The soldiers released Father and he bent down to grab the sword. He stood up in a defensive position, holding the blade.

The look of my gentle, loving Father vanished in an instant. The man I saw holding the sword no longer resembled the one who raised me from childhood. I saw a seasoned, hardened man with a lifetime of combat experience. His eyes danced briefly around every inch of the tavern, taking it all in. A warrior of Aleph always sees every part of his environment in a split second, memorizing the surroundings. Because when the battle begins, he moves and becomes in sync with everything around him. There is no longer a need to see with the eye because his spirit is entrenched in the atmosphere.

I could see the fear in Agus Tull's eyes. He took a step back and held up his sword. He had the look of a child who had rattled the hornets' nest one too many times and knew the outcome of his mistake.

Without warning, he screamed and began the fight with a vicious stab of his sword. Father, quick as lightning, parried the blow which was meant to impale him and sidestepped. As he moved, his foot flashed out, catching Agus in the mid-section and knocking the wind from his lungs. Father then came down on top of Agus's head with a powerful chop. It landed right on his cheek, bringing gravity into effect. His body flew back into his own soldiers, knocking them down in the process.

Agus screamed in rage again and ran towards Father with multiple swings of his sword. Father danced lightly around each attempt with ease. I noticed Father had not swung his sword offensively. He only used it to parry Agus's drunken battle maneuvers.

Quickly, Father ended the fight by ducking a horizontal swipe of his opponent's sword and sweeping his leg into Agus' unbalanced lower body. In humiliation, Agus Tull's body hit the floor.

Father stepped back to allow his enemy to get back on his feet. With a gesture of grace, he motioned for Agus to stand and continue. Agus was speechless. He just looked at his soldiers and nodded at them. That was a mistake. Father moved like the wind. He jumped and flipped in the air. He defended and attacked. One against two, then one against three. Every feeble attempt to cut him down was routed with elegance and precision. Father's sword moved through the air and found its enemy before they knew it. Everywhere they moved, he moved. Every slice and chop of their swords was answered by ten of his own. But not one of them was cut in any way. It was the most perfect display of defense I have ever seen.

Once again, I felt cold steel against my throat. The sharp edge of another dagger was drawing blood from me as I heard the raspy whisper in my ear.

"Stand up now," Agus spat.

The bodies of the soldier's were strewn across the tavern floor. The crowd looked on the scene in absolute abandonment.

I let out a shriek as Agus pressed the dagger into the skin of my throat. Father whirled around in a storm of power and before my enemy knew it, Father's blade was against his throat. Agus was beyond confused at the events which had just transpired. He continued to hold me and looked down in fear at the blade that could so easily sever his lifeline.

"It's over Captain," Father said gently.

Suddenly, a scream of agony left Agus. He immediately released his grip on me and dropped his dagger. I moved quickly away from him, running into Father. His body staggered back, his hands clutching his chest. The tip of a sword protruded slightly from his breastplate. The hand that held the sword twisted and Agus's head whipped back. He looked at his slayer in horror.

"Please, Lucien! I need more time!" He gasped as the end of his life approached. The assailant was hooded in a cowl. His cloak was solid black with red trim at the bottom. It looked like a counterfeit to the order's robes. The newcomer gripped the hilt of the sword tightly, grabbed Agus's shoulder, and pushed roughly. The sword went deeper.

"The time that was given to you by the almighty, Baelor, is now expired, Agus. You are not a cleric; therefore, I have no use for you! It has been spoken!" The sinister voice carried a cold chill that filled the entire room. Agus screamed one last time as his final breath escaped, and his body fell to the floor of the tavern with a solid lifeless thud.

The unknown assailant turned his attention to Father. He pulled back his cowl. It had the look of a man, dark and mysterious. His skin was pale, and his hair jet black flowing loosely down his shoulders. Around his head was a band of unknown material that glowed red. It looked like it was crafted of some beautiful jewel. His face was chiseled with perfect, beautiful features. There were no blemishes or faults of any kind on the face of this handsome man. His chest was well built and fully muscled. He wore no armor of any kind. He was clothed in all black from head to toe. Around his waist was a band of the same material that adorned his forehead. He moved like liquid, with precision and grace. He stood a few feet away from Father and took several minutes to look deep into Father's eyes. I saw a glimpse of recognition on the face of the newcomer as he studied Father. Then he spoke.

"Anlace. It has been a while."

"You shut your mouth, foul spirit! You are in the presence of a keeper of the light." Father sternly retorted.

"Aye, but I have all authority to be here. I will not be moved by any words. If you wish to vanquish me, raise your sword, and let Aleph himself touch it. Then we will dance!" The dark man replied as he positioned himself into a defensive stance. He raised his sword, which was still dripping Agus's blood to the floor.

"What do you want? You now have this soul. Let these people go. They have seen enough!" Father took a step back from the dark man.

"I have come to bring a message to all the people of Shalistar," The stranger boomed. "The king and his family are dead, and his soldiers have taken their lives. The magistrate's army has now been commissioned to maintain law and order. As a gift to you this night, Baelor has seen your suffering from the rule of this sinister man." The stranger spoke, pointing to Agus Tull's lifeless body. You are now rid of this vile Captain forever."

The people in the audience listened to the Dark Man's words as if they were in a trance. "Because of these events, you have nobody to lead you, and Aleph has forever turned his back on you. The only way forward is to surrender to the mercy of Baelor. In response to your obedience, he will impart a gift to all of you. Until now, only his select few have been allowed to know the power of his might. The time has come for each of you to bow the knee and learn the greatness of Baelor." I couldn't stand there another second in silence.

"He is lying to all of you! The true power comes only from…" Suddenly I felt an unseen hand tighten around my throat. It was icy cold and burning hot all at once and filled me with a shudder. The rest of my words were lost. The grip tightened to the point of agony. The feeling of ice and fire traveled throughout my entire body. If I could have screamed, I would have. The people continued to sit there and stare, locked in a trance. The Dark Man walked slowly up to me, gazing into the depths of my soul.

I looked into his eyes and saw endless fires and piles of bodies in torment. Then I heard the terrifying screech and there flashed before me the outline of a creature with immense wings. His head was massive, with beaked jaws. The eyes of this creature glowed red, just like the band around the Dark Man's head and waist. The creature opened his mouth, and I saw rows of razor-sharp teeth. His body and talons looked like they were carved out of glowing rock. I closed my eyes and tried to scream. The vision would not stop. The Dark Man came in close. His breath smelled like sulfur. He spoke softly to me in a voice just above a whisper.

"What's this? You can see me? Who are you?"

"Let him go now!" Father commanded the Dark Man.

"Baelor can use your gift of sight, my young one. He can show you things you cannot imagine. He will give everything that Aleph cannot."

"I command you..." Father began.

"You command nothing!" The Dark Man shouted looking into my eyes. He then took his gaze off me. The horrific images immediately ceased. I fell to the floor gasping for air. All my strength had left me. The Dark Man then addressed the people in the tavern.

"Each of you will be visited. Simply kneel to the messenger who comes to you, and all will be done. If you resist...well..." The Dark Man let these final words hang in the air as he walked around the room, looking into the eyes of several people. They simply stared back, dreamlike, as he finished his announcement. "It would be better if you were tied to a concrete statue and thrown into the Parulin River, than to refuse an invitation from Baelor. That is all."

Then as quickly as it came, all the pain around my neck subsided. The Dark Man was gone. All the demonic presence lifted. The people looked dazedly at one another. It was as if they had awakened from a dream, or rather a nightmare. I stumbled to Father and wrapped my arms around him. Women began crying. Several people came up and knelt for him to pray for them. They stepped over the unconscious bodies of the soldiers and huddled close to us. I looked up at Father and saw him staring with glazed eyes into eternity. Then after several minutes, he returned to the people in front of him. He prayed over them.

The still unconscious soldiers were picked up and placed outside the back of the tavern in a pile. Agus Tull's lifeless corpse was removed as well. After each person had been attended to, we were politely escorted outside and given some bread for our journey back to the sanctuary. As we were standing alone in front of the tavern, Father turned and looked at me. I noticed that the look he gave me was not as a son, but as a brother. I saw not a humble servant, but a war-seasoned General. When he spoke the next words, it was from one soldier to another, a call to arms.

"There is not going to be much time. We must be quick. Baelor has made his move. It has begun."

CHAPTER

6

The night was a whirlwind. Father and I were being led by Aleph into homes throughout the entire town. We would enter and pray for protection over the house, then leave to the sound of screaming from the building next door. The first time I heard it, my body jolted into a defensive posture, and I started to run towards the front door. Father grabbed me and calmly told me.

"It's too late. They have refused Baelor's offer." I felt a pang of sorrow for the people who met the messenger and refused. Aleph, however, had those he wished to protect and sent us expeditiously to pray over them. As they knelt before us, Father placed his hands on them and spoke.

"The holy touch of Aleph is upon you. There is no evil that can befall you. The enemy will not come to your house. Receive now Aleph's peace and have great courage. He will tell you where to go next. Hear his voice and obey. Be blessed, and may Aleph be praised."

From one house after the next, we flew. We ascended flights of stairs, and ran over bridges and rooftops to find the people, marking them with protection. Everywhere we went, we heard the messengers of Baelor nearby. No mercy would be shown to those who did not side with the enemy. It was as if Aleph and Baelor were racing through the town side by side, gathering as many people as possible before time ran out. Suddenly, I stopped. I saw the vision again of the woman huddled in the dark room of hay and barrels. She continued to weep and rock back and forth.

"Father! Please, I am seeing the woman again. Shouldn't we take this as a sign?" Father took a second to think about what I had said.

"Is this the same woman you saw before?"

"Yes, I was shown a vision of her in a dark room with hay and barrels. She was rocking back and forth, sobbing and holding a dagger to her wrist." I concluded.

"Okay, Daeric. Where is she?"

"I don't know. All I saw was…"

"I understand that part…you need to ask Aleph where she is." If he wants us to go to her…he will show you the way. Take a minute to close your eyes so you are not distracted by your surroundings. Then ask him as if you were talking to me right now."

I followed Father's instructions. I closed my eyes and asked. Instantly, I knew where I was to go, as if I had already been there.

"She is in the barn next to the farm by the river." Father and I ran through the main streets. People were out in droves. Screams could be heard everywhere, in each building. The town was being harvested by Aleph and Baelor. People were choosing sides. Faces flew by as we continued running towards the edge of town. I started to feel a tingling in my palms, as though a flicker of flame had just danced across my skin. My palms also felt damp, and I moved my fingers back and forth across them as I ran. The tingling flame had moved up my arms towards my shoulders.

Father and I continued the relentless pace all the way to the barn at the edge of town. As we showed up, we could hear a raspy voice through the door.

"Baelor has a gift to bestow to all who follow and are surrendered to his will...You will not thwart his plans!" Father did not hesitate to kick in the door and spoke in an authoritative voice.

"Release her, foul spirit. She is Aleph's child," Father commanded.

"I think not, monk!" Spat the messenger. "Baelor has laid claim to her soul."

"Baelor claims nothing because her soul cannot be owned by another." Father returned. The messenger took a second to think about the words and then quickly bent down and grabbed the woman by the hair. He brought her up in front of him with a knife to her throat.

"Wise words indeed, monk. I think we will just steal her soul then!"

The messenger made a move to cut the woman's throat and suddenly there was a rush of wind that filled the entire barn. The messenger was thrown back into the wall, knocked completely off his feet. The darkness in the barn bowed to a bright radiant light. There in the barn appeared a large figure, dressed completely in light. Father and I both stared in amazement. The figure moved toward the messenger of Baelor. The messenger backed away in cowardice. The figure pointed at the messenger and spoke.

"Go!" The messenger disappeared instantly. The woman collapsed to the floor, and the newly arrived figure bent down and lifted her up. She was shaking uncontrollably as he placed his hand on her forehead.

"Child...have no fear. The torment has ceased. Aleph has heard your cry." I recognized the voice that came from the visitor in white.

"I'm so sorry. I'm so sorry." The woman continued to sob.

"That is in the past. But you must listen to me now. You are in great danger. These men will take you to safety, and you must follow them." The visitor then stood up and turned around to face us. The radiance was blinding at first, then began to dissipate. I was now able to see the face of the woman's rescuer. It was Jeru.

"You are a guardian! I knew..." I exclaimed.

"There will be time for that later." Jeru cut me off.

"Ride north back to the sanctuary. They are coming under attack and will need your help. All the people in this town who have been marked by Aleph have left and are on their way to a safe place at the Rift. It will be a long walk for them, but Aleph is with them and guiding them to safety. Those who have received Baelor's gift are being assembled for transport to Raithe. They will be trained for Balafas's army. Father Anlace, I cannot stress the importance of young Daeric's safety. Watch after him and protect him at all costs. Now go!"

I had so many questions that I wanted to ask Jeru. Before I could speak any of them aloud, he was gone.

The young woman with us was named Esgar. She was of medium height for a girl and moved with agility, completely silent on her feet. As she ran, her long dark hair billowed behind her. She looked as if she were only a few years older than me. She'd hardly said a word since we had left the barn except to help Father with which way to go. Father and I decided not to bring up her recent experiences.

We came out of an alley and swiftly crossed the street. We could hear in the center of town a large crowd rustling and murmuring as one of Baelor's messengers spoke about the gift they had received. I heard words about "Illusion" and "Alteration" but could not quite grasp the meaning. I was curious to hear what was being said and began to turn away from Father and Esgar toward the center of town. Suddenly, Father grabbed me.

"What they are saying is abomination. We care nothing for the gifts of Baelor. We must get back to the sanctuary. Don't be distracted, Daeric."

Together we stealthily moved back to the wagon and our horses. Although we had to dodge the lifeless bodies of the unfortunate victims of Baelor's wrath, our path was clear all the way to the stables. "They must have had great courage to say no to the messenger," I thought to myself.

"Yes, they did." I heard a soft voice say.

"Did you just say something to me?" I asked. Father and Esgar stopped running and looked at me quizzically.

"No," Father replied. We then continued onward, and I put the voice out of my mind for the time being.

I helped Father load our bags, and Esgar proved extremely useful as she saddled our horses for the trip back. She performed the task with an excellence not seen even in the sanctuary. She knew how to calm the animals with her touch and a soft whisper in their ear. She then gently but diligently placed the bridle over the horse's heads and attached the reins to the bit. Father watched her as she finished.

"I see you have had some experience with horses." Father stated.

"A little," she replied. She turned away from him, letting her body language state that she did not want to discuss it. As she was tucking in several straps to the side of the saddle, I saw Father's eyes catch a glimpse of a mark on her right forearm. He quietly gasped at what he saw. I nudged him and he went right back to work.

The weather turned cold as evening turned to early morning. It was a beautiful night. On display were the heavens and stars as far the eye could see. They were shining brightly all around us as we were carried by our horses over many hills, traveling southeast. It was dark, yet the horses did not stumble. They dodged every tree and bush in our path. Their hooves treaded lightly over the rocks in the road. It was as if their path was illuminated in the black of night. It was mostly quiet the entire trip. Each one of us were busy with our own thoughts until Esgar broke the silence.

"Thank you both for saving me."

"You are welcome," Father and I answered together.

"So, what are you guys, some sort of monks?" she asked.

"We are Brothers of the Elect. We dedicate our lives to the will of Aleph," Father replied.

"Really? Where are your cloaks?" Father's eyes looked over to me and then back to our new companion.

"They are under the boards of the front seat. We will don them once again when we are safely away from Sommerset. Our sanctuary is still further south."

"I didn't know you had to live completely isolated from society to be in the will of Aleph?" Esgar countered.

"We choose to study his personality without any distractions. It has been this way for the order since the beginning," responded Father.

"So, do you come out of your shell once a month and help the people in Sommerset?"

"Sort of. I have made a promise to a certain few over the years."

"So, do you fight as well? You are the Order of the Elect, right?" Esgar asked and Father looked at her in awe once more.

There was something different about this girl, I thought. There were not many people in Shalistar who knew of our order by name.

"Yes, we are," Father answered. "And yes, we do. We study the will of Aleph and dedicate ourselves to training in combat."

"Sounds lonely." I watched her stare out into the darkness. Her eyes were pressed into the night, asking for an answer to an unspoken question. I could not help but stare at her. Her face was so soft, yet her features were hardened. Life must have taken a lot from her. But she was so beautiful. I again saw her sitting in the dark barn weeping, with the dagger close to her wrist. What could have happened? Why would she want to kill herself? Then she turned right to me. Distracted by my thoughts, I was not quick enough to avert my gaze from her. I had been caught looking. I could feel my body blush in embarrassment. She gave a slight smile and patted my knee. Her touch was incendiary. I felt warmth like I had never experienced before encompassing my entire being.

Then she looked toward the heavens and said something in her flinty voice that took me completely by surprise. "Just like Aleph. I guess the joke is on me." She sighed, shaking her head. "When he said he was sending me help, I never in a million years would have guessed this."

CHAPTER

7

We kept a steady pace all the way back to the sanctuary. I was nervous about what Jeru had said. When a guardian gives you an order, you had best jump to it. Esgar was curled up into a ball with her head down between her knees. I could see she did not want to be bothered by anyone, so I was sure to give her some space. Father sat in the front, directing our horses. He was calm and collected, singing songs aloud to Aleph. I loved hearing Father sing. His voice always brought peace to any atmosphere he was in. There was an urgency, but Father did not show any anxiety on his face or in his actions. He remained calm and collected.

As we crossed the bridge and came over the hill, I began to smell the smoke in the air. My stomach tightened into a large knot as we approached the grounds to the sound of soldiers and horses. Then as we came into view of the sanctuary, I looked in horror at the sight of the only home I had ever known, completely set on fire. The flames consumed every square inch of the property. It was like hell had landed right into the center of the sanctuary.

We stopped the cart and crept to a cover of trees, west of the entrance. Below the leaves was an outcropping of large rocks I had climbed on my whole life. We ducked behind them stealthily to keep us hidden from view. From there, I watched a battalion approach the perimeter like an army of hungry ants. The dark-cloaked messengers, clothed in human bodies, were shouting the orders from horseback. I could not believe what I was seeing. Our brothers came running out of the building, blinded by the smoke and coughing in a desperate attempt to breathe in fresh air.

I saw Lionel run out first, with his white cloak whipping in the wind. He knew he had no chance against a battalion of this magnitude, but he put up a valiant fight, cutting down several soldiers as they were commanded to take him out. After Lionel made short work of them, the messengers halted the attack for a moment. Next came Mark and Gareth, together running into the fray and joining Lionel. The messengers gave the command, and more soldiers charged my brothers. Lionel, Gareth, and Mark moved beautifully together and shortly later had laid all their assailants down. They quickly regrouped themselves together, breathing deeply, awaiting the next assault.

I looked desperately to Father, and he responded, "All we can do is pray." Then we met eyes, and his emotion became mine. He knew my thoughts and shook his head no. Then he turned back to the intense scene before us.

The soldiers, being much, greater in number, had now decided to make sport of this and formed a circle around the entrance of the flaming building. Haywood came running out, coughing the smoke out of his lungs. He joined rank with his brothers, his sword raised.

The messengers gave the order, and more of their black-cloaked human minions battled to the death with this far superior group of warriors. The cruel trick they were playing became evident. It was like watching a lion play with a baby gazelle before devouring its prey.

Merwin, Geoffrey, Stewart, Renton, and Halsey all joined the battle as well. The messengers sent more and more soldiers, not caring for any of their lives and knowing they did not stand a chance against the order. They sent them anyway, if only to wear down and tire out my brothers.

The scene was intense, and when I thought I could not take any more, I saw my best friend Samuel run out into the circle. I was about to scream when Father grabbed me and clapped his hand over my mouth. I swore curses on the magistrate's army at the top of my lungs. All that came out were tiny quiet muffled squeals. I closed my eyes and screamed silently, begging for Aleph's mercy on my brothers.

I felt a soft, tender hand placed on my shoulder, and a sweet, gentle voice whispered in my ear.

"It's going to be okay." I looked up and saw the beautiful face of Esgar looking into my eyes. At that word, courage and hope enveloped me in a cloak. I slowly turned my head back toward the sanctuary.

Samuel stood with his brothers in the center of the ring of soldiers. They were all cloaked in white, standing battle-ready in the middle of a black circle. Their swords were drawn and held in a defensive position. The messengers shouted the command, and twenty soldiers rushed in from all directions. Samuel and his brothers met them with a clash and a swirl of steel. Feet whipped around, catching the chins of attackers. I saw my brothers leap through the air and attack, taking soldiers completely off guard.

There were only ten warriors in the middle of the unholy black circle, but the way they moved and fought together made it seem like a 100. Another round of soldiers and then another tried to dispatch my brothers a bit more cautiously. But they were able to finish them off in a flurry of movement that made even the messengers begin to doubt whether this was possible.

As if in response to my thoughts, I heard the loud, agitated cry of a messenger. He cried out for his soldiers to grab their bows and pin cushion our brothers with a barrage of arrows. The soldiers, in an unholy synchronous motion, pulled back on their bowstrings. The white-cloaked warriors looked around at the ring of soldiers and glanced at each other. In agreement and as one, they threw their swords down into the grass. The blade bit deep into the ground, waving back and forth. My brothers stood up tall and straight, raised their hands toward the heavens, and cried out the name of Aleph as the arrows were loosed.

Suddenly a brilliant flash of light appeared from nowhere. As the arrows traveled into the light, they became no more. The light burst into the ring of soldiers, knocking every one of them off their feet.

There appeared in the midst of the group a large man with shimmering, free flowing robes, with a flaming sword in his hands. The soldiers quickly got back up on their feet and picked up their bows. The messengers screamed for them to launch their arrows quickly. The arrows flew and never found their mark.

Once again, a blinding light traveled from my brothers in white into the black ring of soldiers, once again knocking them down.

Suddenly again, there appeared out of eternity another large man, carrying a flaming sword. The soldiers got to their feet again and stared dazedly at the two large men. The messengers shouted a charge command to the ring of soldiers. All at once, the entire battalion charged my brothers and the two newcomers. In unison, all the warriors in the center grabbed their swords and pulled them out of the ground.

I looked one last time at Father, pleading with him. In response, he looked at me and told me to wait here. He drew his sword and ran towards the fray.

The Order of the Elect and the guardians made themselves battle ready as the soldiers came near. A loud war cry erupted that could be heard all the way in Sommerset! As the armies clashed, a brilliant sphere of light encompassed the entire ring of battle. I heard screams and battle cries, including Father, from within the light. My brothers moved their bodies and steel together, and one after another the enemy soldiers were defeated. I could hear steel and grunts. Bodies were flying through the air. It was an impressive display of combat, to say the least. A lifetime of training was clearly seen by all the soldiers outside the ring.

Replacements were hesitant to join the battle, knowing that to do so would be their death, but to refuse would put their lives in the hands of the unmerciful messengers. So they ran in, trying to route the eternal force in the middle of the ring of light. It was a fruitless pursuit. As the combat continued, the cries became fewer and fewer until all was silent.

Then the light vanished and standing in the center of all the dead soldiers were my Father, my brothers, and the guardians. Without another word, they all began charging through the bodies towards the messengers on horses. The horses began to buck and neigh. My Father raised his sword above his head, and the brothers followed suit. Instantly, their swords burst into flame. The messengers then looked at each other in utter astonishment. In an act of cowardice, they turned their horses from the sanctuary and galloped away as fast as they could.

I could see streaks of light as the guardians abandoned their human form and went into the air, giving chase. The shrieks from the messengers could be heard in the distance as they met the guardians in the air. There were several minutes of noise that cannot be described, except to say that the eternals were doing battle. Unworldly shrieks came from the messengers as they were defeated, until all was completely silent.

Father was helping and tending to some wounds that Haywood had received. Esgar and I decided it was safe and came into the entrance. My brothers were winded and tired, leaning on each other and staring, open-mouthed at their home, completely caught up in flames. Samuel looked over and saw Father. He ran into his arms and collapsed.

"They came from nowhere. We were not prepared. What were we supposed to do?" Samuel asked.

"Nothing, brother." Father replied. "You could not have known. But now you are safe. Father assembled the group together and instructed them. "Come, we must go quickly. The rest of the army is nearby. A lot has happened, and we have great work ahead of us. We will travel east towards Rivertown. Once we are away from here and safe, we can have some rest. You have all fought well. Let's travel quickly to Rivertown and figure out supplies. Once we are prepared, we will make our way towards the Rift. Aleph is gathering his people there," Father explained.

"I don't understand. Why is this happening?" Samuel asked anxiously.

"Samuel, the end is near. We are the abeyance being called in for the final battle. As you know, this war has gone on for centuries. Aleph is about to do a new thing here, and we have been called." Samuel was about to respond, but Father, knowing his thoughts, cut him off. "It is not for us to know why. I am sure the revelation of Aleph's purposes will come soon. But for now, we must trust him in everything. Do not question why he chose you. We are simply going to put our foot forth and walk before him," Father rebuked him.

"I'm sorry, Anlace," said Samuel. "It's not my place to question Aleph. Forgive me."

"All is forgiven. Now, are you able to get in the cart? Rivertown is a half a day away, and we need to be on the move. Baelor's servants are not far behind us and are probably mustering many together to ride us down."

"Yes, sir. I am okay."

"Good—then get into the cart and have your sword ready."

We traveled hard the rest of the night, heading southeast towards Rivertown. As the sun rose in the east, we decided to stop for a short break. Lionel, Mark, and Halsey decided they didn't need the rest and volunteered for hunting duty. They came back with a nice haul of rabbit and herbs. Aleph's provision was a blessing to us all, and everyone had a nice breakfast under a grove of trees. Shortly after, we continued down the road.

Before we knew it, we were on the outskirts of a small village that sat on the banks of the Antioch River. The village did not have much to offer. It was a tightly formed line of short buildings made of sod and some brick, lining the riverbank. In the center of the group of buildings was a square with a well and a stage. I could tell this was where the community gathered to fellowship. As we walked to the square, people were commenting to each other about our group. Father and I had now joined the rest of the brothers by putting our white cloaks back on, and the sight of the order in the town caused quite the commotion. The townspeople stood there pointing and whispering, not with menace, but curiosity.

Father and I went into the store to negotiate provisions. The threshold was low, and we had to duck under it to keep our heads from hitting it. The first thing we noticed was the quality of goods. The wares were all common. This community worked hard for everything they had, and nothing on the shelves came cheap. However, my brothers had the foresight to grab their coin before running out of the burning sanctuary. We were able to put all our money together and negotiate a fair deal with the store owner.

He entered from the back room and stood a foot taller than Father. He had to constantly duck to make himself fit in the ceiling space. It was funny to watch, and I could not keep myself from thinking about why he had not fixed the ceiling to accommodate his height. The storekeeper came up and introduced himself, pumping our hands up and down.

"I want to welcome you to our humble town. My name is Groth, and I am the storekeeper here in Rivertown."

"It is an honor to meet you, good sir," Father replied. Groth moved from around the counter, offering assistance to any of our needs. He called out, and from behind the counter came a quick-footed lady who spoke with purpose.

"Greetings, strangers. My name is Loretta. Groth is my husband. We are here to serve you. Please let us know what it is you need, and we would be happy to help. If you need salted pork, we just cut some fresh last night. We have vegetables, bread, clothing, and even some nice wines."

"Thank you, Loretta. You have been most helpful. I think we will be able to make some fine selections with the wares that are available," Father concluded. As we shopped, I looked over at Groth and his wife and saw them just staring at us and whispering to each other from time to time. They were discussing our presence, speaking in hushed voices with no shortage of excitement. I sensed there was no danger and continued shopping.

"Do you have any pens or books, preferably blank, for journaling?" I asked Loretta. She nodded and ducked backed behind the counter. There were some loud noises as she moved product around, but after several minutes of rummaging, she reappeared with several tomes and some pens in her hand.

"I have been sitting on these for years! Rivertown doesn't have too many writers," she replied.

"Thank you, Loretta," Father said. "We will take two books and pens to go with them."

"Please make it three," I corrected. Father turned and looked at me. "Esgar asked me to get her one as well." As I said that, Father smiled and went back to shopping.

We stocked up on the provisions we needed to make it all the way to the Rift. Groth and Loretta were grateful for our business and added several pouches of water to the order in a gesture of generosity. We were overcome with gratitude and blessed them with Aleph's favor. Before we could say another word, they helped us load everything we purchased onto the cart.

◇

The news of our presence got around, and before we knew it, a crowd had gathered in the center of the village by the well to see us off. There were people reaching out their hands to us and begging us to pray over them. There were sick people, too. I was overwhelmed with what I was seeing but did not know what to do.

Father told me to simply have compassion, listen to what they need, and then pray that Aleph would hear their cry. I awkwardly did what Father told me to do. I found myself going from one person to the next, looking them in the eyes and asking them what they needed. My heart flooded with compassion as I listened to them. Father was there in the crowd watching me. He saw emotion overcome me at one moment, and he quickly came to stand behind me. He leaned in and whispered in my ear, "What you are feeling is what Aleph is feeling towards that person." It was all so amazing, the way I was feeling what Aleph was feeling. Father was there sharing it with me.

Suddenly, all of that feeling turned into action.

A boy in the village was walking on a crutch because he had broken his foot. I asked him if he was in pain. He nodded and said he was most of the time. As he responded, I felt a tingling in my fingers and decided that I would pray for him. I placed my hands on his broken foot and spoke some simple words, nothing grand or complicated. I simply asked Aleph to heal him.

My eyes were still closed when I heard a cry of joy and felt the boy's foot move out from under my touch. As I opened my eyes, I saw the boy jumping up and down. His foot had been healed! He had thrown his crutch away and was running in circles, shouting for joy! I was overwhelmed with happiness at that moment. Aleph had just used my hands to perform a miracle on this boy. I looked up through tear-soaked eyes and saw Father standing over me, watching the whole scene. He was grinning and nodding his head in approval. Esgar was looking on as well with wide eyes.

The rest of our time spent in Rivertown was a joyous blur. We were escorted from one home to the next to meet and pray over people. They received our ministry gladly. Some people gave us gifts, others gave us food. Our meager supplies that we had multiplied right before our eyes. People were thankful for Aleph's ministry through us and made sure we were duly blessed for it.

We decided to stay the night in Rivertown and dine with the inhabitants. Groth and Loretta opened their home, which was located behind the store, and several of our company unpacked our sleeping mats, laying them in the small, cozy living area. Several other homes were opened up to us for the rest of our companions to sleep as well. Nobody was allowed to sleep outside tonight. The town made sure there was plenty of room for us to stretch out without intruding upon each other. With sleeping arrangements in order, we went out of the house and into the square.

The inhabitants of Rivertown put together quite the feast for us, and after we had all supped and were ready for bed, I sat up with Father next to Groth's fireplace and asked him about the day.

"Father, what was it that happened?" I asked curiously.

He stopped writing in his journal and looked up at me. "Son, just as Baelor has gifts, so does Aleph. You received a gift today. One of many. Aleph has given you the ability to bless the sick and those who are hurting."

"So, I can heal anyone?" I asked.

"I didn't say that. I haven't seen this gift in operation in a long time, son." Father's eyes began to fill up with tears at the thought of it. Something long ago had happened that he was reminded of. "But it is clear," he said, shaking it off, "Aleph is making himself known once again through this gift. I believe that before all is said and done, you will be manifesting Aleph's presence to the world through many other gifts as well."

I laid down in my bed with that final comment of Father's going through my head. "How many gifts does Aleph have to give?" I asked myself in wonder. Before I knew it, I was asleep.

The next morning, we awoke with the entire town as they gathered to see us off. There were many tears as we departed. I was in awe of how we could make such a difference in such a short period of time. Several families had decided to come with us to the Rift, including Groth and Loretta. Tears were cried for them as well.

Groth took a moment to walk a friend of his through the

store and handed him the keys. I was amazed—Groth and Loretta were leaving everything they had and coming with us! When all goodbyes had been expressed, we were off and on our way. I looked behind me as we went over the hill and saw the remaining inhabitants of the town watching over us until we were completely out of sight.

"That was some gift you had in operation there," Esgar said quietly to me after some time. I turned to her and saw her sitting relaxed across from me, almost studying me.

"I didn't even know what I was doing," I said to her nervously. This was the first conversation we had tried openly together, and I could feel a tightness in my stomach.

"The boy didn't know that. You changed his life."

"But that wasn't me."

"Are you sure about that?" She quickly responded. "Those weren't your hands? That wasn't you on your knees praying?"

"You know what I mean. It wasn't my power that healed him."

"Correct. But Aleph had to have a vessel. And you were the one he filled."

"It just felt like the right thing to do." I replied.

"It wasn't just the boy. The whole town was affected by that. Aleph hasn't shown himself like this in a long time, Daeric," she stated, with an ache in her heart. I could tell this was a hard conversation for her. "You are special for him to use you like that. You should be grateful," she corrected me.

"He will be," Father shouted as he trotted up alongside us on his horse. "He doesn't quite understand all that he has been opened up to. But he will." Father looked right at me and smiled. He then winked one of his eyes and kept on moving towards the front of the caravan.

Esgar and I did not speak again for the rest of the day. We just sat there, awkwardly sitting across from each other, writing in our journals. I tried to open my mouth to speak several times more, but all that came out was a groan. I decided that instead of embarrassing myself again, I would just keep my mouth shut.

I looked back behind me shortly before sunset and saw the expanse of the land behind us. We were going north along the Antioch River, which laid to the east. Somewhere to the west was our destroyed sanctuary. I watched my brothers as they rode beside each other. They were laughing and smiling as they spoke about where we were going and what might lie ahead of us.

"How could they be so calm about all of this?" I wondered. "Our home is gone, and we are on a journey north to a destination unknown. I am not sure I share the same sentiment as the rest of my brothers."

The new families from Rivertown were full of hope and joy as well. I really did not understand that one, either. They had completely left all they had behind and decided to travel with us to the Rift. Why would they do that? We were strangers and had nothing solid to offer them. Still, they packed up and went with us on our adventure.

That evening as we had dinner together, I sat next to Groth and Loretta. I did not want to offend them, but I had to know, so I asked.

"Why did you come with us?"

"It has been a long time coming, young sir," His deep voice replied.

"Can you explain to me why?"

"I sure can." He sat back, relaxing his back and stretching out his long legs. "When we saw you and your brothers come into the village, it was incredible. We felt like this was not the first time we had seen you in our village. And then, when Aleph used you to heal that boy, I was overcome with an even stronger realization."

"What was that?" I asked.

"That we had been here before," Loretta added. I stared open-mouthed from across the fire as she continued. "My mind fought me because I knew it was impossible. But when I looked over at Groth, I knew we were experiencing the same thing."

"We went home and discussed it before you came back for the evening and confirmed we were seeing and sensing the same thing," Groth continued. "It was like Loretta and I had been sharing a dream from before. But the truth was much simpler than that. It was Aleph." He paused a moment, letting those words sink into me.

"What do you mean?" I asked, on the edge of my seat.

"I mean that Aleph had already been there in spirit, and it was He that had already planned for you and your brothers to come through our village. He had already placed his hands on that boy and healed him. In this plane of existence, we were finally catching up to him. Do you understand?"

"Not completely."

ALEPH

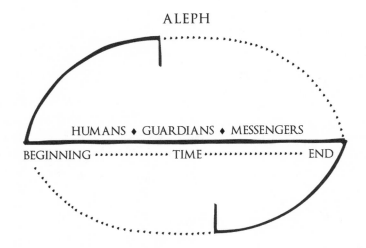

Loretta came and sat next to me. She leaned in and began an explanation. She took her finger and drew a line in the dirt in front of us. She then drew a perpendicular line at each end.

"This line represents time. These two lines at the ends represent the beginning of time and the end of time. We as humans are bound to the constructs and rules of time. Aleph, however, exists outside of time." She drew a circle completely around the line. "He is not bound to the ebb and flow of time, because he is the creator of time. The guardians and messengers themselves were created within time; therefore are bound by its laws. Aleph is not. He can move forward or behind. At times, Aleph is working on our future and his spirit moves on our behalf, ahead of our physical bodies in time. Then as we live our lives, we eventually catch up to where Aleph has already been working. When we reach those important moments where he has already been, he gives us a signal. It feels familiar, like we have already been there before. In those moments, it is important to be sensitive to Aleph and what he is trying to convey."

"And so," I cut her off. "You and Groth were experiencing a moment where your physical bodies were catching up to where Aleph had already been?"

"Yes," Groth affirmed. "We knew He was calling us out to join you all. From there, it was an easy decision. We simply handed our store over to our good friend and came with you."

"But what if you were wrong?" I asked.

"We can't be wrong. Aleph is not to be put in a box. Do you think the only life we could have lived out was in Rivertown? Not so! Aleph has given us many possibilities to live in life. It is like seeing a group of doors! Behind each door is a possible life to live. But what is most incredible about this truth is that Aleph is the God of Possibilities and is standing behind every one of those doors. He has empowered us to choose. Loretta and I have made that choice, and we are now with you," Groth finished.

Over the next several days, Esgar and I made small talk from time to time. She always had a cool smile on her face but was very guarded, not allowing me access to any of her secrets. I could tell she had an intimate knowledge of Aleph but never shared the depth of what she knew. Her comments to me were always on the surface. I had a hard time reading her, which is exactly what she wanted.

At sunset, on the seventh day of travel from Rivertown, we had an unexpected surprise. A skirmish of travelers was on the horizon coming toward us. Father rode up and down the caravan, telling everyone to be on guard but to remain calm. As the travelers drew closer, we could see they were tired and desperate. Several of them were bandaged from wounds.

We stopped fifty yards from each other. Several moments of silence ensued as we scanned each other from a distance. There were about thirty of them. I could see men, women, and children, all tired and hungry. Father and Geoffrey rode out to the middle between us and called for an individual from the other side to join them. A tall, thin man in his forties separated himself from the group and walked out to meet our leaders. As he approached, Geoffrey and Father got off their horses so they were on the same ground as the other man.

They began their meeting, speaking in quiet voices we could not hear. I stood there and watched, anxiously awaiting the outcome. Suddenly, the man cried out, and I saw him collapse into Father's arms, weeping. Father held the man and comforted him there for several minutes. When the man had run out of tears, Father straightened him and continued the discussion. After several more minutes, Father and Geoffrey came back over to us. The tall, thin man went back to his group as well.

Father called us all together to brief us on the meeting. When we were assembled, he began his report.

"They are from Thorne. Baelor's messengers appeared and reaped the city, the same way it happened in Sommerset. The magistrate's army was there as well. He said there were clerics with the messengers.

I looked at Esgar. "What are clerics?"

"Magic users," she quickly replied. I was taken back by the surety of her response.

Father went on to describe how Thorne was overrun by

the army, the inhabitants taken captive and mustered into the center of town. He described a man in black, who wore a red jeweled band over his forehead. As he was describing this villain, my mind went back to the tavern in Sommerset. Agus Tull had called him Lucien, before his life was ended. Then I remembered the vision I'd had as I looked into his eyes and saw him transfigured into a hideous beast. I shuddered at the memory that had come to mind but was able to shake the image loose. Father went on to describe how Lucien had given the people a choice. Those who refused were lined up in front of the whole town. The clerics then used spells of Destruction on them, and they were no more.

I couldn't believe what I was hearing. I looked incredulously over at Esgar. She had a look of anger and frustration as she listened to the report. I felt sorry for her, and I wanted to comfort her. In an act of bravery, I took a step towards her. She saw me approach and turned away from me, walking off into a brush of trees. My stomach twisted as she walked off, refusing any kind of affection.

Father continued telling us about how this remnant was able to escape. The rest of the people of Thorne had either surrendered to Lucien or reached a terrifying end. By the time the report was over, the remnant from Thorne had come over and joined our caravan. My brothers took care to make sure they had plenty of food and fresh bandages if needed. After an hour, everyone was comfortable and supping together around the fire.

I circled the camp looking for Esgar. Having not found her, I decided to walk towards the brush of trees she had retreated to earlier. I found her a short distance away on her knees, sobbing quietly. She was rocking back and forth on the ground repeating the phrase, "I can't do it! I can't do it!"

I took a deep breath and made my move towards Esgar again.

"*Stop, Daeric,*" came a voice from inside me. So faint and quiet, but present. I completely stopped, watching Esgar in the distance. It hurt me to see her crying like that. I knew that any offer of comfort would be refused, so I turned around and left her alone. I went back to the camp to join my brothers and the rest of the caravan for a nice dinner. Afterwards, I laid down and was soon fast asleep.

The green hills grew steeper as we approached the foothills of the Ternion Mountains. I had tried several times to speak with Esgar about the events in Sommerset, but she remained distant.

Father and I had separated briefly from the caravan and were alone walking the horses to a pool of water in a gully. I decided I should open up to him concerning Esgar.

"Do you think she trusts us?" I asked Father.

"Trust is a process, son." Father replied. "If trust has been broken in her life, then the process will take longer. I assume she has had many times in her life when she has trusted others, only to have it shattered."

"So, what do we do?" I inquired.

"We wait, and when the time is right...we listen." That took me off guard.

"Listen?" I asked curiously.

"Yes. Listening is the most powerful form of service we can

provide." Father chuckled. "Do you really think everybody wants to have their problem solved for them? Most of the time, all a person wants is for someone to be quiet and let them simply speak what is on their heart. Very rarely when I am serving another person do they ever ask me for my opinion. Do you think we would have had the outcome in Rivertown if we had not simply listened to their needs?"

"I like her, Father." I completely interrupted Father's lecture and had spoken my heart aloud before I could stop myself. He stopped walking and turned to me.

"Are you sure? You just met her. Is this a physical attraction?"

"Yes, but there is something so incredible inside her as well. I can see a great power just waiting to burst forth. Am I crazy? I have not really been around women, and I don't think I know how to talk to them."

"You talk to them just like anyone else. Aleph created women to be beautiful. They exhibit everything pure and holy about him."

"Have you ever been in love?"

"Yes."

"Who was she?" Father investigated the distance, and I saw a dreamy look on his face like I have never seen before. It was like joy and pain all in one.

"We need to get the horses back to the cart." Father said evasively as he walked away from me. I decided not to press the question anymore.

It began to rain as we continued our journey north. The hills became steeper, and the horses' steady trot began to slow down. I noticed we had gotten away from the river and made mention of it to Haywood, who was in the front of the caravan. He thanked me and turned us back eastward until we could hear the waters flowing.

I was riding with Lionel that day, who described different landmarks to me as we went along. His old age had given him plenty of time to explore our world. As the waters flowed beside us, Lionel explained some amazing facts to me.

"It has been said that the four great rivers of Shalistar were formed from the tears of Aleph, as he sat on the peak of Shaddyia, the highest of the tri-peaks of Ternion." Lionel said as he pointed north. "There is where Aleph watched the great wars being fought in the ancient days. As his tears fell down the mountain, they created the Parulin, Antioch, Tabal and Analyd rivers that flow to the Southern Sea. The tears that formed the Antioch were so powerful that they cracked the Shelf in half and formed the Rift."

We decided to rest for the night beside the river. The rain had stopped, the clouds had moved on, and we were blessed with a starry night. We decided to split the night watch so that all could rest. Father went first, and Esgar had the second shift.

It felt like only minutes had passed before Esgar gently touched me and shook me awake. I awoke to see her sapphire blue eyes. "It's your turn," she spoke. I yawned and nodded.

"Okay," I said.

Esgar walked to the other side of the camp, laid down and curled up next to the fire. I took my blanket and went over to where Esgar lay. She smiled briefly and said thank you as I draped the cover over her. Then I walked back to the other side of the fire and sat down.

Everyone was fast asleep. I could feel the cool breeze blowing and hear the sounds of night everywhere. I decided to grab my journal and walk to the edge of camp. Several foxes had come out of hiding and were playing chase near me. It was an incredibly peaceful night. I looked east toward the river. Our camp was at the top of a steep cliff overlooking the rough waters of Antioch. I watched as the water flowed endlessly by. I imagined what it would be like to fall into the current. What kind of power did Antioch have to tire me out and drown me? It was a morbid thought, but I could not stop my mind from thinking about it.

"Daeric," I heard in a whisper. I jumped up and looked behind me. All my companions were sleeping. This was the same voice I had heard in the streets of Sommerset and several evenings before when I'd approached Esgar. I felt breathless in that moment, yet my entire body was filled with warmth and peace. I decided I would not be rude.

"Hello?" I asked awkwardly.

"Hello," the voice replied in a whisper. Again, I jumped back in surprise. I looked around dumbly for the source of the voice. Then I settled on the fact that the voice did not come from anywhere around me. I tried again.

"Are you a guardian?"

"No."

"Okay. If you are not a guardian then who are you?" I asked.

"I have many names. You have experienced several of my personalities, which are as vast as the treasuries of snow. My love for you, Daeric, has been since the beginning of time,"

the voice answered.

"Aleph?"

"*Yes.*"

"Aleph? The Aleph?"

"*Yes. I am.*"

"Why are you speaking to me? Why now?"

"*Because our relationship is going to be more intimate from here on out. You will hear my voice within you. I have been waiting for this moment your whole life. Now you can hear me, and we can talk.*"

"Does Father talk to you like this? Does Father hear you like this?"

"*Yes. But our intimacy will be different than his.*"

"I figured that. So... are you going to talk to me all the time?"

"*I might. Will that bother you?*"

"No... I do not think so. It is just new. I'm not used to the creator of the world speaking to me."

"*Until now, Daeric, your connection to me has been through your father and the order. But I have always desired a more excellent way of communication with all my children. Now that you are here with me, let us talk. Be honest with me.*" Suddenly, I felt surging white-hot anger boiling up within me. "*Tell me, Daeric. What's going on?*" The anger could not stop. It continued to surface on my features. My hands clenched into fists. I began to pound the ground. "*I'm here, Daeric. What's going on?*"

"Why?" I cried. "Why did you let this happen? Why are all

these people suffering? Why did the order almost completely vanish? Why were you silent for eighteen years in my life? What is the point of all of this? Why me? This is insane— you know that. None of it makes sense! One second, I am plowing the earth, the next I am running from soldiers led by demons to God knows where... to do God knows what!? It's crazy. Then all a sudden, you decide you are going to whisper to me, and we are going to talk from here on out like friends and all will be well. Well, it is not that simple Aleph! I am in pain, and you seem to have been out of the picture for a while. What do you want me to say? Sure. Absolutely. Let's do it. Let us march right into hell itself and do battle with Baelor." I decided to pause for effect. "How about I ask you a question? WHY THE HELL SHOULD I?" There was silence. That silence was louder than anything around me. Did Aleph leave? Did I make him mad? Did I go too far in my questioning?

That is when I heard it in my mind. The answer blasted forth in great power. My heart burst with emotion. The peace and gentleness that invaded my being could not be staved off with any amount of anger in all of Shalistar. I collapsed as Aleph's words were whispered to me. The weight and power of his voice made my legs give way from under me. I could feel his breath tangibly as he came near to me. The light that enveloped me as he spoke was brighter than the sun yet emitted no heat. The glory of his being was so heavy upon me I felt myself sinking into the ground.

I lay in a fetal position and could feel his awesome presence like never before. My breath was not my own. The words coming from my mouth were in a language I had never heard in the world. He filled my heart with a longing to know him more, a passion to go further, a desire to seek for deeper meaning. My head was so heavy I could not lift it. I could feel every hair on my head tingling. Then Aleph touched my heart and tears flooded from my eyes. I could not stop weeping. All I could say was, "Whatever you want. I will do it. Whatever you want. I will do it. I surrender." There was no denying anything anymore. I had no excuse, nor any right to question Aleph. Whatever his will was for me, I wanted to be a part of it. "Whatever you want. I will do it. I surrender."

"I know." His words penetrated deeper than ever. I could feel his presence through closed eyelids. He was so near to me. My skin felt like it was on fire. But the burn was not painful, outwardly. The burn was deep from within. It felt like my heart was on fire. I tried to open my eyes, but they were heavy and would not budge. I could still see the brightness of his being on the other side of my closed eyelids. Then I asked him a question. Not in anger, but in anticipation of an assignment and a yearning to please him in whatever he asked.

"What do you want me to do?"

"Come to me."

"Where are you?"

"You will find me at the top of my mountain. Walk through the door, and we will be together. I will teach you what you need to know."

"Will I be alone?"

"No. I will be with you."

"I mean, will I be alone as far as my companions? Can they

come with me?"

"Only Esgar." A cold shudder passed through me. *"Trust me, my son. Do not let fear guide your emotions. Have your heart bent toward me, and I will tell you what to do. Where you are going, your father and your companions will not be coming."*

"What will happen to them?"

"They have their own path to walk. Your Father understands this well and will not deter you from your purpose. I have been guiding your father for a long time. Trust me, Daeric." I took a moment to examine my heart. Then I responded.

"I do."

"Good. Good. Now, awake."

I opened my eyes and saw the current of the Antioch flowing by. The animals continued singing and chirping. The cool night breeze blew by. How long had I been with Aleph? It seemed like a lot of time had passed, but looking up, I noticed the position of the moon had not moved in the sky. The fire had hardly smoldered in our camp. It seemed like it had only been several minutes.

I looked across the river, and I saw it. There on the other side were two flaming swords dancing in the night, separating, and then clashing. As they clashed, a huge, brilliant flame erupted from the blades. Holding the hilt of the swords were two guardians. They were training right before my eyes. I watched them dance in combat. Their combat mirrored the order's moves—or was it vice versa? It was absolutely mesmerizing to watch these two challenge each other. Then they stopped and looked across at me. Both waved and then vanished.

I spent the rest of my watch thinking and journaling about what I had experienced tonight. I was face to face with the creator of Shalistar, the one who commands all and is all in all. At that moment, nothing else in the world mattered in the least.

CHAPTER
8

The morning came. I awoke refreshed and full of vigor. My time last night spent with Aleph had completely regenerated me for today's journey to the Rift. As we packed up camp, I noticed Esgar looking over at me. It seemed as though she had been wrestling internally. I decided now was not the time to talk to her and continued breaking down the camp.

Samuel and Father had the horses fed and bridled as the sun was rising in the east. The backdrop of the Ternion Shelf was silhouetted as the sun came up. The sharp peaks of the smaller mountain range looked quite daunting. But after last night, it felt like there was no task I could not complete today. The birds were singing as they caught their breakfast. We ate dried beef and corn cakes as we sat on the cart, about to push off. A simple, quick breakfast was all we needed to kindle the fire burning within us.

Finally, the cart began to move, and our caravan traveled north once again. As the morning turned to noon, clouds began to gather from the south. We could tell we might soon be caught in a rainstorm and pushed the horses a little harder. The foothills began to get rockier and more uncomfortable for the horses the further we went. The Antioch River became even more chaotic as we approached the North Road.

When the rains fell on us, our travel became difficult. The torrential storm blew in, draining all morale and stamina from our horses. Esgar and I jumped off the cart and covered the supplies with a tarp that we had rolled up in the back. We tied it down amid the stinging rain. The ground had turned to mud, and I slipped while fastening the cords together, falling face down into the sludge. That made Esgar laugh as she came over and helped me up. As she was steadying me, she slipped, and we both went back down into the mud.

Joy overtook us in this crazy circumstance, and we laughed together. We spent several minutes giggling on the ground next to each other before we got up. As we finally got our footing, we looked into each other's eyes. There was a feeling like I had never felt before. My stomach felt light and heavy all at once. She smiled at me and quickly lowered her gaze. Then she brought it back to rest, looking into my eyes once again. I found myself completely lost. It was my turn to look down nervously. But then I summoned a shred of courage and gazed back up into her eyes.

Samuel looked back from the front of the cart.

"You two okay?" I turned to Esgar and smiled.

"Yes. We are fine," I replied to Samuel.

I held Esgar's hand as she climbed into the cart, and she turned around and helped me up. We sat together on the tail gate of the cart with the tarp over us. The rain fell off in small rivers and splashed our boots that hung only a couple feet from the ground. Our clothes were completely drenched to the skin in water and mud. We both continued to look at our path, marked by the cart's wheels. Nothing had prepared me for the feeling I was experiencing. Being in Aleph's presence last night was amazing in every sense of the word. But this feeling was a different amazing, and it completely enveloped me. I could hear more clearly, smell more acutely, and even taste the rain in the air. My body had become completely sensitized to the atmosphere around me.

There she was, in the center of it all. Her hand was only inches from my own, and I wanted to reach out and touch it. What would she say? Would she pull away from me? Was I going crazy? I had only met her a week ago. I hardly even knew her. But at the same time, I felt like we had known each other our whole lives. I imagined how it would feel if she threw me off the back of the cart. Would I hit a rock? Break a leg? It did not matter. I could not help myself.

Esgar was sitting there staring out at the countryside breathing softly. I slowly reached out my hand and touched hers. I could feel a tremor of movement as she began to pull her hand away. I realized she was looking into my eyes. My heart was pounding in my chest, awaiting the force of gravity to take me to the ground. Esgar looked down at my hand on hers, then looked back at my face. Her lips formed a beautiful smile, and she pulled her hand out from under mine. My heart stopped. I felt a split second of nausea. And then I felt her fingers close completely around my hand and squeeze gently. A whole new wave of nausea came over me. The feeling was like a roaring fire. I thought my heart was going to burst out of my chest. When Esgar scooted over and rested her head on my shoulder, I felt a sudden release of blessed peace. I could sit here forever holding her hand and never move. The world could go completely away, and I would be satisfied. We sat together in that moment of time in a world all our own, talking about where we are going. I told her about last night in Aleph's presence and what he said to me. I did decide to leave out the part about Esgar for the time being.

As Esgar spoke, I took Father's advice and simply sat there listening. We had created a place where nobody could find us or bother us. Somewhere far away in the distance, Father and Samuel were talking and laughing as the rain poured down on them. But in the back of the cart, under the tarp, in a place known only by the two of us, I continued my first full conversation with a girl.

Hours passed in the blink of an eye. The rain had stopped some time ago, and Esgar and I continued our conversation all the way to the North Road. She did not mention much about her family except that she was from Raithe. I didn't press her for information. She told me about her love for athletics, how she loved to run obstacle courses. Her friends would play games when she was young by setting up courses around the house, and they would run them day after day. She also liked to swim and told me about how she had learned that technique. I told her I had never swum in my life, and she smiled, saying she would have to show me one day.

Then I felt a knot in my stomach and a burden to ask her about the night we found her. I mustered a shred of courage and decided.

"Esgar?"

"Yes?"

"Why were you trying to kill yourself?" I gently asked. She looked me in the eyes and held her gaze. She was searching me. I could feel it. She was asking herself questions in her heart. Her eyes squinted quickly, and she released her hand from under mine. She turned briskly away from me and looked at the road we were traveling over. Without looking at me, she answered.

"I'm not who you think I am."

"What do you mean?" I asked.

"I mean just that. I am not who you think I am," she replied quickly.

"Well then...tell me. Who are you?"

"I am putting your life in danger. I was hiding in the barn because they were looking for me."

"Who?"

"The soldiers. The Captain, Agus Tull. The foul creature he is." I decided to tell her what had happened at the tavern before we met her.

"Daeric...it would probably be best for us all if I got off the cart right now."

"I'm sorry, but that's not going to happen." I replied.

"You don't understand..." I cut her off.

"No, you don't understand. I saw you before I met you. Aleph showed me where you were. He wanted us to meet. Now here we are together. I understand you are probably scared. So am I. My whole sanctuary has been burned. All of Father's books containing our existence have been burned to cinders, and my life has been turned upside down." I could see tears start to form in her eyes. "Look...I'm sorry..." I began.

"No, you are right." She composed herself and took my hand back in hers. "I got away. They came out of nowhere and untied me, and I ran."

"Esgar...please. Don't talk in riddles. Tell me what happened," I asked soothingly.

"My family was taken captive by the magistrate. We were on holiday in Shelbye at our waterfront cabin, and they stormed in out of nowhere. We were all thrown on a cart and were being taken back to Raithe. As we were on the edge of the Elder Woods at night, a heavy fog covered everything. That was when I was cut loose and able to run away. I followed a soft voice that spoke to me from my heart. He told me where to go and what to do."

"I made my way to Sommerset and stayed hidden in the barn you found me in. Every day, the stable boy brought me food and water. Then the magistrate's soldiers came through town and wreaked havoc. The night you found me was the day the stable boy got confronted out front of the barn about my whereabouts. He told them nothing, and because they were drunk and bored...She stopped to wipe the tears from her eyes. "That was when I decided my life was not worth the suffering of all these people. But no matter how hard I tried, I couldn't do it."

"Aleph's voice was gentle and calm, telling me to put down the dagger. He told me he had a plan for me and to trust him. He told me he was sending me help, someone to lead me out. Shortly after, out of nowhere, appeared a messenger of Baelor. He was so soothing and calm. He promised me amazing power to control lives and lead the nations. He showed me a display of sorcery. He told me if I kneeled and kissed his hand, it would all be mine. That was when I spit on him and told him I would sooner burn in hell, and he grabbed me. You know the rest of the story." She finished.

As she looked into my eyes, I recalled the day, not too long ago before my eighteenth birthday. The cart had stopped before the sanctuary, and I ran out as the boy was falling. Then I saw the number of bodies in the back of the cart. There were six. My mind was now racing as I recalled the vision of the execution. In that horrific memory, I recalled that the axe fell only five times. My thoughts ended as soon as they had come. I was again looking into the beautiful face of the girl we had rescued. I looked down and saw that our hands were still interlocked. I gazed back into her eyes, and everything clicked.

"You are Princess Kristina? Daughter of Remus?" I asked haltingly.

Her grip tightened to the point of pain. She looked me directly in the eyes and spoke. "It's Esgar. You got me?"

"Yes. But…"

"Nothing more to be said, Daeric." She let go of my hand and scooted away from me. I sat in silence, looking at her for several minutes and contemplating my options in my head. Having finally come to a decision, I gently patted her hand, leaned over smiling, and whispered softly into her left ear.

"Your secret is safe with me, Your Highness."

That evening, we supped in a grove of trees. The sky was full of radiant stars, and a breeze blew gently. The rest of the caravan had gathered away from us. Father just wanted Samuel, me, and Esgar to eat alone, away from the rest of the group. I had been watching Father wrestle with thoughts that afternoon, and after camp was set up, he retreated from all of us. There was something happening inside him that I wanted to help with, but I knew he would not let me be a part of his private burdens.

Esgar sat next to me by the fire. I couldn't believe I was sitting next to King Remus' daughter! Samuel and Father sat across from us, completely oblivious to the fact that we had a princess in our midst. Father ended supper and sat back looking up at the sky. We were all quiet, letting dinner settle in our stomachs.

"I want you to know, your secret will always be safe with us, Princess," He looked right at Esgar as he said those words. She looked at me with fire in her eyes and jabbed her fist into my shoulder.

"It wasn't me!" I exclaimed. "I didn't say a word, I swear!" Esgar was about to unleash another assault on my arm when Father came to my defense.

"It wasn't Daeric. I've known for a while now." Father stated bluntly.

"How did you know?" Esgar asked.

"On your arm. You have the mark." Father pointed to Esgar's forearm." I leaned over and nudged her to show me what he was talking about. "It's okay. You can show him. You are safe with us."

Esgar rolled up her sleeve, and I saw it. It was a small brand, almost like a tattoo, of a silver star. Father continued. "I have met you before. You were much younger at the time and probably don't remember it. But you were there, with Her." I saw a look of pain come over Father's face. Clearly, highlighted from the light of the fire.

"Who was she?" I asked.

"The most beautiful woman I have ever known." He said dreamily.

"Tell me about her, Father." I nudged. I could see this was a painful memory for him. I had asked several times before about this time in his life and had gotten no response. In all honesty, I expected the same here. Father got up and walked away from the fire. "Well, that was that," I thought. He came back a moment later with several logs of wood.

"We're going to need some more fire to get us to morning." He placed the wood strategically into the fire pit and sat back down. He then looked over at me. "I'm sorry, Daeric."

"Why are you apologizing, Father?"

"Because I never told you about my past," Father said as he bent down and opened his backpack. "You must understand—it is a painful time in my life. But, nevertheless, it is important for you to hear. You need to know everything." He reached in and pulled out a rugged black book.

"I understand, Father. We can do it another time."

"No!" Father exclaimed. "We will do this now. I have to testify. If I don't, then the wound in my heart will continue to fester. After you came to the sanctuary, Aleph led me to write everything down. My story and my pain is all in here," Father said, patting the front cover of the book. "This tome has been with me your whole life. It has never been on any of my shelves, but stored safely with me in my backpack, going with me at all times. It is time I opened this book and read the contents to you."

"Okay, Father," I replied. "We are listening."

"It's not just about me, Daeric. This book reveals everything about you and her," Father said, pointing to Esgar. "It reveals Balafas and King Remus, Esgar's father. It reveals the truth about our specific order. It reveals HER. I have carried so many secrets, son. I'm sorry I never told you.

"It's okay. We are here now. Tell us Father," I concluded. Father settled himself on the ground and opened the black book. He took another deep breath, and I saw the inward battle within Father's heart come to an end. He opened his mouth, and all the nervous speech from before had vanished. For the next hour or so, I heard Father read his personal testimony from so many years ago. As he began his story, I smiled. This is my Father, whom I have loved for so many years.

PART II

CHAPTER
9

"It seems ages ago," Father began.

I was twenty-one years old and a foot soldier in Chisenhall. This was during the War of Kings, a time in our history when the noble families of the land spent years battling and spilling blood all over the world. They fought for control. It was maniacal. Every family wanted the throne in Raithe and would stop at nothing to have their heirs seated on the throne of Rian, the great King who protected the realm for many years.

His family line, though it began with righteousness, had been tainted over the years. His heirs had forgotten their heritage and went seeking temporary riches and pleasures, instead of serving the will of Aleph. This led to conquests in the coastal regions and slavery of its people. The kings listened to the short-sighted words of men in prominent positions of authority.

Balafas, the magistrate of Raithe, who held judicial order in the city, conducted meetings in private with influential people. In these secret places, they would conjure demons and bind the influential men and women within their witchcraft, spreading disorder throughout and bringing Baelor's chaos to its peak. Using magic and sorcery, Balafas, through the manipulation of the throne, had control of Rivertown and the crossroads of Cruces. Raithe could now attack.

King Tark ruled the throne of Raithe at the time. He and his son, Prince Remus, made their move on Shelbye. The soldiers there could not muster their defenses before they were taken. The nobles and their families were beheaded by the magistrate. Tark then set his eyes on Chisenhall. I was a soldier in the city guard at that time, and we were made aware of the onslaught that was coming towards our lands. We prepared ourselves as best we could.

We met Tark's army at the Bridge of Sarayu that divided the Analyd River, which flowed through the Sarayu Forest. The battle ensued for weeks until we finally fled back to Chisenhall. Tark's army could not be defeated. Their numbers grew as they continued to conquer town after town. With our backs to the Eastern Sea, we fought one last battle on the walls of Chisenhall. There was no victory that day. I watched as all my friends and our families were killed without mercy. Balafas beheaded our nobles and their families after a pathetic trial. Those few soldiers who remained alive were rewarded with a place in Tark's army.

I was young and reckless at that time and did not have many loyalties. I knew full well that to refuse was to embrace death, so I accepted my position on the lines of Tark's army. We continued the rest of the conquest without much resistance at all. Those who did were killed mercilessly. I was numb to it all, not caring one way or another. I simply kept my eyes focused forward and went with the tide. It took me back to Raithe, to Her.

◇

I was drunk, belligerently drunk, the first time I saw her. We were having another endless party to celebrate our man-made deity King Tark. We were taking turns throwing knives at peasants against a wall. I stepped up to the line with a dagger in my hand. The man who was my target was pleading with me to stop, begging for his life and the well-being of his children. After so much blood and war, I could no longer hear the cries of people in torment, nor did I feel much of anything. In a haze I lifted the dagger and looked forward, poised to throw.

Suddenly I felt soft fingers close around my throwing hand, and the sweetest voice whispered in my ear.

"Please stop," She spoke.

I was stunned. I had never felt anything like it. I could feel the wind blow through the entire courtyard, yet the leaves never wavered in the trees on this still, quiet night. Instantly, I felt all the effects of the party and the beer I had consumed that evening lift off me. I looked at this hooded woman and saw that she had several locks of dark hair falling down the side of her face. As I looked into her emerald green eyes, I was momentarily lost in her magnificent beauty. I felt completely separated from my body.

She continued to look directly at me and said with a sweet, yet authoritative voice, "I commanded you to stop. Please obey me." The words were not important. She could have told me to slit my throat, and I would have done it. I released the dagger, and it fell into the ground, hilt up. She placed her hand on my shoulder, thanked me, and walked off.

I then realized where I was. I looked in front of me at the

peasant tied to the post against the wall. I felt a sickness in my stomach and decided it was time to untie him. As I let him free of his bonds, I turned around and noticed my comrades looking blankly at me as if they were having an inward conflict of their own. One thing was for sure, we were all ice cold sober at that moment.

"What had just happened?" I thought to myself. "Who was that woman?" I looked around the courtyard for her but could not find her. She must have gotten lost in the crowd.

I continued in my stupidity for several more weeks. I had not a merciful bone in my body. I didn't care for anyone or anything other than myself. If there was someone who got in my way, I cut them down with my blade. This was the way it was with me, until that fateful day.

I was on watch, high upon the walls of the common sector of the city. Our beer allowance had been cut off due to the sluggish morale of the company I was in, which really made our blood come to a boil. My comrades and I were bored beyond belief looking into the crowded streets below. It was a busy day, regardless of the weather, and chill in the air. The city was stirring with activity, vendors going back and forth selling wares to people passing through. There were soldiers and peasants, maidens, families, and prostitutes.

Up to that point in my life, I had seen it all and experienced every form of murder you can think of, and I still ask myself to this day why I cared about what was happening below me.

There were two peasants being forced into the street by two of my fellow soldiers. I watched on for several moments with a steady grin on my face, and then suddenly I felt a burning sensation rise within me. Without another thought, I jumped off the high wall and landed with a thud onto a wooden scaffold. Carefully, I leapt from the top platform to the next level below it. I continued the process until my feet had landed on the solid ground. Without any hesitancy, I quickly moved up behind the violator and grabbed him in a tight hold.

"What the—" he cried. I tightened my grip, pulling viciously, and his body went airborne into the street. He collapsed to the side with a clang as his sword hit the stone pavement. He was immediately up on his feet with his blade drawn. He whirled around to face me and looked at me in shock.

"Anlace?" He exclaimed. "Are you out of your mind?" I had my own sword in front of me, made ready to defend.

"Why don't you move along, Roderick?" I commanded. "Leave these peasants alone." Roderick continued to stare at me, aghast.

"You are crazy," Roderick countered. He knew he could not compete against my skill and decided to sheath his sword. I never took my eyes off him for a second. He smiled at me and quickly nodded to his fellow soldier behind me who intended to put his sword into my back. I was too quick for him and sidestepped as the blade traveled forward. The tip found only air. The momentum of the thrust propelled the soldier forward as well, and I performed a vicious chop with the hilt of my sword to the back of his head. Roderick then pounced on me. The full weight of his body slammed into my side, knocking the breath out of me, and sending the two of us into the street. He was on top of me with a flurry of punches to the face.

Tumultuous thoughts coursed through me like a tidal wave.

"Why did I stop Roderick from having his way with the peasant woman? What was going to happen to me now? Am I going to have to kill a fellow soldier?" Then I heard a shout from the road.

"ENOUGH!" It was Captain Zant, my commanding officer. Roderick got off me and stood up at attention. I was a little slower to rise. I made it to my feet as Zant stopped before us. He stood there in silence, looking at the two of us in disgust. He then looked around at the crowd that had gathered to see the scene.

Zant stepped up. I could smell the beer on his breath and see what shreds of roast beef were left in his teeth from the lunch he had eaten minutes before. He opened his mouth to speak but no words came forth. That was when I felt his cold fist across my face. The blow almost knocked me off my feet. I could taste the blood pouring out of the cut he had created to the side of my mouth. Then Roderick grunted just like me as he was struck by our captain. My mind was having a hard time imagining what would happen next. Fighting among soldiers was a serious offense in Tark's kingdom.

I slowly made my way to a standing position again, and my eyes looked past my captain into the crowd of onlookers. That was when I saw her, the peasant woman I had rescued. It was Her! It was the hooded woman! I could see the same locks of dark hair falling down the side of her face! This was the one with the sweet voice who had stopped my heart from beating only weeks earlier. She looked back at me, and I saw the recognition in her emerald green eyes. She scanned quickly to the right and left without moving her head. She then moved her index finger up and placed the tip of it on her lips, signaling me not to say a word about her. In the raucous fight, she had been able to blend in with the crowd and go unnoticed.

Once again, the world seemed to stop. I could faintly hear Zant proclaiming our sentence to the crowd, and somewhere in his muddled words he called for a whipping post to be brought to the spot where we were standing. I just stood there dazed, looking into the crowd, into her eyes which totally wrapped me in a hypnotic embrace. She held my gaze for several more moments, turned away, and disappeared once again into the crowd.

I was awakened from my trance when rough, mailed hands grabbed me and threw me into the street. Roderick was thrown down right beside me with a clank. Several soldiers were on us ripping the armor and uniform from our bodies until all that remained was loin cloth covering our privates. I felt the cold air biting me down to the bone as the shivers took over my body.

Suddenly, the crowd parted, and I watched as more soldiers came into view carrying a wooden post and base, along with several hand tools. Fear began to seep into my mind as I watched them erect a whipping post in front of me. I looked over at Roderick and saw the same emotion pouring from him as well. Then our eyes met, and his look of fear was disguised by one of burning hatred. I couldn't care less what Roderick thought of me and did not look away from his gaze. Now that I knew whom I had protected from my comrades' perverse desires, I reasoned that if Zant had not broken up the fight, I would not have minded in the least running him through with my sword.

Zant continued his dramatic speech about the standards of

Tark's army. He raged on about how fighting would not be tolerated among our ranks and deemed that our punishment was to be carried out immediately. Once again, we were roughly handled by our fellow soldiers. My heart began to pound unmercifully as they pushed my chest up against the right side of the large wooden post. Roderick was pressed firmly up against the left side. Together we stood on either side, pressed against the wood, our faces only inches from one another. The soldiers then took my hands and pulled them tightly around the lower back of Roderick. They pulled harder, and I felt the rough splinters burying themselves into my skin as my hands were tied together behind Roderick. The soldiers then did the same with Roderick's hands, creating a twisted image for all to see. Roderick and I were locked in an unholy embrace. Then the slack was tightened, and our foreheads were pushed into place, with our temples buried into the wooden post.

I could see nothing but the crowd around me and Her. She was standing right in the middle of my peripheral vision. I smelled Roderick's stale breath centimeters from my mouth and heard nothing except the curses that issued from it. I sensed movement from the soldiers behind me and heard the loud crack of a whip. Fear flooded me as I awaited the agonizing pain that was about to shoot through my entire body.

It seemed like a lifetime passed in the next moment. All I could do was wait. It was agony. Yet, she was there with me. It was an odd sort of comfort, considering the situation I was in.

"Anlace," Roderick said calmly, evilly. "I want you to know you will forever be my enemy. I make it my mission for the rest of my life to take away everything from you. If we are in battle and I see an opportunity, I will murder you. I curse you, Anlace, and the ground you walk on. Go to hell you coward!"

"Fifteen lashes!" erupted Captain Zant.

The pain that followed cannot be put into words. I was so grateful that I passed out after I heard the whip crack for the eighth time.

As I gained consciousness, I found myself lying face down on a bed in the infirmary. After a quick inspection, I noticed I was all alone. They must have put Roderick somewhere else. The soft, cool light coming through the window told me it was night. I tried to lift myself up from the bed and felt agonizing pain shoot through me. I cried out and collapsed back into the mattress. My back was on fire from the lashes I had received earlier. I was sweating from every pore of my body as a fever was breaking loose. It hurt terribly to even lift myself up an inch, and when I tried, I found myself right back where I started.

I noticed the quarters were empty of all personnel, and I was about to try another attempt to rise, when I felt a soft hand on my forehead. As the contact was made, I felt a gentle warmth spread throughout my entire being. The pain in my back lessened, and I was able to think clearly. A soft, soothing voice was speaking just above a whisper in a language I had never heard before. The words she spoke were so eloquent and pure. I could feel a presence in the room I had not known was there. It was as if the presence was responding to this sweet prayer. I felt a breeze from nowhere blow across my bleeding back. As the soft wind traveled along the deep cuts, I could feel the cool breath fill the riven flesh. There was a short tremor of pain, followed by a terrible itch that I wanted to scratch. I moved to touch the gashes, and the soft hand came to rest upon the back of my neck.

"Relax," the female voice said. "Aleph is doing a mighty work on you right now. Let him finish." The itching was driving me to insanity. The owner of the beautiful voice continued to speak in the unknown language, and the presence responded once again. It now felt like a soothing ointment was being spread over each of the gashes. The itching almost immediately subsided. All I could think about now was the exhaustion that I felt, and I began to slip once again into a realm of sleep. Right before I lost consciousness, I saw the face of the voice in the room. It was her, the hooded woman with locks of dark hair. I felt her lips kiss my forehead.

"Thank you for saving my life," she whispered. "Aleph thanks you, too. You have found favor with him, and he is pleased with you. Now...sleep." There was nothing left in me. I instantly fell into a peaceful, uninterrupted slumber.

A week later, I was issued an official document to present myself before the magistrate and his court. I was to give testimony to what had happened in the street between Roderick and the peasant. At midnight, after receiving the note, I was dragged out of bed by my commanding officer and taken outside the barracks. It was pouring rain outside that evening. One look at Zant told me he meant business. He looked me right in the eyes and spoke.

"You are to tell the magistrate that the peasant started the raucous." He then grabbed me by the back of the neck and pulled me closer. "Do you understand, soldier?"

"Yes, sir." I replied.

"Good," he said and without another word, went back into the barracks.

I cleaned myself up and got back into bed. As my head hit the pillow and my breath escaped me, I had a thought in my mind I could not shake away. I knew in my heart that the thought was not anything I could dream up on my own. I was confused. Why was I having conflicting thoughts and emotions about what Zant had ordered me to do? I was a soldier, and he was my commanding officer. There were to be no arguments. I was to be obedient and follow through with the orders given to me. Any refusal or deviation from his command in court would result in contempt.

I stayed awake listening to the thought in my head. It was a simple sentence crashing through my mind, will, and emotions like a tidal wave. It was one simple sentence, keeping me from sleeping. I couldn't turn it off. When I closed my eyes, I could see the sentence written out in the darkness.

I had heard somewhere that if you had a hard time falling asleep, it was good to write. I decided to give it a try and opened my footlocker next to my bed. I pulled out my notebook and filled the writing jar with a generous portion of ink. Then I found my pen at the bottom of the container. I was now sitting up in my bed, using the light coming in from the sconce outside the window to see what I was doing.

I began writing my first sentence on the blank sheet of paper in my lap. After I was done, I gasped and dropped the pen. The sentence on the paper was not what I had planned to write. I tried again. The same text came out. These thoughts were not my thoughts. I found myself scribbling furiously with my pen trying to change the words on the paper. I wrote the same line over and over until the entire paper was filled with the same sentence that had haunted my thoughts and kept me from sleeping.

I had enough. Trying to write was pointless. I crumpled the paper and threw it across the room. Like a helpless child, I pulled my knees up to my chest and began rocking back and forth in my bed. I felt like my mind was being pulled apart. I couldn't keep any thoughts in my head besides that one. That was when I heard His voice.

"Anlace." The whisper seemed to have come from inside of me.

"Leave me alone," was all I could reply. I looked around to make sure my comrades were not sitting up in their beds looking at me like a crazy man. They were all asleep.

I waited in silence, expecting to hear the voice respond. I never heard it again that night. The one whisper I had heard was more than enough. I had never in my life heard a voice that carried such supreme authority. What I heard would have put Zant on his knees in a second. At that moment I had my doubts about whether I was really in control of my life. However, because I was a stubborn, self-seeking individual with an anger problem, I decided not to acknowledge what my heart was trying to speak to me.

I laid my head back down and made peace with the fact that the words had been permanently ingrained in my thoughts. I closed my eyes and saw again the same simple sentence that was written all over the crumpled paper in the corner of the

room. It read,
"YOU HAVE FOUND FAVOR WITH ALEPH."

CHAPTER
10

The day had finally come, and the entire city was full of buzzing. I made my way to sit before Balafas, the magistrate. I had no doubt in my mind that my soul was torn in half. I had strict orders from Zant to lie and blame the peasant, however, Aleph, or "the Voice," as I had come to call him, had invaded my inner man, making sure I would not forget the words I received the night before. They burned in my heart and mind as if they had been branded there.

I walked through the Common Sector of the city with Captain Zant, Roderick, and several other soldiers who were witnesses. As we passed the taverns and merchant stalls, I snuck a glance over at Roderick. He kept his gaze forward, never looking my way. I thought for an instant that maybe he had gotten over our ordeal, but then I remembered his words to me as we were about to receive corporal punishment for our actions. No, the insult would never be forgotten.

We came to a large gate that led into the Prestige Sector. The atmosphere had changed all around me. This area of the city held large homes and offices for the wealthy. At the far end, past the plaza, was the entrance to the Palace Sector. The stone of the streets in the Prestige Sector looked newly paved, without any cracks. The shops and homes were laid neatly side by side and built with the finest stone. All the ruckus of the Common Sector seemed to vanish and was replaced with idle chatter from high lords and ladies. It was pathetic to look at them. They walked about with their noses stuck up, talking about meaningless topics that had no bearing on everyday life.

As we continued our way to the palace, I looked over again at Roderick, but he kept that same cool gaze, looking straight ahead. The streets suddenly expanded into a clearing which held the great plaza. The plaza had been built in the shape of a wheel, with a man-made river flowing through it, in a large circle. Stone-paved walkways branched out from the center in all directions and smaller bridges arched over the water, connecting the central point to the rest of the plaza.

As I passed over a bridge, I looked in awe at the large fountain that had stood the test of time. The Guardians Fountain was built of marble, and carved into the rock were two of Aleph's servants holding the pitiful figure of Baelor down in a bowing posture. The fountain had been built by the guardians themselves. The marble was indestructible, having withstood all previous kings' attempts to destroy it. Water sprayed over the three figures in a holy arch, into the massive bowl below. The sound of the water splashing into the bowl was peaceful and serene. Hearing it made you want to stop every task and rest peacefully beside the fountain. All types of artists, musicians, theologians, and other gifted individuals were gathered, taking part in the tranquility that seemed to rest permanently in the plaza.

My escorts kept on walking across the northern bridge, towards the far end of the plaza. I stopped at the fountain and investigated the water in the bowl. Without thinking, I scooped my hand into the crystal-clear liquid and brought it back out. The cool water sprayed out in all directions as it met my face. When the water hit me, my breath left me. I had never in my life felt anything so refreshing.

The company had stopped and turned to look at me. I could see they were annoyed with my attention to other things and decided it would be best to join them in the ranks immediately. As one, we continued to approach the far side of the plaza.

Several moments later, after we had crossed the bridge, I looked up into the morning shadows of the two massive structures, the palace, and the temple. The two buildings had stood for over 2,000 years, long before Tark had been on the throne. Built in front of the southern sea, towering above every other structure in Raithe, the grandest sight in all of Shalistar could be seen for miles away. The Palace sat on the top of the Impossible Cliffs, a sheer face of rock set at a near 90-degree angle all the way down to the shores, nestled on a pinnacle of rock that stretched out over the water and overlooked the vast ocean depths hundreds of feet below.

My eyes followed a large staircase made entirely of marble that led upward to the front door and the outer courts beyond. Marble statues of the past kings were built on either side of the staircase, all the way to the top. As we made our way up and I passed these ornate statues, I noticed the care and detail that was taken to carve accurate images of the kings of old. Each one of them depicted a figure of great strength and courage. However, all that I had heard about the kings was the total opposite. They were cruel and cowardly, hiding behind religion and the people they had sworn to serve and protect.

The long staircase finally leveled out into flat solid ground, and we found ourselves in front of the palace gates. I looked up and noticed the soldiers of the palace looking down at me through the murder holes on either side of the gate. They looked at us with steady gazes. I could instantly tell that these soldiers would dispatch us in an instant if needed. The soldiers of the palace were the best in Tark's army, having gone through a harsh gauntlet of tasks to prove themselves worthy of the honor to guard the king's keep. Very few soldiers finished these trials with their lives, and those who did were worthy of the position to guard the palace and temple.

Zant stopped our march and spoke to the soldiers positioned above us. "Captain Elric Zant and company, summoned for court!" he bellowed.

After several moments of silence, the gates slowly opened inward. Together, we walked into the keep. The first thing I saw upon entering the outer courts of the palace was the great statue of Rian, the king who had saved Shalistar from The Evil One, centuries ago. It stood around twenty feet, made of marble, again by the hands of the guardians themselves. It showed Rian standing tall and proud with his sword raised towards the sky, just like that day so many years ago when Aleph had kissed his blade and set it on fire before the armies of Baelor. Many kings had also tried to destroy the statue; however, Aleph's unseen protection kept it from being harmed. Many chains had snapped, and sledgehammers had broken in any attempt to defile the statue, forever reminding anyone who resided in the palace who Aleph's chosen king was.

The palace was built in the shape of a horseshoe with the

courtyard in the center. There were three main entrances from the place where we stood. To the south, was the entry to the throne room. It was guarded by two of the strongest guards. To cross blades with one of them would certainly lead to one's death.

Huddled together in several groups were people standing outside the throne room, awaiting their time in court. Just like me, each group was chaperoned by several soldiers. The citizens in each group had a different temperament. Some were nervous, others were bored. None of them were criminals. The ones, who were to be "judged" by the magistrate, entered the throne room through another door. In Tark's kingdom, if you entered the throne room through the "Door of Guilt," it usually meant your life was at stake. As a criminal in Raithe, under the judgment of Balafas, you were guilty until proven innocent.

We waited in the courtyard for several more moments before the throne room doors were open, and there to meet us were two individuals. One appeared to be a man, dressed in all black with a glowing red band around his forehead, and the other was Balafas, the magistrate, himself. The two important men looked at the group below them in the courtyard and spoke in whispers. Balafas leaned his ear towards the dark man, and I noticed him point his gloved finger at me and nod in approval to an unheard dialogue.

The magistrate was the embodiment of stone. His chiseled face was solid. He never forced a smile or gave any indication of unnecessary emotion. His movements were precise and calculated. He knew the authority he carried. Balafas never wasted a moment on petty gestures or wasted a breath with idle chatter. He was all business. His tall stature gave him a commanding presence over those around him, including the elite guard. I could tell he enjoyed every bit of his burdensome position. At around 40 years of age, with only a handful of gray hairs in his short, jet-black hair, it would seem the office of magistrate had not taken its toll on him.

His companion had the look of a man with a sinister agenda. His chiseled arms and legs revealed he was athletic in every sense of the word. I noticed a sword that hung from the belt and made a note not to pick a fight with this figure. His flowing dark hair fell past his shoulders on both sides and was held neatly in place by the glowing red band on his forehead. The magistrate continued to whisper to the dark man, and as he listened to Balafas's words, I noticed his face cast a smirk several times at the soft-spoken words entering his ears. He looked up, and as he locked his gaze with my own, I felt something cold come over me. This man was looking at me with a sense of recognition, like he knew me well. It was as if he could see through me.

After several more minutes of hushed conversation, the two men came down the marble steps, into the courtyard where we were waiting. Balafas moved one step closer to us and addressed the crowd. "Good day to you all. I am Balafas, the chief magistrate of His Majesty. You have come here to have an audience with the court. I will now meet with you one group at a time. Once my ruling is spoken, you may leave. Be assured, whatever I decide regarding your circumstance will be carried out in the swiftest manner." Balafas turned his attention towards our group. "Captain Zant!" My captain stood immediately at attention when he heard his name called. "These instructions do not pertain to you. My inquiry for you and your misfit soldiers will be heard in the privacy of His majesty's throne room." Balafas placed a hand on the dark man's shoulder next to him. "As soon as business is concluded with this rabble, you will follow Lucien and me through those doors behind me."

It was agony to wait. Balafas was very thorough with each case presented to him. Convincing arguments were given from the groups over small claims of larceny, thievery, payments owed, and other trivial matters. As one group was dismissed and the next came before Balafas to argue their case, the courtyard became less populated, which meant I was one step closer to my inquisition. I felt sweat begin to drip from under my arms and thighs. I tried to keep a thought in my mind for longer than a second. What was I going to say, and how was I going to say it? However, my mind would not allow any sentences to stay—except for one.

The statement I had seen on the piece of paper, which flooded my soul endlessly, would not go away. "You have found favor with Aleph." This was when I started to argue with myself within my mind.

"I hope that's true," I thought to myself. "Captain made his point loud and clear regarding what he wanted me to say, yet I haven't heard anything further from you since you scarred my mind with that drivel." I waited for several moments for a response of some kind, another thought perhaps. There was nothing.

The magistrate had finished with the second and third group. Only one other group remained before me. How long had I been standing there debating my situation? Minutes? Hours?

Balafas dismissed the final group and turned towards us. "Captain Zant, you and your men please follow me." Together, we climbed the staircase to the large oak doors that led to the throne room. They slowly opened, revealing the heart of the city of Raithe.

As the doors opened to the room, the first sight revealed to my eyes were the massive marble steps leading to the lower dais. To the right and left of the hall were enormous pillars, raised to hold the base of arches which led up to the ceiling. The ceiling was constructed of oak beams flowing upward into a large dome, which flooded natural light into the keep. Large, ornate tables were set beside the steps leading to the lower dais. Here sat diplomats and historians from all over Shalistar, who happened to be in session with the king's court that day. They were all silent, writing scripts and amending documents to be read and approved by his majesty when he returned.

We waited a moment at the foot of the marble stairs as Balafas and Lucien climbed the stairs to the lower dais. He stopped at another table and removed a document. Taking a moment to scan the contents, he took a dramatic pause before lifting his head, looking at us. Lucien stood beside Balafas with his arms across his chest. After another agonizing moment, Balafas' voice boomed throughout the entire throne room.

"Captain Zant!" Hear now the instructions of this court. You will not speak unless you are spoken to and will only give information that is relevant to this case. I will not tolerate any deviations from the truth in any way, shape, or form. I hold you all under oath before the supreme authority of His

Majesty, Tark II, ruler of the realm of Shalistar and all its inhabitants. You and your men may approach the judicial table."

Together, we climbed the large marble staircase to the second floor. When we reached the top, the rest of the throne room was revealed. Straight ahead was a smaller marble staircase that led to the upper dais, which held the throne of the king, now empty. Three massive arches were cut out of the southern wall behind the lower dais. These arches were held in place by massive pillars. The southern wall was wide open to the world behind it. The ocean breeze billowed in and filled the air with the smell of salt. The expanse displayed through the arches was the great blue sea, as far as the eye could see.

Below the steps leading to the King's throne, to the right and the left were two smaller thrones. The one to the left seated Balafas, and the one to the right was, at this moment, empty. Beyond the arches to the right was a door that led to the Palace's royal quarters, and to the left was the Door of Guilt that led to the dungeons.

Lucien gestured for Captain Zant, Roderick, and me to be seated at the large table several feet in front of him. We each sat in ornately decorated oak chairs that were outfitted with a soft cushion. My heart pounded through my chest as I placed my sweaty palms on the wood of the table.

The magistrate stood up and paced before the three of us, his eyes looking directly into ours, searching within us for that most critical determining factor of guilt—fear. I felt courage rise from within me as his eyes met mine. This courage came from nowhere, and I was able to look directly back into the eyes of the magistrate without any shred of guilt. I knew the truth, and it was my hope that the courage within me would partner with the unknown words that Aleph had yet to give me. Then Balafas began to speak.

"The court of his majesty, Tark II, will now hear the details of this event. Please understand this: if any lies are spoken in my presence, you will be subject to contempt, and your punishment will be carried out in the swiftest manner. I do not tolerate liars." His speech was different in the throne room. Outside this room, Balafas was cordial and polite, with every word spoken according to protocol. Here in the throne room, however, it felt and sounded personal. There were no formalities in his speech. I knew I was in his domain. Putting any of his declarations to the test would result in severe repercussions.

"So, gentlemen," Balafas began his inquiry. "You are here for fighting?" He shot a disgusted look at Roderick and me. "That is very disappointing. How am I to maintain order and control over these subjects if my soldiers are fighting each other, publicly in the streets?! This spectacle resulted in immediate corporal punishment, correct Captain Zant?"

"Yes, sir," replied Zant quickly.

"Good. However, if I find you guilty today, that will seem like a summer holiday compared to what I do to you." Balafas looked again at Zant. "You mentioned in your report, a peasant woman."

"That is correct."

"The report stated she was harassing one of the accused and that she was quickly dealt with for the insult?" Balafas asked.

"That is correct, sir. I'm sure Roderick can give an accurate account of what happened, regarding the peasant woman."

Roderick began his recount of the event. His voice was steady without any quivering as he stood before the magistrate and lied. I found myself admiring his talent. He did exactly as Captain Zant had instructed and spoke of how the peasant had come on to him, asking him for illicit favors. Roderick told Balafas how he tried to get the peasant off himself so he could continue his patrol. Then he mentioned the peasant having a knife and suddenly lashing out at him. That was when he was forced to put her into the street.

For the first time that day, Roderick looked briefly my way and met my gaze. Instantly, I saw the white-hot flame of hatred. He continued his false testimony. "As for my fellow soldier here," he said, pointing at me. "He decided he wanted a piece of the woman and tried to keep me from detaining her."

Instantly, anger was ignited within me. Roderick was lying about my actions as well. It took everything within me not to jump up and wrap my hands around his throat. I mustered all my will just to stay calm. I was extremely frustrated with the situation that was quickly getting away from me. The voice had not spoken any words to me, and I was undoubtedly confused as to how I should proceed.

Roderick continued his monologue of lies and spewed out of his mouth false witness about me. I couldn't take it anymore. I began to open my mouth in objection, when suddenly I felt an invisible hand press against my chest with a great amount of pressure. Then I heard the voice speak to me from the inside.

"Be still," it softly said.

My mind was racing with thoughts.

"It's going to be okay."

My thoughts responded to the contrary.

"I am with you, Anlace. Right here in this room."

I thought about that for a moment and wondered why the voice did not appear.

"My time of revealing has not yet come," the voice responded.

"What do I do?" I wondered. "Roderick is lying, and my captain told me to do the same. I can't disobey his orders."

"That is true. You cannot. But I can. It is time, Anlace. We will now become one. My thoughts are now going to be your thoughts. Say what I tell you to say."

My internal conversation was suddenly interrupted, and I noticed that Balafas, Lucien, and the entire congregation were looking directly at me. Roderick had finished and they were awaiting my testimony.

I felt something. My heart pounded as though it were coming through my chest. The palms of my hands were sensitively soft and moist. I felt warmth all over my being, and with it came courage. I knew in that moment I could obey the voice, regardless of the outcome, no matter how brutal it was.

This time as I stepped forward, I did not feel the invisible hand on my chest. With my decision made, I opened my mouth and spoke.

"Your honor, everything Roderick testified to is a lie..." That was as far as I got in my testimony. Before I could say anything else, the doors to the throne room were flung open, and a cadre of the king's soldiers poured into the room. Balafas was extremely disturbed by the presence of these enlisted men and asked for the meaning of the intrusion.

Last to enter the throne room was a smaller group of men. They were a different type of soldier by the look of them. Their different colored capes told me they were from the other cities in Shalistar. Following in their wake were two final figures. One was a heavily clad knight that no person in the realm would want to tangle with. He was escorting the final attendee, a beautiful woman with long locks of flowing, dark hair and emerald green eyes.

CHAPTER
11

"Princess Iska? Why are you in the palace? This is most irregular!" cried Balafas.

"No sir! What is irregular is the fact that you are holding court for such a simple misdemeanor as fighting! Don't we allow these minor infractions to be handled by their superior officers? What is even more irregular is that you have summoned one of my personal guards to court without an authorization from me!" replied Iska.

"I don't understand," stated Balafas with a look of confusion on his face.

"No, you wouldn't. A magistrate usually has no dealings in the personal matters of royalty. Nevertheless, you have detained my personal guard, and I want him returned." She then pointed directly to me. "Hand this man over to me now!"

Captain Zant took one step forward and bowed his head. "My lady, this man is guilty of..."

"I command you in the name of the King to hand him over, now!"

Zant boldly continued his protest. "My lady, this man hasn't been properly released from my command. Papers must be signed, and an agreement must be…"

The princess cut him off for the second time. "You will find all the required papers are already on your desk. He has been promoted to the royal guard." I could not believe what I was hearing. It was all moving so fast. With a snap of her fingers, a royal ambassador appeared with another document and placed it in the magistrate's hand. Iska continued. "Another copy has been prepared for the court as well. You will see everything is in order."

All eyes were on Balafas as he opened the document. I followed every trail of his eyes as he scanned the ink on the paper. After several moments, he looked up.

"This document is legitimate. Please release soldier Anlace." Balafas commanded.

Roderick and Zant looked at each other in horror. Their plot had been spoiled. I was still reeling from what had just happened, unable to believe I had been saved. The king's daughter had just pardoned me, for it had been Her the whole time. She was the one Roderick had been forcing himself on. She had been the one in the garden at the party. She had visited me in the infirmary. Everyone watched as two of the royal guards came up to me. They stood on either side and marched me across the room to the midst of the elite, most decorated soldiers in the kingdom.

Princess Iska gracefully raised her hand and motioned for her cadre to move out of the room, with me in their tow. "The rest of the day is yours, magistrate." She then turned, and we all exited through the door to the right of the dais.

The wooden door shut, and I was escorted through many

passageways and stairwells. Then, the halls opened into the large center room of the royal quarters. The pillars that held the multi-storied levels were massive and made of dark marble. There were many passages on both sides of the great hall going off to different areas. We stood before a grand staircase that stretched to the top level.

Princess Iska stood before me. I felt so small in her presence. I had a hard time even bringing myself to look into her eyes. As I did, I noticed a beautiful smile had spread on her lips.

"Your new comrades will escort you to your living quarters. You will find all your things have been safely brought over and stored in your room for you. Please take the rest of the day to rest and relax. This evening, you will be my guest at dinner. I have wanted to thank you for some time now."

"My lady, I…" The princess gently placed her hand on my shoulder, cutting off my sentence.

"We will speak this evening. Go and rest in your new home." She then turned around and gracefully climbed the royal staircase with her two personal guards by her side. I was left alone with my new squadron of comrades.

"This way, captain." I quickly turned my head. Did he just call me captain? I decided it would be best not to speak to this, but to go with it.

We walked across the grand hall to a large wooden door. It opened, and we went down another smaller staircase, onto a hallway turning sharply to the left. There was another stairwell and another door, which opened into a living area.

The room held a large common area with a fireplace and sitting chairs. Varied bookcases were filled with literature from all over the land. Tables held dice and other games. It was an inviting, warm area that put a smile on my face. In the center of the room was a dining room table that was already laid out with plates, silverware, pitchers, and goblets. Food was being brought to the table, and I suddenly remembered that lunchtime was closely approaching. I watched servants coming to and from a door to the left side of the room. "That must lead to the kitchen," I thought. Along the back wall of the common area were four doors. Several of my fellow soldiers walked to the door farthest to the left, so I followed behind them. As the door opened, it revealed a large barracks with many beds.

There was a good amount of space between each of the beds, with bookcases and cupboards behind—plenty of storage. At the foot of the beds were large chests as well. This was a much nicer barracks than I had been in the previous night, with no moldy smell and beds that looked very soft.

I was smiling brightly and about to ask which bed was mine when one of the soldiers said, "This way to your quarters, sir." I was confused again. Why was this soldier calling me "captain" and "sir"? I decided to go with it and followed him back into the common area.

As he walked me past the other doors along the wall, he quickly pointed out their functions. "The soldier's latrine is through the second door. The captain's latrine is through the third. That door over there to the right goes to the palace kitchens. We don't really go in there. We are served directly from the kitchens by the palace servants. The food is pretty darn good, too." He stopped in front of the fourth door. These are the captain's quarters. He opened the door, and it revealed another smaller hall. There were four smaller doors, two to the right and two to the left. "Your room is the last door on the right." I looked at him blankly. "I'm honored to serve with you. Thank you for saving my lady."

He then saluted me and left my side, walking back to the first door and entering the barracks room. I slowly walked through the door and down the smaller hall to the door that led to my room. I opened the door, revealing a room of generous size. Against the left side wall was a large, wood-framed bed and a trunk at the foot. There was a nice sitting chair in the right corner of the room with a side table for reading. A small window was to the left of the table that let a good amount of light into the room. I could smell the salt of the sea coming into the room through the window. The room smelled fresh. Along the right wall was a dresser and cupboard.

I was absolutely in awe of my circumstances. I entered the room and sat down on the corner of the bed. The mattress was soft and full. I quickly got up, closed the door, and removed my outer garments and boots. Without another word, I dove headfirst into the soft bed. I had never felt anything so comfortable in all my life. I rolled over, putting my head into one of the many pillows, and before I knew it, was sound asleep.

I was awakened by a soft knock on the door to my room. "Sir, it is time to get ready for dinner with Princess Iska." I noticed the voice belonged to the soldier who had shown me to my quarters. How long had I been out for? It felt like minutes but must have been hours. I felt refreshed, like I had slept for a day.

I replied, "Thank you. I will be out in a moment."

"The lady has provided a special attire for this evening." The voice on the other side of the door replied. "You will find the clothes for this occasion in the top left drawer of your dresser." I got out of bed and opened the dresser, where I saw a set of soft garments sewn in deep blue and a pair of trousers in a dark gray. Next to the dresser was a pair of elegant shoes as well.

I put on the outfit and tousled my brown hair with a comb that was in the cupboard, trying to create a part in the middle. After several futile attempts, I abandoned the primping, tucked my blue tunic into the gray trousers, and opened the door. The soldier from before was standing against the back wall, giving me plenty of room. He saluted as I came into the hall. I was not used to this honor, but I had been in the presence of Captain Zant enough to know the appropriate commands. "At ease," I replied.

I walked up the hall and through the door into the common room. My soldiers were all enjoying the early evening around the fire, playing games at the tables and talking loudly. They created a good amount of laughter and commotion. Next to the door of the kitchen was a barrel of ale, where several soldiers were filling their mugs. I was shocked. The soldier, sensing my thoughts, replied.

"The last evening of the month, Princess Iska provides us with a keg of ale and the night off. You came into the company on a good night, sir. A remnant of soldiers is still on duty, and we rotate that responsibility among ourselves each month." The soldier gestured to the keg. "Can I fill your cup, sir? We have a little bit of time before you are expected."

"Not right now. What is your name, soldier?"

"Michael, sir," he replied. "I am your personal assistant. If you need anything at all, please let me know."

"How old are you, Michael?"

"Twenty-eight years as of last week."

"How did you become an elite soldier for the Princess?"

"Just like you. She chose me, sir. It is an honor to serve and protect the lady."

"How many of us are there?"

"In this cadre, twelve."

"How many captains?"

"We are the newest addition to my lady, and we needed leadership. You must be honored that she selected you."

"I am. Was there anyone else up for the promotion?"

"Yes. Your own captain, Elric Zant. He was recommended by Balafas himself to my lady, numerous times." I felt a cold shudder at the mention of my old captain's name. It seemed so long ago that I had been standing by his side, but only several hours had passed.

"Why don't you introduce me around?" I asked Michael.

He took me around the room, and I greeted each of the men. There was a tall, gruff man named Geoffrey. A shorter, lean, young couple of men, who almost appeared to be related, were named Gareth and Mark. Then there was a much older soldier named Lionel. Michael told me not to tangle with him. "Age means nothing, and he could whip you good."

Playing dice at the table near the fire was a group that was composed of three soldiers. Their names were Haywood, Merwin, and Stewart. Three other soldiers named Renton,

Tobin, and Fletch were asleep. Michael told me they were going to be on the night watch soon, and it would be best to not disturb them. I was sure I would have plenty of time to get to know everyone, so we moved on to a table and sat down.

"So, what exactly do we do, as soldiers of the lady?" I asked.

Michael did not meet my eyes as he responded, "Secret tasks."

"Secret?" I probed.

"Yes."

"Like what kind of secret tasks?"

"Well, our squad is the newest addition, and we have only been established for several months. That time has been spent recruiting members."

"What are we recruiting for?" I asked Michael.

I looked into Michael's eyes and saw that he was trying to stall this conversation. "Sir, it's not my place to reveal…" Our conversation was cut off as another soldier came into our quarters. He crossed over to our table and saluted.

"I apologize for the intrusion, captain, but it is time for me to escort you to the Lady's table." Michael placed a hand on my shoulder.

"You will have your answers tonight, sir."

CHAPTER
12

I looked around the grand hall once more as we climbed the staircase towards the Lady's quarters. There were servants moving with all kinds of plates, drinks, and trays. Commands were being shouted politely but firmly from the head servant, always ending in the phrase, "We're running out of time. The dinner will start soon!"

Elite soldiers were checking the trays as they passed into private quarters. There was obviously some great importance to this evening and the Lady's dinner. I instantly felt a flush of pride come over me. She had invited me to be a part of this—the Lady herself, with beautiful green eyes and long locks of dark hair. I thought about the sweet, soft voice that had spoken over me that night in the infirmary, the way she prayed, and how all my fear and pain had melted into the night. I could feel my body begin to get warm as the thoughts invaded my mind.

"Sir, we are here." A voice shook me loose from the tranquil memories, and I found myself standing before a massive double oak door with two elite soldiers standing guard. The escorting soldier nodded to his comrades, and they moved to open the door. My escort looked me in the eyes and smiled.

He then gave a slight bow. "Enjoy your evening, highly favored one."

Then with a quick turn of his heel, he walked away, leaving me standing in front of a half-opened door to the Royal Dining Room. I looked at the soldiers on either side of the door and gave a slight nod to each of them—they in turn nodded back. "Enjoy your evening, highly favored one," they stated as well.

The doors opened, and the dining room's expanse was fully revealed to me. The first thing I saw were the immense, marble pillars that framed the sides and held the high ceiling into place. My eyes traveled to the top of the room, where a large, domed glass window showed a beautiful starry sky this evening. The moon's radiance filled the dimly lit room with natural, colorful light. Such a peaceful feeling pervaded the air.

In the back of the room was a small dais, and at the top were three small thrones in front of an impressive table. These were inhabited during parties by the king and his heirs. They would observe their guests from this table and make announcements from a place of honor.

This evening, the large dining table in the center was laid out for only half the table. Several guests were milling about whom I did not know. They were wearing cloaks around their shoulders that went all the way down to their knees. One of the cloaks was white with red trim on the bottom. The other guest's cloak was white with blue trim on the bottom.

Suddenly, I heard an excited child's laughter erupt from the end of the dining room table. I saw a little girl who looked to be the age of two or three years being chased around. Upon a second inspection, I saw that it was Her! She playfully ran around in circles with the little girl. "I'm going to get you," she boomed in a silly, deep monster voice. The threat to the little girl only made her giggle more. The game continued, and I watched with a beaming smile on my face. Finally, the little girl was caught, at which point the giggling came to a climax, and the Lady lifted the little girl up into the air to give her hugs and kisses.

She noticed us standing there watching and blushed. She was slightly winded as she carried her sweet little prisoner over to us. "Captain Anlace!" That was the first time I had heard her say my name, and it just about took my breath away. "Thank you for coming to dine with us this evening!" As she came near, I stood at attention and saluted. "Oh, enough of that!" she mildly rebuked. "No formalities exist between me and Aleph's favored ones." I felt slightly embarrassed and confused. I had heard several times that evening from several people the title "Aleph's favored one." I wondered what it meant. "Please relax, Anlace," the Lady commanded, out of breath.

"Thank you, my Lady," I responded. "May I ask who this beautiful little girl may be?" The Lady had the girl hanging upside down, holding onto her by the waist.

"This is my lovely niece, Kristina! She is a whole bundle of fun! She likes apples and horses and a nightly game of tag." I reached out to shake her small hand.

She looked into my eyes from the upside-down position and giggled out the word, "Hi!"

"The honor is mine, my lady," I stumbled.

The Lady then turned Kristina back upright and placed her feet on the ground. She called her assistant over and received a handkerchief to dab her face. Her long locks of dark hair were slightly disheveled.

The assistant nodded a bow to me. "This is my assistant, Abigail. Well, we are more like sisters. We have been friends for life, and there is nobody I presently care more for than her."

I looked at the face of the assistant named Abigail and realized immediately that this was the other woman who had accompanied the Lady, the night Roderick had tried to "take her" in the street.

"You may know her husband?" the Lady continued. "He is now your personal assistant."

Recognition fired in my brain. "You are married to Michael?"

"Yes, I am. Has he helped you get settled?" Abigail asked.

"He has, thank you," I replied. "I look forward to getting to know him more over the next few months. And may I say, congratulations on your baby."

Abigail blushed at that comment and placed her hands on her protruding belly. "Yah. We are ready to come out any day now. He has been kicking up a storm. Hopefully, she decides not to be a night owl when she finally comes into the world."

"And which do you prefer? A boy or girl?" I asked curiously.

"I don't mind either. I know Michael wants a boy." He wants to name him after his Father, Daeric. But for me, I am content either way."

"Well, it looks like the two of you are hitting it off well." The Lady interrupted. "Abigail, can you please take Kristina back to her quarters. I am sure my brother is worried, wondering where she is. After that, you can have the rest of the evening off. Go home and relax."

"Thank you, my lady," Abigail concluded, and she took little Kristina by the hand. "Say goodnight to the captain."

Kristina gave a large swoop of her hand, and I noticed a small, star-shaped crest marked on the skin of her forearm. "Night! Night!" She said and skipped out of the dining room through one of the doors on the left, with Abigail several steps behind.

I then realized I was standing next to her, and nobody else was in our circle of conversation—just her and I. I could feel my throat start to dry up. I did not want to look at her, because I knew if I did, she would expect me to say something. But before I could help it, I turned and found myself looking directly into the emerald green eyes of Lady Iska, Princess of Raithe.

"My Lady, I want to thank you for everything you have done," I said nervously. "I am forever in your debt, for saving me from the magistrate."

"Anlace, you have got to relax. You are highly favored, and we may speak as friends. And besides, it is I who am in your debt. I am forever grateful to you."

We shared an awkward silence for moments. We looked into each other's eyes several times and quickly looked away before I decided to break the quiet. "If I may ask, my Lady, what do you mean when you say that I am highly favored by Aleph?"

The Lady seemed excited to answer the question. "First it means you may call me by my name and not some silly title like "my lady." So, let us try that one on for size."

She turned away from me to pantomime leaving and quickly turned back towards me with her hand out, offering a greeting. "Hello, it is a lovely evening don't you think? May I introduce myself? My name is Iska."

I took her hand gently and shook it. "Hi. My name is Anlace," I said awkwardly. "Nice to meet you my la...Iska."

"NOW WAS THAT SO HARD?" A booming, deep voice resounded behind me, and I suddenly felt a large, strong-arm wrap around my shoulder. The other large arm had wrapped around the Lady's shoulder, embracing us at the same time. We were both at the mercy of this massive intruder. I looked up at the face and saw a jovial smile covered in a thick, bushy black beard. I quickly looked over at the Lady and saw a look of pure joy, with laughter coming from her mouth.

"Jeru! You made it!" she exclaimed.

"Wouldn't miss meeting Aleph's highly favored!" Jeru then turned completely towards me and bowed deeply. "It is an honor." I took a step back from the large man.

"Okay. What is going on?!" I stammered. "This is really hard to grasp right now. Only hours ago, I was on my way to a lifelong prison sentence, and now I am in a dining room with the princess of Raithe and...you, whoever you are. I demand to know what is going on!" I just realized what had come out of my mouth and was mortified at what I had said to the princess. I bowed my head. "I apologize, my lady. My temper has gotten me in trouble quite a few times in my life. I should just keep my mouth shut. It was wrong of me to question your motives."

Several seconds of silence ensued before the Lady and Jeru

both burst out laughing. "Well, now...it's about time!" the Lady exclaimed.

"There's the spunk Aleph was talking about!" added Jeru. "I see why he favors you! Wouldn't want to cross swords with you!" They both continued laughing together.

I felt so out of place. Jeru read my thoughts and said, "Don't worry about it, Anlace. Your place is here. Consider us your family now. We are not going to keep any secrets from you. Everything will be revealed in time. You must give us the pleasure of teasing you and dragging it out a little bit longer."

"You know my name? But who are you?" I asked the stranger.

"Oh my. I apologize. My manners...I have gone by many names, but you may call me Jeru. I am your humble servant, from Aleph, the Most High. And you, sir, have found favor with Him, so He has sent me to you." Jeru bowed deeply as he finished his introduction.

"Who is Aleph?" As I asked the question, it felt like all other conversations in the room had ceased and all attention was on the three of us.

Jeru seemed so pleased that I had asked that question. "Young Anlace, that is why you are here. This next season of your life will be a season of revelation, in which The Great One will reveal Himself and show you who He is."

"Yes. But who IS Aleph?" I asked again.

The Lady interjected. "Jeru, allow me?" Jeru nodded his approval. "Aleph is your creator. Before you were in your mother's womb, Aleph knew you. He knew what you were to become. He chose you before time began and put His mark of favor upon you before you ever existed."

"Mark of approval? For what am I approved?"

"Service, young Anlace. You are favored to serve Him," Jeru continued.

"And why would I want to serve him?" I asked. The Lady and Jeru looked at each other and smiled. Jeru waved his hand for Iska to answer.

"That is not something that anyone can answer. The only one who can answer that is Aleph, himself. When he appears to you, you will know."

That conversation was closed for the time being. Jeru moved to another group in the room, giving them the same intrusive hug he had bestowed upon the Lady and myself only minutes earlier. The Lady took me around the room to meet several other guests. A tall, well-built gentleman with thinning hair from Shelbye was the owner of the white cloak with red trim. His name was Seth, and he was a gardening aficionado. He and the Lady spent some time talking about flowers of the season and different techniques for winterizing flower beds.

Next, we met a shorter but still muscled gentleman with long, dark hair graying at the sides, wearing a white cloak with blue trim. His name was Marec, and he hailed from Chisenhall. The lady and he spoke about the books they had read lately and Marec's own work in progress, a history book.

Just before we sat down, Michael came into the dining room and approached us. "Evening, sir. Everything is in order. The men are enjoying the evening now. Have you had a chance to meet everyone?"

"Yes, Michael, I have," I responded, "including your beautiful wife and unborn baby. Congratulations."

"Yes. We are excited. I hope it is a boy, so I can name him after his late grandfather, Daeric." Michael announced.

"I am sure you will be blessed, and he will grow up to be a fine young man," I concluded.

Before we could continue, the head servant for the evening announced that it was time for us to dine. The commotion in the room reached its peak because everyone was ready to eat. The servants gently moved forward and ushered us to our seats. The Lady sat at the head of the table, and I was seated to her right. Jeru was seated directly across from me, to the Lady's left. Next to me was Michael, then Seth, while Marec was seated next to Jeru.

Conversation during dinner was casual. The guests asked me where I was from and how I had ended up in King Tark's army. I thought it best to leave all the bloody details out of my story. Nobody was really interested in my past, anyway. I heard all about summers in Shelbye and how I must take some time to go there someday. According to everyone at the table, it was the premier destination for vacation and relaxation.

We continued to talk over a meal of pheasant and potato pie. Michael was asked about his unborn child and whether the nursery was ready yet. He said that he and Abigail had just finished last night. When asked about her health, he said she was very active, taking walks to prepare for the birth.

Marec shared about the historical book he was writing on the War of the Kings, beginning with Rian, the High King. He had hired a historian named Artour to help him with his research and was making great progress. He hoped to have it finished by the end of the summer. Marec was a very well-spoken individual who never wasted any words or lacked emphasis for any description. He was an astute storyteller, and I enjoyed sitting at the table listening to him.

The entire group gathered at the table was extraordinary—everyone except me! I felt so out of place even being in their presence. They all had such amazing talents and accomplishments. Each one of them carried dreams and desires with a concrete plan to fulfill them. I got lost in all that was spoken and just sat there, soaking it all in. From time to time, I looked across the table and saw Jeru looking at me with a calm smile on his face. It was as though he was seeing through me and into my thoughts. He was holding something back, waiting for something.

After dessert was cleared, the servants brought out a carafe of fine port wine from Marthyla on the east coast. This was a gift from Marec for the rest of the guests. He explained, "The sweetest grapes were grown in that area from a number of vineyards that overlooked the Eastern Sea."

I had only heard of such delicacies, never taking part in them. But here I was, sitting in the King's palace at the table of Princess Iska. The servant presented the carafe to Marec. He looked at the bottle and nodded. A small wine glass was immediately placed in front of Marec. I observed him closely and witnessed the proper way to sample this fine port.

The servant poured a small amount of dark red liquid into the glass, barely filling the bottom. Marec placed his fingers on the stem of the glass, never picking it up, and moved the glass on the table in a circular motion. The motion caused the wine to splash the sides of the glass, never spilling over the rim. He let the wine settle a moment and then raised it, looking at the areas of the glass where the wine had splashed. He said he was "inspecting" what he called "the legs." After another second or so, he deemed that the port had a "very good consistency." He again raised the rim of the glass to his nose and breathed through his nostrils. Finally, he brought the glass to his lips and took a sip. I was on the edge of my seat in anticipation.

After several seconds, he nodded again to the servant who had poured, and glasses were placed in front of all of us. The servant then poured Marec a generous amount that filled ¾ of his glass. He did the same for each of us at the table. We each took a turn sampling the port and gave a sound of enjoyment as we took a drink. I raised the glass as I had seen Marec do earlier and put my nose above the glass. I sniffed it once or twice and took a quick drink. The port's flavor exploded in my mouth, filling it with flavors of fruit, caramel, cinnamon, and chocolate. I had never tasted anything so delicious in all my life. I tipped the glass back and emptied it completely with my next drink. As the glass came back to the table, I looked around and noticed everyone looking at me, smiling.

"What?" I spoke.

"Son, that's one way of drinking port," Marec explained, "but let us just say, not the proper way. A good port is best enjoyed with small sips. It is like a dessert—don't rush it. Enjoy it slowly, as if it were the last port you will ever have." Marec motioned to the servant, and I was given another generous pour. This time I decided to follow the "Master of Wine." I took small sips, letting it sit inside my mouth for several seconds before swallowing. He was right. The flavors were so much more clearly defined in my palette. I even took to swishing it around the inside of my mouth before swallowing, and that brought even more flavor out of the wine. I was truly enjoying this new experience.

We were all relaxing and sitting back in our chairs when the Lady called the head servant over and thanked the servants for all their hard work. She gave them the order to take tomorrow off for rest and asked them to leave us alone for the night. The servants in turn thanked the Lady and dismissed themselves through the side door that led to the kitchens. When we were completely alone, the Lady stood and addressed the group.

"I thank each of you for being here this evening. Your attendance is most important. I thank you, Father Seth and Father Marec, for coming a great distance to be here today. We have had such a wonderful time in conversation and fellowship over an amazing meal. But now we must attend to the business at hand."

I saw a look of pain come over The Lady's face as she looked at each of us. It was as though a shadow had crept into the room, and all the joy and laughter was frozen in time. I saw Princess Iska age five years in the blink of an eye. She leaned forward over the table and placed her hands on the solid wood to steady herself. Jeru reached out and placed his hand over hers, comforting her.

For a second, I thought she was going to fall over, but she remained steady and straightened herself. "I am sad this evening. I knew this moment would come. But it doesn't make what I have to say any easier."

"We are with you, Iska," Seth encouraged her. "Aleph has

brought us together for such a time as this. Please tell us what is on your heart so we can share the burden together." The Lady looked over to Seth with tear-soaked eyes and smiled.

"Thank you," she replied. "You are all so special and important to me right now. I can't do this without you." She then looked right at me with her beautiful emerald green eyes. "I can't do this without you." A heaviness dropped into my heart. Along with that came warmth and a wave of courage. All I wanted to do was help this woman and stand by her side. Before I could stop myself, I reached out my hand and placed it over hers, just as Jeru had done earlier. Feeling the warmth of her skin made me dizzy and overcome with emotion. I think my touch did the same for her, because she began crying more and smiled simultaneously. She looked at me again and mouthed the words, "Thank you."

Several moments later, she straightened herself and addressed the group seated alone in the royal dining hall. "Friends. It is with great sadness that I must tell you our world is coming to an end."

CHAPTER
13

Across the table, the news swept us up and took our breath away. We sat there motionless, letting that word settle into our hearts. The finality of it was overwhelming. After moments of silence, Michael spoke. "How do you know this?"

"Aleph has shown me," replied Princess Iska. "For over half of my life, I have served Him. He has shown me visions as I walk around in the day and given me dreams during the night. I have known for some time what my purpose in His plan was to be. It is now clearer than ever before that the fulfillment of my purpose is drawing near."

"Please, Iska. Can you speak plainly to us?" Seth asked. "Tell us about your purpose and what you mean when you say, 'Our world is coming to an end?'"

The Lady looked over at Jeru, and I saw him nod his approval. She then took her seat and removed her hands from beneath mine and Jeru's. "Aleph has charged me to usher in the end of days. I am to establish his leaders and prepare a safe path for the chosen one. That is what I have written in my journal and reflected upon with Aleph for as long as I can remember. You gentlemen sitting here at this table are my leaders. This one here," she said, gesturing to

Jeru. "He is a guardian, sent by Aleph to facilitate the end of days." A burst of excitement exploded from the table at the mention of Jeru. All eyes were upon him as I calmly raised my hand.

"What is a guardian?" I softly asked. Another abrupt sound of excitement erupted from the group as I asked my question. Jeru simply raised his hand, and all went quiet immediately.

"You gentlemen must understand, not all of Aleph's highly favored ones come from a studied background," rebuked Jeru. "Young Anlace here was raised in an environment far from the truth of Aleph. The words of life were never allowed to enter into his ears. He has only known of survival and has lived a life in the pursuit of self, as have many others in times past. It matters not to Aleph. He chooses who He wills and reveals himself to them in His own way."

Jeru then turned to look directly at me. "Your question is good. I appreciate your honesty, and I will respond. A guardian is simply a servant of Aleph. We go where He tells us to go and do what He tells us to do. We serve his chosen people and protect them from the enemy. Those who know the heart of Aleph and obey his commands can also command us."

"How old are you?" I continued with my questioning.

"Ageless. I have no age. The only existence I have is in Aleph. Aleph is ageless. Before the beginning of time, He was." Jeru saw the puzzled look on my face and decided to help me. "Don't worry Anlace. Your brain cannot comprehend it. It is far above even my understanding."

"So, you are a servant?" I asked.

"Yes. I am a servant of the light. I am here to put men

into place before the end of the age." Jeru stopped suddenly and thought for a moment. He made some kind of mental decision and stood up. "I tell you what—allow me to give you a peak of the light. I think seeing is worth a thousand words. If it is too bright, you may want to cover your eyes."

Jeru then stood up, and a piercing, blinding light began to radiate from his being, as if he were surrounded with light. The light also came from inside him. I had never seen anything so bright and beautiful in all my life. The light went into every corner of the dining hall, illuminating the darkness. I had to cover my eyes from the brilliance. And then it was gone. We all sat back in silence, trying to comprehend what we had just experienced.

"I have known Jeru all my life," the Lady stated calmly. "He has come to me on several occasions, to serve me and help me." We were all coming back to the reality of the situation and asking each other if we had just seen the same thing.

"Truly, you are from Aleph!" Marec burst out. "All hail the Creator!" Marec jumped out of his seat and began to bow before Jeru.

"Stop this at once!" He harshly rebuked Marec. "I am NOT to be worshiped! I am a servant. Do not bow before me!" Marec was taken back by the rebuke, and a sorrowful look came over his face.

"Aleph, forgive me!" Jeru quickly placed a hand on the weeping, broken man at his feet.

"It is understood. But the power and light you saw was not my own. That comes from Aleph. He alone is worthy of our admiration." Jeru reached down and took a staggering Marec by the arm, lifting him up onto his feet. He then gently helped him collapse back into his chair.

I was completely in awe of what I had just witnessed and heard. The world I knew had so quickly been tipped upside down. So much had happened in a brief period of time. I still had so many questions to ask. I directed my next question to the Lady.

"Tell us more about the end of the age?" I felt so full of courage and strength at that moment. I felt awake and my senses were heightened. I was ready to learn more.

"Aleph is a creator. He is an artist and an engineer. He has created the heavens and the universe around us. Shalistar is not the only world, for He has created thousands of worlds within universes.

"Marec," Lady Iska said, looking to her left. "The vintners of Marthyla, they are the best in the world at what they do? They grow grapes and produce wine. Is there any better?"

"No ma'am. Not to my knowledge," Marec stated, still slightly out of breath.

"It is the same with Aleph. There is no better creator than him. He is a master at His craft. He creates worlds. He creates a world with every living creature, including man and woman and then allows the world to play out until the end. Our world is at its end."

"How do you know this?" questioned Seth.

"It has been revealed to me."

"No offense, my Lady," Michael carefully stated. "But why has none of this been revealed to the King?"

"My Father is selfish. He has always been about the pursuit of Himself. Ever since my mother died, he has gone further inward, caring less about his family and more about his conquests. I have made peace with it. Aleph has been my comfort."

"What about Prince Remus?" asked Michael.

"Remus is captured by fear. He is afraid to speak up to Father and wants no conflict of any kind on his doorstep. He would rather bury his head in the sand and pretend that nothing is happening."

"That's a shame," concluded Seth.

"With Father out conquering land and a Prince struck with fear of his own shadow, our kingdom has been left in the hands of a magistrate who has been holding secret meetings." Commotion began to boil among the inhabitants at the table.

"What kind of meetings?" asked Marec.

"I have sent spies to infiltrate the ranks of society over the past year, and they have dined with those in the prestige sector. These people of influence are led by none other than our magistrate himself, Balafas. They have come back with reports of unspeakable evil. These meetings are used to conjure demons from hell and receive the power of magic. The prestige has bowed before minions of Baelor and received these gifts in these meetings." I will not go into more detail, for it is truly appalling what happens in these rituals. I will say that what was once in secret is now coming out into the open."

Iska closed her eyes and shook her head. She struggled with the next part of her report. "Some schools are entirely dedicated to the distribution and education of magic. Baelor's gifts are being given to our children!" There was a groan of despair from the group. "Seth, perhaps you may be able to give us a better understanding about what we are dealing with here."

Seth leaned forward and spoke. "Some of you may or may not know this about me. When Aleph found me, I was surrendered to Baelor and practiced these dark arts myself. I was completely enthralled by the power and manipulation of it all. It is nothing I look back on with pride, but I believe it needs to be said, and I may be able to help us understand more about our enemy." Seth took a deep breath and continued his explanation. You could tell it was not a happy memory for him, and he had a hard time relating the story.

"I was adept at Conjuration and Alteration. I had learned many spells. I always loved to levitate and open locked doors with my mind. I enjoyed manipulating the thoughts of others, but the greatest high I had was in conjuring spirits. Demons from the other realm. It took the most out of me and was a great challenge but was the dark art I favored most. The spirits would speak to me and tell me things about others—secrets that only they could know. They would do errands for me as well." Marec leaned forward.

"Did you ever learn the art of Destruction?" he asked.

"No. I never had the courage. I don't really care too much for fire!" Seth replied. "I was always afraid I would lose control and set fire to my own house." Everyone laughed, Seth included. But he quickly regained his composure and continued. "As funny as that seems, it is very real. You can learn to summon fire, hurl it at an enemy, and burn them alive. This is not a joke, people. These spells are an abomination, and it just about destroyed my life and the life of my family. These powers come into you, and you feel strong! But what you find at the end of this road is an emptiness. There is no end to the want! You cannot ever have enough. You must have more and learn more. You must open yourself up to more spells so you can be more powerful! And then, Baelor sends a messenger." Seth was really having a hard time with this part.

"It's okay, Seth. You don't have to tell us." Michael placed his hand on Seth's shoulder to comfort him.

"No. You need to hear."

Seth began to tell us about a moment in his life in which he met a demon face to face. "When the messenger comes, it's not friendly. It is not polite. I remember it clearly. I was levitating right outside of town in the dark of night, so nobody could see me. I had gotten about 30 ft from off the ground, and my power was starting to wane. That is when I heard the loud piercing screech in my mind. I felt like my head was going to explode. I clamped my ears with my hands and screamed, but the pain in my mind wouldn't end.

"Then I saw, as clear as day, the demon levitating right in front of me. Its taloned hand wrapped around my throat, choking me!" Seth's face clouded over in a look of horror. "The voice that came from the demon was from another world, not this one. "SURRENDER!" It screeched. "SURRENDER, AND ALL THE POWER IS YOURS!" I looked into the face of a hideous creature with glowing red eyes. It looked like a raptor with a long beak full of razor-sharp teeth. "SURRENDER!" It screeched again. I was terrified and couldn't speak.

"I could feel my power failing, and I looked down in terror, afraid of falling at this height. I opened my mouth to say the words the demon commanded me to say, and then all the sudden, there was a flash of brilliant light. The demon screamed, "HE'S MINE! GO AWAY!" I couldn't see who the demon was addressing.

"Again, there was another flash of light, and I felt the grip around my throat release. I took gasping breaths of air, grateful for the breath of life filling my lungs. I was completely spent from the encounter and felt like I was about to pass out. Then, I remembered I was still levitating in the air. The demon screeched one last time and then was gone. All the pain in my head immediately subsided. And then I realized, to my horror, my power had run out and I was falling. I screamed as my body fell and screamed again as I heard the dry snap of the bone in my right leg being broken when I hit the ground. My parents heard me screaming and found me. Of course, I did not tell them the truth of what had happened.

"That week, Aleph appeared to me and told me he had greater responsibilities to offer me. I surrendered my life to Him, and the rest is history." We were all on the edge of our seats as he finished his testimony.

"I say all this to tell you. This is not a joke. Baelor cares nothing for people. He will entice them with spells and incantations. They will dabble a little and then hunger for more. Baelor will continue to give them what they desire until he has them completely. Then, he sends the messenger. At that point there is no way out, and they surrender. Yes, they will receive more power. But they will find themselves a slave to an unmerciful master. He will then rule them through fear. He will send messengers to torment them into doing his will, threatening to remove their power and prestige if he is not obeyed. With no other choice and the desperation of an addict, they will surrender, and then it will be too late.

"This is a dangerous enemy, not to be taken lightly." Seth concluded his remarks and sat back. He looked tired. Michael leaned forward, addressing Jeru.

"Why doesn't Aleph just stop this?" He asked.

"Young one, that is the question most asked of Aleph. Why, if he is the creator of all life, does he let these things happen? The answer is simply this. He prefers true love over automation. He wants someone to come to him out of love and choice. He wants the people to have that choice. When they surrender to him, then they have chosen to love him by choice. That is true love. A love of choice.

"Baelor, on the other hand, cares nothing of love or choice. All he wants to do is conquer. He will force submission on you no matter what the cost. He will break you and bend you until you have no other choice but to surrender. You are nothing but a trophy for him—a trophy that is his and not Aleph's." Michael decided that the answer was sufficient and sat back.

"We are here at this table to discuss a strategy for these final days." Iska began. "Our enemy Balafas is influential in the spread of this doctrine. My Father is blinded to it, and my brother is too afraid. I have my suspicions that he may be compromised. With this growing threat, I would like to propose the addition of the Final Order!"

CHAPTER
14

Commotion reached its peak, and the Lady had to calm everyone down. "Please, let us stay on task here. I understand your hesitancy. But the need is here, and the time is now. I think it is time we take a moment and reveal to Anlace the identities of his fellow members sitting at this table." I looked around at each of the men and a thousand questions entered my brain all at once. As if she read my thoughts, the Lady continued.

"I know you must have a lot of questions. Allow me to help you. You have heard me address Seth and Marec as "Father," correct?" I nodded my acknowledgment. "Since King Rian's reign, he established a secret order that would serve the crown, but most importantly, carry out the will of Aleph. This elite group would carry out missions of the utmost importance and fight beside him on the battlefield whenever he called for them. They are to this day known as the Order of the Elect. King Rian had these fantastic soldiers disperse to the east and west, with his orders. They were to secretly remain in their sanctuaries, waiting for orders from the King.

"It was like a well-oiled machine for many years. From one king to the next, the order continued—one sanctuary in

Chisenhall and one in Shelbye. From one generation to the next, members were sought after and placed within the order. Those members in the Order would grow in strength as they waited to hear from the King. They would master sword craft and battle tactics as they studied the Will of Aleph. It was truly a high calling.

"As time went on, kings became more corrupt and self-seeking, and the order was almost forgotten. Then came the Age of Renewal, and the order was reborn with more strength than before." I raised my hand to interrupt. Again, the Lady read my thoughts and replied. "That's a long story for another time."

She then continued. "I don't want to lose you in this explanation. So, sitting next to you are Father Marec and Father Seth. They are the current Masters of the Order of the Elect. Father Marec is from the sanctuary in Chisenhall, and Father Seth is the current Master of the sanctuary in Shelbye." I looked at both and they nodded to me, reintroducing themselves. "I have asked them to be here today because I believe that the time is upon us to open the Final Order of the Elect, and I require their blessing to proceed. Up until this moment, only two sanctuaries have been in existence, but the time is upon us for the third."

"What is the significance of the third sanctuary?" Michael asked.

"The third sanctuary is to be established to protect the chosen one until he is called out." The Lady continued as she looked out over mine and Michael's puzzled faces. "I know this is a lot to process, but you have to trust me, and Aleph has sent Jeru here to endorse my words." Jeru leaned forward to speak.

"Lady Iska speaks the truth. She has been given Aleph's wisdom and has been allowed to see into the future so that she can be an effective leader. Aleph has not shown her everything, but only what she needs to move forward. Have no fear in following her, my friends. She will not lead you astray."

"Who is the chosen one?" I asked.

The Lady continued, "The chosen one will go to Aleph himself and be trained. Not since King Rian has Aleph spoken face to face with any of us. The training we have has only been a shadow of what is to come. But the chosen one will find a way to Aleph and sit before him. He will be taught all that is needed and come back to us with the knowledge, rallying a final remnant to defeat Baelor and his minions once and for all." All of us leaned forward on the edge of our seats, waiting to hear more.

"Have you seen who the chosen one is?" Marec asked. Lady Iska nodded her head gently and looked directly at Michael with tears of joy pouring out of her eyes. "Congratulations, Michael."

Everyone's eyes were on my new friend sitting next to me. "What? No. It can't be." The understanding and immensity of the situation flooded Michael, and he stood up and stepped away from the table. His hands were rubbing his temples as the information seeped into his brain. He quickly turned back around. "My unborn child is the chosen one?" He asked this question looking not at Lady Iska but at Jeru, seeking an answer from the source, Aleph.

"It is true, Michael. You and Abigail have found favor with Aleph, and he has blessed you both with a son. This boy will do and see things nobody in this world has seen or done, and he will learn from Aleph Himself. It is the highest calling of this age, and it is my honor tonight to share this wondrous news with you."

"I don't know what to say. I'm completely at a loss for words." Michael stumbled back to his chair and collapsed into his seat. He sat slumped with his hands on either side of his face. "Why us? We are nobodies. Not royal blood, we have very little. It doesn't make sense."

"Maybe not to you," Jeru encouraged him. "Aleph does not see men and women like we do. You say you are small, but Aleph has put something great into you and Abigail. He has revealed many things to you over your life span, but then there are other things he put into you that have remained secret. These are the mysterious gifts that only Aleph can bring into the world and only he can see them. You say you are small, but Aleph has made you great. You say, "Why me?" Aleph says, "You are chosen." Most everything about Aleph is a mystery to the world and is only revealed to his most beloved. You and Abigail have spent your lives in service and pursuit of HIM. Because of that, you are favored and have been chosen to bring young Daeric into the world." Michael's head shot up with bright eyes at the mention of his son's name. "That is correct. It is a good name you have chosen."

Michael took a few more moments before speaking again. "Will the enemy know of his existence?" Lady Iska answered the next question.

"Yes, which is why we are all gathered here today. We need to establish the Third Order. This sanctuary is where Daeric will be raised until it is time for him to go find Aleph. I have spent time gathering its members into my circle of trust. All that was missing was its Master. Until tonight."

I realized at that moment that she was looking at me. "Me? A Master? Clearly you are mistaken. I am nothing like Seth or Marec. I have a bad temper. I run into situations before thinking. I am not a strategist. I don't even know who Aleph is!"

Jeru leaned forward. "Which is exactly why Aleph has chosen you. You are a clean slate. You have no preconceived ideas as to who He is or what His will is. He can use you. Just like Michael, you feel unworthy, and that is okay. None of us is worthy. It is He who makes us worthy. It is He who brings us through everything, and when we come out the other side, we are changed. Aleph knows what you will look like when you come out the other end, Anlace. And what he sees is a strong, confident, patient, and prepared man, full of wisdom and knowledge. Do you think Seth and Marec were anything like they are today? No! They were both stubborn and quick to anger. They never wanted to face problems and ran the other way. Aleph has shaped and molded them over the years into mighty men of valor. He will do the same for you.

Thoughts of my future and what it might hold were clouded, and I had a hard time in that moment wrapping my head around the weight of what had been revealed. But something in my heart yearned for more, and a clear thought made its way to the top of mind. "What do I do?" I asked Jeru. The question made him smile.

"You say, 'yes' and Aleph will take care of the rest," concluded Jeru.

"Yes," I replied, though little did I know at the time what that meant.

Lady Iska smiled and continued, "You honor us all with your decision." The Lady stood and stepped away from the table. She gestured for me to join her. I slowly got up and walked over to where she was standing. The Lady then asked Jeru to join us. A massive smile beamed from his lips as he came over. "The sword, please?" the Lady asked Jeru, holding out her hand. Jeru unsheathed a beautiful sword from his scabbard and handed it to the Lady Iska, hilt first. The Lady turned to me and asked me to kneel before her.

My breath had completely left me, and I felt as though I were in a dream. Knowing there was no turning back, I got down on one knee and bowed my head.

"Join me, friends," the Lady asked of those in the room. They each drew closer. "Let Aleph kiss this blade, and may His glory be upon you now and forever." I looked up to see a flash of light, and the tip of the blade that Lady Iska held ignited into flame. Everyone around me had their hands stretched out towards me and they were speaking to Aleph in another language I had only heard once before, when the Lady had prayed over me in the infirmary.

They continued speaking in this unknown language together. I felt the power of the words I did not know and realized this was an important moment. The words they spoke were inviting Aleph to come and be a part of this. I closed my eyes again and leaned my head down, exposing my neck to the Lady. "I pray that the love of Aleph penetrates deep into your heart. I pray the wisdom of Aleph guides your thoughts, and the strength of Aleph moves your body as you surrender to him every day, from now until you stand before him face to face. May His favor always be upon you and His life course through you.

"I proclaim before all eternity, that this day, before friends and witnessed by the guardians themselves, you, Anlace, are Father of the Chosen. You will be the Master to watch over the sanctuary housing the chosen one until Aleph calls him out into the world. I speak prosperity over you and the members of your order. I bless you all in the name of Aleph, the author and finisher of your story!"

I felt the warmth of the blade as it came near. I kept my eyes closed but could feel the tip only centimeters from my head. Then the blade touched, and I felt the warmth of the flame come into my being. It began from the top of my head and spread all the way to the soles of my feet. I was filled with warmth throughout every part of my body.

My thoughts became clear at that moment. There was no more confusion. I knew who I was and what I had to do. I was caught up, and my spirit left my body. I was taken into the future, where I saw the sanctuary on a hill overlooking a town at the crossroads. I saw circular pits and men fighting in them, training for combat and battle. I saw myself walking amongst these circles, instructing these men in the correct stance and technique. I saw myself sitting at the head of a table, laughing merrily with these men all around me. As I was sitting at the table, I looked up and saw the sky above me as though there was no roof over my head, and I saw a garment floating down. The wind was whipping the fabric back and forth, and I stared hypnotically as the garment came closer. I could see it clearly now and recognized it as a white cloak, except at the very bottom was a trim of emerald green. The cloak slowed its fall and draped itself over my shoulders. Then I heard the voice, so soft, but the weight of it could shatter a mountain.

"Thank you, my son. Thank you for saying yes."

Suddenly, the dream ended, and I found myself back in the room, my spirit returned. How long had it been? Only moments from what I gathered. Everyone still had their hands outstretched. The blade had just lifted off my forehead. I looked up and saw my Lady's beautiful green eyes staring deep into mine; she was absolutely overjoyed with what had just happened. Then I noticed something had changed. I felt something, like a garment had been placed over me. I looked at my shoulders and saw I was now wearing a white cloak flowing all the way to my knees. I took the fabric in my hands and moved the soft folds of cloth through my fingers. There at the bottom of the cloak was a line of emerald green trim, the same color as Lady Iska's eyes. I looked next to me, and Michael had the same shocked look on his face, as he was holding the same cloak in his hands. It seems my friend had received the same gift from Aleph's presence and was holding it in awe.

Then I heard the booming voice of the guardian standing next to Lady Iska. "It is confirmed! Aleph has clothed you both with power! You are now Father Anlace, Master of the Order of the Elect!" Everyone cheered and praised Aleph all around me. Jeru came forth and offered me his hand. As I took it, he pulled me up and into his arms. I was completely buried in his mass as he gave me a grand hug.

"He is so proud of you, do you know that. He looks forward to getting to know you intimately and personally, Anlace. He will not be the father who abandoned you. He will show you that he is the Father who knows you best." The hug ended, and I was met with more affection from my fellow brothers in the order. Marec and Seth both hugged me and gave me their congratulations. Then Michael came and offered his support. I, in turn, congratulated him as well and helped him put the cloak over his shoulders.

We were all in high spirits and spent the rest of the evening getting to know each other a little more until the Lady dismissed us for the evening. The last word she said that evening was to me. "I am glad Aleph chose you, Anlace. I look forward to working closely with you. I will send for you tomorrow afternoon. We have a lot of work to do in a short amount of time."

Those words of gratitude from my Lady made me feel warm inside. My stomach churned at the thought of spending time with her tomorrow and working closely with her in the days ahead. I decided it would be best for everyone if I simply turned off my emotions for now. To be working near the Princess of Raithe was a serious charge, and I needed to keep my wits about me. I decided from this moment forward, I would put aside any feelings I had for her and keep to the business at hand. But what I realized is this was much easier said than done.

CHAPTER
15

The rest of the summer flew by in the blink of any eye. So much had happened in a short period of time. Daeric was born only a month later and Michael had taken up residence at his home in the city with Abigail. This left me with a lot of day-to-day responsibility with the elite soldiers that would normally fall on Michael, my first in command. I did not mind, though. The soldiers respected me, and it made my job much easier. Everyone knew their job and did it with excellence.

The Lady had taken great care in selecting the members of my team. They were hard-working strong men but humble as well. They all loved Aleph and had given their lives to Him. I took the next several months learning from each of them and hearing their testimony of how Aleph had revealed himself to them. Some stories were dramatic, to say the least. It was an honor to lead these warriors and serve beside them.

Day after day we would walk the palace and the city in observation. My eyes were opened to everything around me. It was like a shadow over my eyes had been removed, and suddenly, I could see. Life was bursting at the seams in all areas of Raithe.

As I patrolled with my men, donned in my white cloak—the one that Michael and I hardly ever removed—I was observing life. Aleph's handiwork could be seen in everything and everyone. It was all so overwhelming—I could see Him everywhere. He spoke to me, too. We would have long, inward conversations.

Lionel, one of my favorite soldiers, though the one you would not want to cross swords with, had taught me how to listen to Aleph's voice. He said, "Aleph sounds a lot like us. Often you will find yourself mistaking His voice for your own. It takes time, but when you quiet your mind, you will hear him clearly." So, I learned over the months how to quiet my mind and listen to His voice, speaking from within. Lionel was right--it did sound like me.

Daily patrols were a great time to walk around and listen, not only to the bustling city around me, but to the soft voice of my creator inside me. He would tell me all sorts of interesting things about people. I was enthralled with this gift I never knew I had. I didn't say anything out loud, but just kept the inward dialogue going.

If we weren't patrolling, we would train in the barracks courtyard. If I wasn't training, I was taking a trip up to the crossroads to oversee the construction of the sanctuary. Little by little, the building was coming together. I was excited every time I came up the hill and saw the progress. One day soon, this would make a fine home.

The routine continued day by day, month by month. My favorite time of day was the afternoon. That was usually when

I was relieved from my shift and met with Princess Iska.

She and I met regularly throughout the week as well. Each meeting was different. Sometimes it was she and I in the garden, just walking and talking about the progress of the construction of the sanctuary. Other times we would be interviewing her spies in the dead of night, who had infiltrated the secret meetings. Iska called for me at all hours of the day, and I never minded in the least. As time went on, my feelings for her had grown stronger, and I couldn't wait to be around her. Whenever I saw the escort come into view, I always smiled because I knew he was coming to take me to her.

I had never felt this way towards another person in all my life. I had heard about being in love and even read about it in books, but to experience it was another thing entirely. I thought about her all the time and what I would say when I finally did share my feelings with her. I did not have to wait that long at all.

On that fateful evening, we were meeting with our spies in the royal office in the dead of night. They were extremely anxious about recent events and needed a great amount of encouragement to continue. The description of the most recent meeting left me with a sick feeling in my stomach. These leaders were performing detestable rituals in the darkness, right under our noses. I erupted during the meeting, and my temper flared. "Why don't we raid these meetings and put an end to it? What they are practicing is an abomination!"

Iska wisely answered. "Anlace, please sit down and calm

yourself. If we were to go in now, we would not be dealing with this evil by the root but merely stoking the flames and causing more rebellion. What we are seeing is only the surface. Our battle is not against flesh and blood, but against the unseen forces of darkness from Baelor himself. The way forward must be carefully planned out and executed with caution. The enemy is already entrenched in our society, but even worse in the minds of our youth. The youth are hungering for these powers. We must be watchful because around every corner is deceit."

I received her rebuke and turned to Hamlin and Margaret, the spies who were with us. "I apologize for my temper. The Lady is wise in her words." I sat down and let them continue with their briefing.

The report only confirmed her words even more. We were playing a dangerous game, and the spies across from us were afraid. I could see in their eyes how tired they were. Hamlin and Margaret had been in the Lady's service as spies for more than a year now, and it was taking its toll on them for sure. The married couple feared for their lives. Iska encouraged them to hold on only a little longer, and after several hours of ministry, they agreed. The atmosphere was heavy as they were dismissed and the door to the office closed. Iska looked up at me after they had left. Her eyes had started to form "bags" under them from sleepless nights. She was weary.

"I can't do this, Anlace!" She began to weep. These are people with families we are sending into the putrid darkness. I can't take much more of this!" She cupped her hand over her mouth to keep a cry from coming out. It didn't work, and she began weeping. I couldn't stand to see the woman I loved in pain. I stood up and moved over to her, holding out my hand to her. She took it. As her hand clasped mine, warmth spread throughout my entire being. She began to weep harder. She struggled to stand, and I helped get her onto her feet.

We were within an arm's length of each other. She looked into my eyes, and I could see that she wanted me to hold her. I put my arms around her, and all the remaining strength completely left her. She collapsed into me, weeping. I held her closely, telling her repeatedly that it was going to be alright. She stayed in my embrace for several moments and then wrapped her arms tightly around me, returning my embrace.

"Oh, Anlace! Thank you for being here. I couldn't do this without you," she cried.

"I'm here, Iska." I replied.

"We are sending these people to death! You know that, right? It's only a matter of time before Hamlin and Margaret are compromised."

"It's going to be okay," I continued to console her.

"If not now, someday soon. They are going to be revealed, and then what?"

A knot was in my throat, and my legs felt like jelly. As Iska continued to rant, I held her closer. My heart was beating so fast I thought it was going to come out of my chest. I couldn't go another moment without her knowing my feelings.

"What are we going to do then, huh? They will be compromised!" She continued. "They will be compromised, and it will be all my fault!"

The agony of my feelings coming to the surface was too

much to hold. I was losing this battle fast. "Iska…" I began.

"They will not be merciful if they find out they are spies." She continued not hearing me.

"Iska!" I said boldly and loudly, getting her full attention. Her tear-soaked eyes were locked into mine; it was now or never. "I love you." Iska just looked at me with her mouth slightly open. There were more than several dreadful moments of silence. "Is she going to reply?" I wondered. "Did I just doom this relationship? Can we ever go back from this moment?" And then she responded.

"Thank you," she replied, looking away from me. I could see she was shocked at what I had just said and needed a minute to process it, but I was filled with courage, and nothing was going to keep me from making it very clear to this woman the depth of my feelings for her. I adjusted her position in my arms, looking right into her emerald green eyes and spoke again.

"I love you, Iska," I said to her boldly. Again, she looked away and then came back to staring into my eyes. I could see the battle within her between her royal responsibility and the longing to be loved and cared for. The battle was playing out in her mind. She was thinking about the consequences of her next choice and the words that followed. After several moments that felt like two eternities, she smiled at me and made the decision.

"I love you, too," she tenderly replied. My heart was flooded with emotion, and I couldn't hold it back. We embraced again and stayed in each other's arms for several hours, enjoying the peace and joy that came with our love for each other, letting the words we had said soak into the depths of our hearts. We said it repeatedly to each other, never wanting this moment to end, but staying there, with each other, away from all the evil and hatred of this world.

The rest of our time that evening was spent in the garden. We walked side by side, speaking not of any of the current events in our lives, but instead sharing our hopes and dreams and where Aleph would take us after all this evil had been dealt with. It was the most incredible night of my life, and one I would never forget.

The morning came quickly and with it, a dose of reality. We met for breakfast together and made several hard decisions. We decided that our relationship had to be kept a secret. She was a princess, and I was the captain of her royal guard. It was a slippery slope we found ourselves on, and from that moment forward, we were careful to hide our emotions in public, only stealing quick glances at each other from across the room. That was enough to keep me going. I was a simple man and had very little all my life. Just one look from the woman I loved could tide me over for a week.

The months turned into years. I had been in the Lady's service for two years now. The sanctuary was reaching its final construction, and I spent a lot of time with Iska. Our love had blossomed to a place we could not have imagined. She even talked about confronting her Father, the king, and asking his blessing on our marriage.

"That will be impossible, my love," I calmly stated. "You are royalty, and your father would have me executed."

"I want to be with you, Anlace. Openly, where everyone

can see." She cried.

"I know. But we both knew from the beginning that our love would be in secret." I came over and held her in my arms, comforting her.

"This gets harder every day, you know that?" Iska said.

"Yes. But it is what we must do."

We decided from that moment forward, we would not discuss marriage again. I will admit it was hard not to go there in my mind, but we agreed that there were bigger pieces of the puzzle around us in need of solving. Aleph had given us a mission, and we were close to finishing the sanctuary.

Hamlin and Margaret kept coming to our secret meetings with horrific reports. More schools were opening in the city dedicated to magic and sorcery. Balafas was gaining more power and influence over the Prestige Sector. I had a hard time some days, seeing the darkness creep in before our very eyes. Iska had to correct me when my temper flared. I found myself apologizing often to the spies. It was so regular they had gotten used to my short fuse. It was my iniquity, a vestige of lordship I had not given over to Aleph. It was a familiar spirit that I continued to hang on to. However, no matter the outburst, Aleph's voice continued to comfort me and help me through it. He would tell me repeatedly to trust him. I found myself having to surrender my need to control and my temper to him daily.

The men and I would also find comfort in training. As the world grew dark around us, we would circle each other in the pits, two against one, challenging and strengthening each other in the sword. Each one of us brought a different skill and style to the pit, and over time, you could see the skills combining, creating a beautiful corporate form. We were unified in combat.

Each evening we sat together as a group and dined. The men had grown accustomed to giving me a space of time to speak to them about the events of the day and what I had heard from Lady Iska. I would gladly brief them and encourage them. Then I opened the conversation to all of them, allowing them to reflect on what Aleph was teaching them or whatever thoughts they wanted to share for the day. It was completely opposite from the experience I had in the king's army when we would chew our food in almost complete silence. The fellowship we enjoyed here was completely different. These were not just my men; they were my brothers.

Time continued throughout the rest of the year in the same fashion, except for increasing occurrences of sorcery, some ending in death. We could feel a tangible shadow over the entire city, like it was at its breaking point. I was on edge as I patrolled the Common Sector one fateful day. It was two years to the day since I had been rescued by Princess Iska, since I had seen the hateful face of my self-proclaimed nemesis, Roderick.

I was at a vendor's stall, observing some fine jewelry. I was thinking to myself how beautiful this would look on my Lady, when I heard a scream from down the street. I quickly placed the jewelry back and looked to my fellow brother, Tobin, who was on patrol with me that day. Nobody in the street even noticed the sound, but we were both of the same mindset and began running towards the direction of the screams. We turned the corner into an alley and ducked low behind a cart of spoiled food. Then, I saw him. He had aged over the past couple years and had streams of gray hair and a thick beard, but there was no doubt in my mind who was at the back of the alley.

Roderick had a man pinned down in the street. A fellow soldier was kneeling at the man's head and held a short blade only inches from his throat. We had not been seen, and I asked Aleph what we should do.

"Stay hidden and listen," Aleph immediately replied.

Tobin almost gave up our position, but I reached out and pulled him back before it was too late. I put a finger to my lips, gesturing to him to be silent.

Roderick was muffled due to all the noise from the main street behind us, but I was able to hear what he was saying.

"My master needs the blood for the meeting tonight! Do not try to back out now! You made a promise to Baelor!"

"I know I did!" cried the man. "But you must understand! It is all I have! The goat is one of a kind! I have raised it for years, and I cannot just give it up."

"Oh yes you will!" Roderick threatened, leaning his face closer, within an inch of the other man's face. "You most definitely will. There is a ceremony tonight that is of the utmost importance. We will confer several members to the highest authority. They will drink the blood; the oath will be spoken, and the power given! Nothing is going to stop Baelor's plans! Nothing!" The minion with the knife then shouted "BLESSED BAELOR!"

"I'm sorry my Lord, I can't!" the man cried even harder.

"Perhaps he may need a demonstration?" Another voice spoke from across the alley, and I felt a shudder of cold come over me. I looked over and saw the owner of the voice. It was the man called Lucien who had been with Balafas during my trial. He was perched calmly at the top of a stack of crates, like a raptor looking down on prey he was going to devour. The red band on his head was softly glowing, creating a dramatic effect along with his all-black attire. Seeing him perched like that in the streets made him look even more menacing than before.

Roderick looked back at Lucien and after a moment of thought, bowed his head. "Yes, my Lord." He responded.

Roderick quickly got off the man and commanded his fellow soldier to stand him up. As Roderick stood, he turned directly towards us, revealing his attire. He was not dressed in the armor of the king's army. He wore a black cloak with a cowl drawn back over his shoulders. His armor was also black and engraved with a golden dragon upon the cuirass.

Lucien turned his attention towards the man and spoke menacingly. "You really don't understand who you are dealing with, do you? I think it's about time you did." The dark man hopped down from the crates and stood next to Roderick. "Show him what you have learned, cleric." He spoke evilly.

Roderick took a step towards the frightened vendor and softly spoke out of his mouth a word or two in an arcane language, then snapped his fingers. Suddenly, a small flame erupted from his fingers. I could not believe what I was seeing.

"Let me tell you about the power of Destruction!" Lucien

began. "My apprentice controls the flame at the end of his fingers. The flame will obey him! The flame will go where he directs it. Do you understand?" He asked the man menacingly. "If you do not tell us where the animal is, he will unleash the flame from both of his hands, and it will engulf you and burn you. There will be no mercy for you, and you will scream in agony until you die! You see, he is a cleric! Baelor has given him this power, and he will use it to destroy you!"

The man was trying to get away, but he was held in place by Roderick's minion. He had a look of horror on his face as he stared at the flame protruding from Roderick fingers. "Last chance!" Lucien cried. Where did you hide the goat?" The man said nothing. He was completely frozen in fear. Roderick looked over to Lucien, giving the man several more seconds. "It is a shame." Lucien stated, nodding to the minion who was still standing behind the man. The minion quickly moved away from the man. The poor man backed away from Roderick, looking for a way to escape but finding none.

I watched from my concealment as Roderick looked one more time to Lucien. "Do it!" the dark man shouted. Roderick outstretched both of his arms. He spoke a word, and out of his hands came two unholy streams of fire.

The rest of the scene was beyond description. When the "demonstration" was over, Roderick stopped his spell and the fire ceased. "Stupid fool," Lucien cursed over the body. He looked at Roderick, and the minion who was entranced by the immensity of power that had just been displayed. "I guess now his sister will have to tell us. I hope she is smarter than her brother."

The three of them turned to walk toward us, and I decided

we had better get out of there now. We quickly moved out of the alley, staying low and concealed behind the cart. We made our way back out into the main boulevard of the Common Sector, ducked into a store to our immediate right, and closed the door behind us. After several minutes, we decided it was safe and went back out into the market.

Tobin and I walked quickly back to the palace, not saying a word to each other about what we had just seen. I kept playing it over in my head. Why hadn't I tried to stop him? The man had nowhere to go and was cornered. I had just sat there and let him die! Then I thought of my nemesis. Roderick had learned the art of Destruction and was adept at the wielding of it. He had obviously surrendered to Baelor and received the gift. But who was this man called Lucien? Why had Roderick called him Lord? I shuddered at the thought of having to come face to face with him again.

Eventually we found ourselves safely back in our quarters. That evening, we discussed what had happened with our brothers around the dinner table. They were as shocked as we were.

Discussion flowed that night into the early hours of morning. We talked about what we needed to do to prepare for a confrontation with this power. The discussion was reaching its climax when I saw my Lady's escort enter the room. I was relieved to know that I would soon be in my Lady's presence.

We met with Hamlin and Margaret again later that evening. Because of what I had experienced earlier that day, I had a new question to ask.

"Who is the man called Lucien?"

Hamlin's face went pale at the mention of his name. "He is mostly seen with Balafas. Nobody seems to have any answers as to who he is or where he came from. He is not to be trifled with. All we know is he oversees the training of the clerics."

"There was a blood ceremony tonight." Margaret continued. "Three members were receiving the highest rank in Destruction, Conjuration, and Enchantment. Lucien was there to confer the rank upon them. Balafas gave him the floor, and Lucien spoke to all of us. It was the first time he had ever spoken openly to the members." She stopped and looked at her husband before continuing. "There is something more going on. Something big is about to happen. Lucien spoke of the chosen one. They know he has been born." Iska and I leaned forward.

"Do they know who it is?" I asked anxiously, thinking about young Daeric.

"I don't think so. But I'm not sure." Margaret stated. "There's more. Lucien spoke about "the Shift."

"What is the shift?" Iska asked.

"The shift is when Baelor makes his move."

"On what?" I pressured.

"Society. It is when all at once, everything that was secret will be made known. All that was in the dark will be revealed."

I could not believe what I was hearing. But I knew all too well that what they said was true. Iska had already spoken to all of us about the age we were coming into, the end of the age. It was not going to be pleasant. I decided to share the events of my day with those in the room. As I finished my tale of the unfortunate man, Iska grabbed my hand. I saw the look from the spies across the room. They were shocked to see the princess grab my hand. I looked at my lady and then down at my hand. Iska, realizing her moment of weakness, quickly removed it. Hamlin and Margaret looked at us and smiled.

"It's okay, my Lady. You are worthy of love and affection, just like all of us. And you too, my Lord," they said, looking at me. "Don't worry. We will not tell anyone. We are now keepers of each other's secrets."

"I appreciate your secrecy." She said to the spies. "Concerning the events of today, this is unfortunate for all of us. They are moving quickly, and we are not safe here. I think it would be best for us to prepare to leave."

"Where will we go?" The spies asked together.

"I think it is time for us to go to the sanctuary," Iska stated, looking at me. "A little bit of construction still remains to be done, but for the most part, it is finished and habitable. You two will leave immediately and make your home in the town of Sommerset. It should be safe enough for you to live in peace. I had one of my trusted soldiers place a generous amount of coin in a chest under your bed this evening. It will take care of your needs for many years. You two have done an admirable job and from this moment forth, are relieved of your duty," Iska finished.

"Thank you, my Lady."

Then the door burst open, and two of the king's soldiers came into the office. I immediately stood and drew my sword, holding it out in front of me towards the intruders. The soldiers did not draw their own, so I surmised that we were not in danger. They were tired and sweating. From behind them came two more of the Lady's elite soldiers.

"Please forgive the intrusion, my Lady." Their words were broken and hollow. I could tell something was wrong.

"What is this about?! Out with it!" I commanded.

"Yes, my Lord," The soldier replied. "I don't know how to say this. I can't believe I'm saying this." He stuttered. He was delirious.

"OUT WITH IT!" I shouted.

"My lady. My Lord," the soldier stammered. The king is… dead."

CHAPTER
16

The entire city mourned the loss of King Tark. For the next week, the preparations for his memorial ceremony were at the top of the list for every citizen. All judicial summonses were put on hold, and the government found itself at a complete standstill. In the wake of this tragedy, Iska asked that I be with her at all times. She had family matters to attend to. Her and her brother Remus both had responsibilities that superseded anything else for the time being. I stayed with her as she mourned with her family.

Remus was a nervous wreck, unable to keep his thoughts straight and always looking behind him to see who was coming. He made the whole atmosphere uneasy. His wife, Jessilyn, was no better. The only sane one in their entire family seemed to be their 4-year-old girl, Kristina. She was sad about the loss of her Grandpa but didn't let it ruin her day. She continued to be the life of the party.

We met with the nobles of the city and of course the magistrate himself. Always in Balafas's presence was the dark man called Lucien. The hairs on my arms stiffened every time I was in the man's presence. The thought of him and Balafas leading this underground demonic group made my blood boil.

On the third day following the announcement of the king's death, we were called to the throne room to meet with Balafas and several ambassadors from other lands in Shalistar. A decision was to be made today about who would take the throne, although the right was Remus's by birth.

The doors to the throne room opened, and I entered with Michael and Tobin at my side, escorting Lady Iska. I saw Balafas sitting casually at the table and Lucien leaning calmly against the pillar. My temperature began to rise. Then I saw standing next to him, my nemesis, Roderick. He was dressed in the same black cloak and wore the dark armor with the golden dragon. Tobin and I looked at each other. I saw the same look in his eyes. We had to play this cool. None of our enemies knew we had been there when Roderick unleashed his power of Destruction on the vendor only days ago.

We walked into the center of the room and stopped. I stepped forward and announced my Lady's arrival. Everyone in the room bowed—everyone except Roderick. As my head came back up, I saw his hateful eyes staring into mine. That look made my entire body shiver with cold. Here was my nemesis, in the very throne room. He had only days before obeyed Lucien's command to murder a man using forbidden magic. Now he was standing beside Balafas as his personal guard. Was Roderick the one whom the ceremony was for? Had he been conferred the highest authority? It was too much to take in. I gritted my teeth and stepped forward with my Lady.

Introductions were made, pleasantries exchanged, and the meeting of the royal council began. I had never heard so much arguing among men and women in all my life. It was hard to imagine that these people had kept this world together for so many years. Iska and Remus sat quietly, allowing everyone to have their say. Some believed Remus was right for the throne. Others disagreed. There were some who felt Iska should sit on the throne, but Balafas quickly shut down that argument, stating tradition and the sentiment of birthright.

After what seemed like days but was only several hours, a consensus was reached, and Remus was chosen by the group to take the throne. Of course, this was only a demonstration of theatrics. The throne was always going to go to Remus. The coronation was planned for a week from now, and the meeting was dismissed. I looked to my left and met the gaze of Lucien, still leaning casually against the pillar with a smirk on his face. He nodded to me, and a cold shudder filled me again. I felt Michael's hand grab me and pull me to an abrupt stop. I realized had he not grabbed me, I would have walked right into Balafas, and before I knew it, I was staring into the eyes of Roderick.

"Has it already been two years? You know I just realized I have never congratulated you on your promotion, captain," sneered Balafas. "My Lady has always selected suitable leaders. Don't you think so?" Balafas directed his question to Roderick.

I could feel the hatred emanating from him as he answered, "Yes, my Lord." It took him a second to form the next words. "A fine choice."

"It is a shame, though," continued Balafas. "I had my own plans for you." I couldn't take it anymore. I took a step towards Balafas, and my men were right behind me.

"What's that, magistrate? I need you to speak a little louder! What kind of plans?" The entire room turned into our conversation. Roderick stepped forward to meet me, and we were once again face to face. "What kind of plans?!" I asked again loudly, not caring anymore. I felt Iska's hand on my shoulder and heard her voice.

"No, Anlace." She calmly said. "Not now." Roderick looked at me and then back at her. His eyes were searching us, as if they were seeing right through both of us.

Roderick smiled, but it was not a joyful one. It was a maniacal smirk. "I see," Roderick spoke softly, just above a whisper. "So, royalty is mixing with commoners now?" I whipped out my hand and before Roderick knew it, I had it cupped around his throat, squeezing with a great amount of pressure. He didn't know what had hit him and found himself on his knees, gasping for air but not finding any.

Balafas looked at me with longing. He was enjoying this scene before him. "Please, sir. Don't kill him. Good help is so hard to find these days." Balafas stated nonchalantly. He added an evil laugh at the end as well. I squeezed one last time and then released my hand from around Roderick's throat. His body collapsed into the floor, coughing and heavily breathing the air he had almost permanently lost. I turned around and was about to leave when I heard the magistrate speak.

"It is a shame though…I had such great plans for you." I quickly turned back around and lunged toward Balafas. Tobin and Michael held me back with all their strength. It was too late; I had taken the bait.

"What kind of plans, huh?" Iska again came forward and put her hands on me as well. This time, it did not work. "Tell me, magistrate! Tell everyone here! What plans did you have for me?!" I could see by the look on Balafas's face he had me exactly where he wanted me. I could see Lucien leaning against the pillar behind Balafas with that evil, steady grin on his face. He was overseeing the events and was pleased at the outcome.

I didn't care about any of it. I felt like a cornered dog. The only way out was to bark, bite, and fight. "Was I going to drink blood?" I shouted and heard gasps from all over the room. "Tell me! Were you going to make me a member of your secret club? Were we going to conjure demons and levitate? Were you going to teach me how to walk on water? How about enchanting clothes and weapons? Or better yet, were you going to teach me how to control fire, ice, and electric currents to harm my enemies?" There was a loud commotion in the room now, and soldiers had come in from outside to see what was happening. Roderick was still on the floor, zapped of strength, unable to speak. I turned to my brothers and told them to let me go. They released their hold on me.

The whole room was looking from Balafas to me, waiting for what was going to happen next. Balafas never took his eyes off me. The next words came from the dark man behind the magistrate. "You are a foolish boy who has no idea what he has just unleashed upon himself," Lucien said calmly.

He came over to Roderick and helped him onto his feet. I saw his lips move and words in another dark language come out. Instantly, Roderick's limp form straightened and stood up full of strength. I took a step back, and Roderick started to approach me, but Lucien calmly placed a hand on Roderick's chest. "No, not yet."

The dark man then turned towards the ambassadors and Remus. "Take them all, except the King." His words were spoken to the air. Suddenly, from out of nowhere, ten men in black cloaks appeared, standing behind the ambassadors. They grabbed their victims from behind and brandished a sharp, long dagger, bringing them close to their captives' throats. There were muffled screams. "Take them to a quiet place!" Lucien commanded. And as suddenly as they appeared, they were gone, taking their victims with them.

I heard Iska behind me scream and place a hand over her mouth, having witnessed the horror. "Oh my!" Balafas suddenly laughed maniacally, dancing around like a jester. "Now wasn't that incredible!? I love ILLUSION! The power is so awesome. You can just go…POOF and people vanish. Artifacts of intervention! Voila! You are transported to another place! Can you really believe how amazing this is?" Balafas had changed before all our eyes. The disguise had been dropped; we now saw clearly who he really was—an insane man, driven by fear.

"Now, where were we?" Lucien continued. He had ascended the dais and was perched upon the King's throne. His posture was unholy and altogether wicked. "Oh, yes." Lucien stretched his hands out, said an unknown word, and all around us, the doors locked loudly to the throne room.

Balafas laughed again and praised Lucien's spell. "Alteration, the power to lock doors!" I had seen and heard enough and commanded Michael and Tobin to raise their swords. In unison, we all stood ready for combat in the center of the throne room. Balafas looked at us amused. "Really? Please stop, you are embarrassing yourselves!"

"BALAFAS! You are playing a game you cannot win!" The shout came from Iska. She looked at the dark figure perched on the throne. "Baelor is using you and will toss you aside when he is done."

"Oh, my Lady. You really don't understand, do you? Of course, he is using me! This world is being wrapped up like a napkin, and nobody will be spared the destruction that is coming! Baelor will make me a ruler of this world!"

I looked over and saw Remus lying in a fetal position, rocking himself back and forward with his hands over his ears. He was completely oblivious to anything going on. "What? You think your king will save you? He can't even change his own underpants without me saying so. He is in my thrall, and he will do whatever I tell him to do!"

I looked hopelessly at Iska and saw the disappointment in her eyes. I had made a mistake and blown our cover. My naiveté had put us all in danger, and here we were in the center of the throne room with Baelor's puppet, completely uncovered. Aleph, forgive me!

Balafas danced up the dais and sat down on the smaller throne beside Lucien. "My first order of business, as king, let me think. Ah, I know! Entertainment!" Balafas snapped his finger, and again, another black-cloaked figure appeared from out of nowhere. He lifted the delirious king up off the floor and brought out a long dagger. The dagger went to the throat of the king. "I snap again, and he's dead!" Balafas hissed. The magistrate pointed towards Tobin. "You!"

Tobin looked at me in dread. I screamed for Balafas to pick me, but he would not hear of it. "Another word, and the king will be dead!" he shouted. Tobin slowly climbed the stairs and stood to the right of the throne. I watched as Roderick followed him and stood to the left in front of Tobin. "Now, let us have a 'demonstration' of things to come!"

Tobin held his sword, readying himself for what he feared. Roderick, with an evil grin, held his hands out. As I watched the demonic scene unfold before my eyes, I understood all too well what it all meant. Lucien was perched on the King's throne, feeding off Tobin's fear, which was clearly manifesting on his face and in his body.

Lucien was the master, and Balafas was his puppet. Lucien was the ruler of Shalistar, and Remus would be in his thrall. Lucien was the general and leader of Baelor's army and the manifestation of his power here on Shalistar. It was Lucien who would throw the entire world into chaos.

"Do it!" Lucien shouted from the throne to his apprentice.

"Yes, my Lord," Roderick responded to his master. He turned his attention back to Tobin and spoke an unknown word. Instantly, a flame flickered from both his hands. Tobin stared open-mouthed at the flame. Knowing there was nothing that could save him, he cried a war cry and charged Roderick. Without any further hesitation, Roderick spoke another word, and flames came out of his hands.

CHAPTER
17

I held Iska close to me as Balafas stepped over Tobin's dead body. Michael still stood beside us with his sword out. Iska was weeping uncontrollably, afraid. Once again, our world was being turned upside down. Later on, and for many years to come, I would question Aleph about what happened next. The magistrate continued to walk closer to where we were standing. Roderick, with flames still flickering from his hands, walked behind him.

"Followers of Aleph and the cursed Faith!" Balafas addressed us. "My second decree is that any worship to the dead God is from this moment forth, illegal and punishable by death! It seems you all have been found guilty, and as magistrate of the High King Remus and the land of Shalistar, I condemn you to die by the flames of Baelor, like your comrade before you!" His head turned to Roderick. "You know what to do!" Roderick took a moment and looked back to his true master, still perched on the throne. Lucien nodded his consent.

Roderick, with a pleased look on his face, stepped slowly towards us with his hands raised in front of him. I decided not to look into his eyes but held my gaze in Iska's. Then I felt a warmth and a peace come over me, followed by a quiet voice speaking to me from the inside.

"It's going to be okay. I will protect you," Aleph said.

Roderick unleashed the fury of flames, and we felt the heat hit us like a ton of bricks, but the fire did not singe us. The flames completely engulfed us, but the fire did not harm us. I looked at Michael, and the white cloak around him was glowing with a bright light. The look on his face was one of pure awe! I looked down and saw the white cloaks Iska and I wore were glowing as well—we were protected! Aleph's power was manifesting in the cloaks, keeping the power of the magic from harming us!

I stole a look towards the dais and saw the dead body of Tobin. He wore no cloak. My heart broke at that moment. We had been unprepared and caught off guard. Tobin was dead because of our mistake. Only Michael, Iska and I were donned in the white cloaks. I made a quick mental note to myself, to make sure every member of our order received a white cloak. I would petition Aleph day and night until it was so.

I then looked Iska in the eyes and saw that she had the same revelation about the protective cloak she wore. We broke our embrace, turned towards Balafas and Roderick, and stepped unharmed through the wall of flames.

"No! It cannot be! Impossible!" Roderick shouted. "I burned you! I control the flames! I have been given the gift!" Balafas stepped forward, stretched out his arms, and shouted a magic word. Out of his hands came a long spear made of solid ice. The tip of the spear could impale the skin of a desert buffalo. I winced as the ice spear hit me directly in the chest, but alas, there was no impaling. The cloak had protected me from any effect of magic. Balafas and Roderick both screamed in hatred and hurled one spell of Destruction after another at us. Every magical effect simply failed.

The three of us continued to step in unison towards our adversaries. Balafas cowered backwards toward the stairs to the throne. His steps faltered, and he tripped, falling onto his back side.

Lucien, seeing his puppet in danger, hopped off the throne and shouted, "Ignorant fool! How long must I put up with you!?" He spoke another guttural word into the air, and all around appeared black cloaked figures. They held blades in their hands. We looked all around us. Every direction was covered, and we were surrounded. Michael and I stepped forward, ready for combat.

Then the door to the right of the throne burst open with the force of a mighty blunt object in the hands of several of my men. The rest of my cadre came into the throne room with their weapons raised and a war cry on their lips. Weapons clashed as my warriors met with the black-cloaked figures. I looked at Roderick and Balafas. We had to move quickly and dispatch them before they could unleash another spell on our uncloaked brothers. Michael had the same thought, and together, we charged the dais.

Roderick knew his magic would not work against me and quickly unsheathed a blade from his side. I was on him in a flurry of blows. Roderick parried my attempts with ease at first, lashing out with an attack when he could. I leaped through the air over his head, landing on the steps of the dais. Roderick whirled around in shock at my move.

"What's the matter cleric?" I teased. "Didn't they teach you that one at magic school?" We crossed swords again, but this time I had the advantage and the high ground. My blows were coming down with much more force, and I could sense my enemy was weakening quickly.

To my left, Michael was fighting Balafas, and Iska had been surrounded by several of my men. She was protected for the time being. Michael was raining down blows upon Balafas, who was quickly parrying each one of them. Balafas was not simply a magistrate, but a seasoned warrior. Who knew how or when, but this man had combat training and experience and was winning the clash against my first in command. I had to help him.

I decided the best way to dispatch Roderick would be to open my defense and make myself vulnerable. Roderick saw the opening and attacked. I barely parried in time but felt a spasm of pain along my right arm. The attack had wounded me. The cloak did not protect me from normal weapons. That is what our training in combat was for. I cried out and came down upon Roderick with all my force. His attack left him open, and before he knew it, he was disarmed. He stepped backwards with his hands outstretched. He spoke a word, and flames erupted from his fingers. The flames hit me, blinding me temporarily. As my sight came back, I saw my enemy had retreated away from me and joined Balafas in his battle against Michael. I looked up to see Lucien standing over me, studying me.

"Anlace, you are worthy of all that Baelor would bestow upon you. Give up this foolish errand and join us," Lucien stated soothingly. He stretched out his hand for me to take. "Everything I have, I will give to you. Simply take my hand." His words were hypnotic and put me in a dreamlike state. I found myself starting to reach out and take his outstretched hand.

Then I heard the cry of Michael from across the room, and the trance ended as soon as it had begun. I looked one last time into the eyes of the dark man named Lucien. He looked at me and smiled his deep evil grin. "We will meet again, Anlace." And with those final words, Lucien vanished before my eyes.

My mind was trying to process what I had just seen when I heard my friend cry out for help again. Without any more hesitation, I jumped off the dais and ran to where Michael was fighting both Balafas and Roderick. I got there just in time to see my nemesis, Roderick, impale my best friend.

I screamed as Michael's body hit the throne room floor with a thud and a clang. Roderick quickly removed the sword from his body. Lionel heard my scream and came to my side. Together, we attacked the pair. This time, my sword clashed with Balafas, and Lionel began hammering blows upon Roderick. They barely had time to raise their swords in defense. Several more blows had Balafas retreating backwards. I looked over again at my love and saw she was still standing, protected by several of my men.

That look was nearly fatal. Balafas saw the opening and went from retreat to attack. His skill was much more advanced than I would have imagined, and far more experienced than Roderick. "I see you question my skill with the blade!" Balafas taunted. "I have trained for many years from my master!"

The magistrate reigned down a blow on me that put me on the floor. I expected him to finish me right then and there, but he didn't. He took a step back, spoke a word, and snapped his fingers. His entire being vanished right before my eyes. Before I could figure anything else out, I heard a scream. It was my love, Iska.

Balafas was holding her with a blade to her throat and backing away from her protective soldiers. He had teleported to her side, taking hold of her before we knew what had happened. Looking around the room, I noticed all my men had dispatched the enemy. There were dead black-cloaked bodies scattered all over the throne room. Lionel had backed off from his assault on Roderick and stood next to me. Only Roderick and Balafas were left.

"Leave her alone!" I commanded. "It's over and you lost!"

"Over? No, I don't think so! This is not over! We haven't even begun!" Balafas cried maniacally.

"You have nowhere to go! You are completely surrounded!" Then I heard the explosion of flames from Roderick's hands and saw the body of Fletch fly back, engulfed in flames.

"On the contrary, Anlace, I believe we have a way out. Your men, however, are in deep trouble."

"Stand back, men! Don't engage!" I commanded my troops. The men obeyed, keeping their distance.

"Captain, here is what is about to happen: Roderick and I are going to take your beautiful lady to a safe place. When I return, I will have instructions for you." I began to move forward towards them, and Balafas pressed the blade into Iska's skin. "Move another step closer, Captain, and she is dead!" I quickly halted and held up a hand to my soldiers, signaling them to do the same. "That's better. Now, you sit tight; we will be right back."

At that, with a single word, Balafas, Roderick, and Iska disappeared, leaving us alone in a throne room of dead bodies with a delirious King Remus still rocking back and forth with his hands over his head and ears, completely unaware of any reality.

I immediately ran over to my best friend's body and held Michael. "Are you still there? Wake up Michael!" My assistant's eyes slowly and weakly opened. "There you are. Stay with me, friend. Please." I began crying.

"Anlace," Michael said weakly. "Tell Abigail I love her."

"No! Tell her yourself." I cried.

"I'm not going to make it."

"Don't say that."

"Anlace, take Daeric with you. Remember Iska's words. You are the Father of the Chosen." Michael coughed, and a stream of blood began to form on the right side of his mouth.

"Michael. No, stay here. Please." I realized there was no use. Michael had passed away in my arms. The pain penetrated my heart like a thousand swords. I wept, holding my friend for several minutes before laying him back on the floor of the throne room. I stood weakly to my feet and saw all my brothers kneeling, overcome with sadness—not only for Michael, but for Tobin and Fletch as well.

A strange, magical noise sounded, and once again, Balafas and Roderick appeared. I screamed and ran towards them. "You murdering coward!" Geoffrey and Stewart held me back.

"Hypocritical comment, captain. Look at the dead bodies of my men all around you!"

"Go to Hell!" I screamed. Balafas winced at the comment

and considered his fate. It was too late for him.

"I'm sure I will, one day. But let us not think about such unpleasant times. I came to tell you that your lady is safe, for now."

I knocked Geoffrey back, freeing my injured arm to draw my blade. Balafas continued. "However, captain, I will tell you that the lady's captors have been given specific instructions to kill her if I don't return." Hearing the threat from Balafas and seeing the impossible situation we were in, I slowly sheathed my blade and commanded my men to do the same.

"Good. Now, you and I are going to make a deal. I am going to give you one hour to leave this city. Take your men and leave. Do not ever come back. You are banished. If you and your men are ever seen within the walls of Raithe, your lady's life will be forfeit. Go now, and do not look back. Leave Raithe to me. Don't worry. It's in good hands."

A thousand thoughts crowded my mind. All I wanted to see was the end of Balafas and Roderick's lives. Rage consumed me, and I wanted to run both men through. I could attack them both and cause a distraction so that the rest of the men could overwhelm them without any fear of magic spells. I decided that would not be successful. They could just as easily teleport back before I got to them, and Iska's life would be ended.

I was angry at Aleph for allowing this to happen. He hadn't protected Iska. Why not?! My mind was racing, and I couldn't keep my thoughts straight. Then I felt a hand on my shoulder and a whisper in my ear.

"We have the sanctuary." It was Lionel. "The lady knew and prepared us. Aleph has made provision. Go get the boy.

We will meet you there."

Overcome with emotion, I nodded agreement to this deal, unknowingly sealing the fate of my love. "We agree," I said to Balafas.

"Good. You have one hour. No more. Move quickly, captain."

CHAPTER
18

As a group, we moved through the secret passages of the palace until we were in the streets of the Common Sector. Without any hesitation, I went into Michael's home. Abigail was sitting there with Daeric in her arms. As I came into the house alone, bloodied and beaten, without her husband, she began to cry. "Where is Michael?"

"I'm sorry, Abigail. He didn't make it."

"What's happened?!" she cried.

"I'm so sorry, Abigail. It's all my fault!" I collapsed at her knees and told her everything that had happened. "Please forgive me." Abigail was obviously shaken and overcome with sorrow.

"Why? Why didn't you stay silent? Why did you speak up? Michael would have been alive! Iska would have been safe."

"I know. I am sorry. I'm so sorry, Abigail." I wept.

We were suddenly interrupted by Merwin, one of my brothers. "Captain, we must hurry. King's soldiers are down the street and headed this way. They are looking for us. Our hour is up!"

I looked Abigail in the eyes. "We have to go. Now! We

have to go, and Daeric has to come with us." This bit of information completely undid Abigail. She knew the truth, that Daeric was chosen, but it didn't make this part any easier.

"No. Please let me keep him," she pleaded.

"You know we can't. He is not safe here. They are looking for him, and it is only a matter of time before they discover who he is."

"I know." Abigail stood up and walked over to a cupboard in the corner of the room. She opened the door, reached in, and took a journey bag out. She slowly came back over and handed me the bag for her young boy. "Michael and I have had it packed and ready for a year now." She then looked pleadingly at me. "Can I have one last moment with him alone?" I agreed, and we left them in the house by themselves. A short while later, she appeared and handed Daeric over to me.

The entire city was in a state of alarm. We moved quickly towards the front gates. King's soldiers were everywhere, and we had to duck in and out of the alleys to make our way safely forward. As we moved through the streets, we heard the people sharing a rumor that a group of soldiers had organized an attack on the throne room. The group was supposedly led by Lady Iska, who wanted her brother Remus eliminated so she could take the throne for herself. The rogue group had reputedly tried to murder Remus and steal the throne, kidnapping the ambassadors who were being held captive.

The crowd began moving south, towards the palace. I grabbed a citizen to inquire what was going on. "The magistrate has the Lady! The one who tried to take the throne! He's at the steps to the palace and is about to pronounce judgment on her!" My heart stopped. I couldn't believe what I had created by my words. If only I had kept my mouth shut, Michael would be alive. As if on cue, I felt a tug on my cloak and looked down to see young Daeric looking up at me. "Dada?" he asked me. My heart broke at the question. I could not respond.

I stopped Merwin. "Take young Daeric and escape the city through the sewers. Do not stop until you have met up with Haywood and Lionel at the edge of the Elder Woods. I removed my cloak and placed it over Merwin. "It will protect you if you run into any cleric."

"Wait a minute, sir! Where do you think you are going?" he asked me.

"To her.," I quickly replied. "Don't wait for me. I'll catch up."

"But sir…" I didn't hear the rest of what Merwin had said because I was caught up in the crowd, heading towards the palace. I grabbed a plain brown cloak left unattended at a vendor's stand and put it on. I drew the cowl over my head and let the crowd carry me all the way through the plaza to the foot of the stairs at the palace.

Soldiers were everywhere, moving through the crowd. I am sure Balafas had them patrolling in case we decided to interrupt his proceedings. I kept my head down and covered, remaining towards the back of the crowd that had gathered. Roars of commotion and shouts erupted from the audience. They cried out in unison, "Condemn her! She is guilty!"

The crowd's commotion had risen to the point of riot, and several of the king's soldiers had to display a use of extreme force. Once the people saw the brutality of their actions, they corrected their behavior. The roar of the crowd came to its peak as Balafas and Roderick took the stage. Standing behind them in the shadows, with his arms across his chest, was the man named Lucien. He stood watching the proceedings with great pleasure.

"Faithful people of Raithe! We bless you today!" Balafas shouted as he lifted his hands and moved them back and forth over the audience. "It has been a hard week, with the death of King Tark, and the events of today have not given us any respite. I stand before you today to announce a conspiracy!" The crowd booed and hissed. "Calm down. The conspiracy has been going on for some time now, and we have taken great care to prepare for any kind of attempt at a coup. This group of conspirators has been dealt with, and their leader has been captured. She is none other than Lady Iska!" The crowd roared and began throwing spoiled food and small objects towards the steps.

"Please understand, we are all equally as shocked and appalled as you are. To think that one would lust for power to the degree of murdering one's own brother? Why, it is unthinkable!" The crowd was completely under the spell of Balafas's poisonous words. "My personal guard has uncovered the locations of the ambassadors as well, and they will be safely returned to their families. As for the leader of this conspiracy…" The doors to the palace were thrown open, and there was my love, being led in chains by two soldiers in black cloaks and a chest of golden armor.

My heart sank to see her in such a pitiful state. I had no

possible way to save her. I would be cut down immediately when my foot touched the first step. All I could do was watch and observe as they condemned the most beautiful, pure woman to her fate.

"I have heard the case and examined the evidence. My judgment has been shared with King Remus, and we are in agreement. Lady Iska has been found guilty!" The crowd erupted all around me with cheers and applause. I bit my tongue and closed my eyes. This could not be happening. As my eyelids weakly opened, I could see Lucien staring right through the entire crowd, his eyes locked onto mine. He could see me! He knew I was there! My whole body flooded with cold shivers as my eyes locked onto his. Then as if from around me, I heard him speaking.

"Join us." His words spoke telepathically into my mind. I told myself it was just a dream. The roar of the crowd continued, as Lucien's words echoed in my mind: "join us." I was completely broken, and had no strength left in me. I had lost a lot of blood from the wound in my arm and felt myself falling into the crowd. "Join us." Lucien's words continued over and over. And then, I was falling. But before I could hit the floor of the pavement, I felt a set of arms catch me. Lucien's voice suddenly stopped. It was replaced by a muffled voice above me saying, "I have to get you out of here." There was another loud roar, and I heard, almost as if from another plane of existence, the word "execution" shouted from the steps of the palace, which was followed by an even louder roar.

I was floating; I could not feel my feet under me. I realized with my final waking thought that I had been slung over the back of Geoffrey's large mass. I hovered in and out of consciousness, hearing the crowd roaring in the distance until finally, I was blessed with complete darkness.

As I regained consciousness, again I felt as though I was floating. The sky was just about to receive the morning's first light. I was sore all over, especially my right arm. It had been bandaged, and I couldn't feel anything except the constant tremor of pain from the wound Roderick had given me. My mouth was completely dry and longed for a drink. I leaned forward to look around and saw large trees in the distance, as far as the eye could see. We were coming over the hill, and the Elder Woods loomed across the vista.

Looking to my right, I saw my brother Gareth marching alongside the cart. To the left was his twin, Mark. Sitting at the foot of the cart by my feet was young Daeric. He looked as exhausted as the rest of us. The woods overhead completely blanketed us under its leaves, and we were lost from the view of the eagle's eye. I heard Stewart shout something about staying on the path through the woods or we would be lost and then something again about how it would be safer to go around and not take the main road back to the sanctuary. I looked to my left and saw Geoffrey marching on that side. I was afraid to ask, but I had to know.

"Geoffrey." He looked at me sympathetically.

"Please don't talk, sir. You need to rest," he replied.

"No. Please, Geoffrey. Tell me. Iska...my love..." He looked at me with a sorrowful expression, bowed his head, and shook it to the side.

"She's gone," he simply stated. Again, my heart felt like it had been stabbed with a thousand blades. At that moment,

I would have rather had Roderick's unholy fire consume my body and burn me alive. I was truly lost in that moment, and the only thing I could do was cry. I did. I cried until there were no tears left, and then I passed out once again.

The next days spent under the leaves of the woods were dark and brought no joy. My heart was empty. All the love I'd had in me for another person had been snatched away. My insides hurt, my head hurt, my body ached, and I didn't want to have any kind of conversation with anyone. All I wanted to do was die, but I knew that was not an option. Aleph needed me. Aleph had a purpose for me. I thought of Him as a twisted creator who would give me such joy and pleasure before completely removing it from me. I allowed those thoughts to poison my heart. For days, I sat there. On the cart, even during mealtimes, I stared blankly forward, not caring about anything or anyone. I felt empty and hollow, just like I had been before I had met her.

It was the dead of night and we had just come out of the Elder Woods, approaching the road to Swaltayer. Another days travel east would bring us over the bridge to the sanctuary. We decided to stop for the night and finish the journey in the early morning. Everyone except Haywood and I were asleep.

I was having a hard time sleeping today. All I could think about was her. The birds had been silent for several hours now, and all I could hear was the snoring of my brothers as they slept, and a light breeze as the wind blew. I walked around the camp several times that night, deep in my thoughts, until

I found myself standing just outside the light of the campfire. Everything was still and quiet, as if time had stopped. Then I saw the peaceful, sleeping form of my best friend's son, Daeric. He was curled up with a blanket, sleeping peacefully.

I stood there entranced as I watched him sleep. I felt a stirring in my heart, and a warmth filled me from the top of my head down to the soles of my feet. I smiled and silently wept tears as I saw the boy. My heart was flooded in that moment with love for him. I was reminded of the two years I had spent with his father Michael and the love I had for my first in command.

Something else stirred in me—responsibility, duty, and purpose. All my muddled thoughts became clear right then and there. I knew where my future lay. I quietly leaned down and adjusted the blanket so that it was covering Daeric all the way up to his head. Then I softly placed my hand on his shoulder and whispered a prayer, thanking Aleph for him. I kissed his forehead and whispered in his ear, "Goodnight, my son. I bless you this night as your father. Sleep well, my darling."

The next morning, we found ourselves approaching a rolling green hill as the eastern sunrise was just coming up, illuminating the stone spires of our sanctuary. We all cheered as we made our way towards the front gate. We unloaded our belongings and made our way into the building through the large wooden front door. The first thing I noticed as the interior of the foyer was revealed were ten soft white cloaks with dark green trim, hanging on hooks to the left. Seeing the cloaks made me smile. Aleph had heard my prayer and sent his guardians ahead of us with garments of authority for all of my brothers. Before I entered my new home, I looked back towards Raithe and wept one more time.

"I'm sorry, my love. I'm sorry you couldn't be here." Suddenly, the door burst open and little Daeric was there, pulling on my cloak.

"Da! Big room! Play!" He then ran back inside, leaving the front door open for me. A huge smile came over my face, and I was once again filled with joy. I looked one last time toward Raithe and made a solemn vow.

"I will make this right, my love. I promise." I then entered through the front door of my new home—a home Aleph had provided.

PART III

CHAPTER
19

Father finished his story and closed the book with a sigh of relief, as if a large weight had been released. Esgar was lying down next to me, staring into the flames. She had tears in her eyes as she heard about the tragic end of her aunt's life. "I never knew the truth about her." Mother and Father never told me. Anytime her name came up in conversation, they would quickly change the subject." She then looked over at Father. "Thank you for sharing this with me."

I looked across the fire at Father and let everything he had read just settle in. Here was the man who had raised me, my father. He had made a promise to my birth father as he lay dying in his arms, that he would take care of me. I had a newfound respect and honor for the man. He had opened his heart and shared an intimate and difficult time in his life with us that evening. I was so thankful to be sitting there with him.

But one more piece to the puzzle had yet to be revealed. "What about my mother?" I asked anxiously. "Is she still alive?"

Father looked back at me and shook his head. "I'm not sure. After we escaped Raithe, we never looked back. Your mother had a path set before her, and it was a tremendous sacrifice to release you to me. She told me to go and not look back."

It hurt my heart to hear that. Before any false thoughts could plant themselves in my head, Father said again, "I'm sure Aleph has taken care of her, son. She knew when she birthed you who you were. She did what she had to do when she gave you to me."

"I just wish I knew where she was," I concluded.

Esgar looked up at me. "So, you were the little boy I vaguely remember from my past? It's sad, but those were some of the happiest memories of my life."

"What happened to you after your father took the throne?" I asked innocently. Esgar's face immediately clouded over as I asked that question, and she retreated inward. I saw the change in her appearance and looked over at Father. He was shaking his head, signaling me to stop my questioning.

"I'm sorry. I..."

"It's okay, Daeric. I would rather not discuss this right now. It's late, and we need some rest before the morning." As she said that, a weariness came over me, and a yawn escaped from my lips. We all agreed to turn in for the rest of the night.

The entrance to the valley of the Rift was located to the northeast. We had traveled north from Rivertown along the waters of the Antioch until we reached the foothills. Even though the roads were growing rougher beneath our feet, everyone was in good spirits. Our caravan had grown with the addition of the refugees from Thorne and the inhabitants of Rivertown. Groth and Loretta were a joy to be around. They always had a way of making people smile and were positive in their words. They were also helpful with hunting and provisions. The couple was up early most days, and before I had my boots on, they would return with fresh game slumped over the saddle of their horses. I found myself traveling with them frequently.

Esgar was quiet most of the day. I could sense an inward battle waging within her. She was opening up a little more every day but still would not share anything with me about her upbringing. I thought to myself just how terrifying it must have been to be raised in such a corrupt and evil regime, where magic was everywhere throughout the city, and the magistrate's army had all authority in the kingdom. Her family must have been gripped in a vice of fear, wondering every day if their importance had expired, and they had become expendable.

I walked with Aleph one day and asked him about it.

"Why is it hard for her to trust us?"

"She has been betrayed by the ones she loved the most," he replied from inside me.

"Is there anything I can do to help her?"

"Give her time," Aleph gently said. *"I am working on her heart. She will be vital to your journey. She just needs more time to heal. She has walked through evil unspeakable and had everything taken from her. She feels abandoned."*

"But she's not. We are here," I interrupted my creator.

"Yes, you are, and she will come to you for comfort, so have your heart bent towards me and be ready. She will need you more in the days ahead."

I enjoyed hearing Aleph's soft voice day after day. He was so gentle, and his words carried so much power and authority. Spending time with him through daily encounters gave me strength and courage. Father was right. All his words to me over the years had been sound. I just did not understand. I thought it was all some religious thing that was required by all of us because we were the Order of the Elect, but it was so much more.

Father was showing me more than religion. It was all about me hearing Aleph's voice and spending time with him as a friend. It took eighteen years, but I thought I finally understood what he meant. From then on, I dedicated the first part of my day to walking with Aleph, talking with him and journaling my thoughts.

On the day when everything changed between Father and me, our travels brought us close to the North Road Bridge and waiting there to meet us was our enemy. They had set up a camp and blocked the road that led into the valley. The mountains of Shaddyia loomed high above us on the horizon.

Father had sent Merwin ahead to scout out the area before we gave ourselves away and several days ago he tasked Stewart with going back and locating the enemy if they were behind us. That day, Merwin came to us with a difficult report.

An entire cadre of the magistrate's army was assembled, and amid these warriors was a handful of clerics. They had set up a camp just in front of the bridge. As I heard this, I cursed under my breath because of our misfortune.

We were a good distance away from the bridge and not in any immediate danger. Father gathered the brothers together, and we discussed a strategy for how we would overcome the soldiers. The clerics were going to be the key. They had to be eliminated first. We knew we were safe from their magic because we were all donned in the safety of the guardian's white cloaks. But if we were to direct any attention to ourselves before dispatching the clerics, then we would put the rest of the caravan in danger.

Several of my brothers gave sound wisdom and strategy for how we could make the plan work. Father listened to each of them, giving his full attention and considering their counsel.

Geoffrey stood up first. "I suggest that the element of surprise is most important. We need to attack in full force from all sides. Any able man or woman needs to be a part of the assault. A quick, powerful attack will put them off guard and allow us to focus on eliminating the clerics." The brothers thought about it and looked at several scenarios, but in the end, we agreed that the plan would incur casualties, which is what we could not afford. Father opened the floor for more suggestions.

Merwin stood up next. "I think we should create a diversion. If we made a loud enough noise, then the enemy's camp would send many soldiers to see what the disturbance was and leave a smaller number of soldiers behind for us to overrun." This plan was better than Geoffrey's but still had too many unknown outcomes. We would be relying on chance rather than strategy, so it was tabled for now.

Gareth was next to make a proposal. "I believe we should simply find another way around the blockade. Perhaps if we went northwest and circled back east, we could find a more secluded entrance into the valley." This idea was met with a good amount of approval until Lionel spoke up.

"I would like to say, we are thinking about this too rashly," the elder brother began. "We don't know anything about our enemy's numbers or their whereabouts. How do we know we would not come across a larger cadre further north? Anlace, you said you want to limit casualties at all costs. I agree with you, and for this to happen, I suggest subterfuge."

My brothers in the circle began to talk among themselves about this new idea. Lionel continued. "Two of our brothers need to infiltrate the enemy camp, either by donning a uniform or pretending to be weary travelers. Once they are within the camp, they can find out where the clerics are, eliminate them secretly, and signal us to attack, joining us in the assault from within."

After several moments of clamor, Father stood up. "Does everyone agree this is the best way forward?" All the brothers gave their approval in unison. "I agree as well. But I feel the deception should be that of weary travelers. If we load you up with some of Groth and Loretta's wine, you would be a most welcome visitor to a group of thirsty soldiers. But I will not send you in without special protection. We will sew an outer layer of common cloth over the white cloaks. To the normal eye, your garments will look like tattered, travel worn fabric. But underneath, you will be protected by a guardian's cloak. Now, we must now decide who will be going."

Lionel stood up again. "This part may be difficult for you, Anlace, but I feel like the best chance we have at subterfuge would be to send myself and Daeric." Commotion broke out again from among the group. My heart filled with excitement as I heard my name called out by the elder. I looked over at Father and could see the worry on his face.

"No, Lionel. It's too dangerous," Father rebuked him.

"I understand your concern, Anlace..." Lionel returned.

"It's out of the question!" Father shouted over the rest of the brothers.

Mark stood up. "Lionel is right, Anlace. If we sent an old man and a boy, they would not attract suspicion. Our best chance for success is to send Daeric and Lionel." I continued to observe Father during this exchange. Several other brothers threw in support for me to go. Father would not hear of it and remained closed off from any acceptance of this outcome. I had a hard time seeing him like this. He was being stubborn and selfish and remained unwavering in his decision.

Finally, Lionel stood up and rebuked Father. "I have been with you a long time, Anlace. I know where you have been and the losses you have had. But I want you to know that you are wrong! You are believing lies in your mind. If you decide based on fear, then we are all doomed, and the enemy has already won. Daeric is just as important to me and the rest of us as he is to you. I believe in my heart that my suggestion was sound wisdom from Aleph. Where he leads, he provides. That includes protection. Aleph will be with us, even in the enemy camp. Daeric is our best chance for success. Please do not make your decision in fear. Trust Aleph to protect him."

"You don't understand..." I saw Father begin to tear up, and my heart just about broke.

"Yes, I do...and Iska knew the danger, too, but she accepted her end in peace. Do not carry this burden anymore, Anlace. She is gone! Nothing you could have done would have changed the outcome." Father slumped over and cried.

"Please don't make me do this!" Father cried into the air,

probably to Aleph. The brothers all stood up and surrounded Father, praying for him with words of comfort and peace. I had never seen my father cry like that, and it hurt my heart deeply to see a strong, wise, and courageous man brought so low. It was all because of me. Father loved me, and all he wanted to do was protect me. But I could sense that Aleph was working in my father. Hearing Lionel and him exchange words had brought to the surface feelings and emotions Father had carried for a long time. I had never seen him in such pain. Aleph was using Lionel and my brothers to bring healing if Father would receive it.

Father continued to cry into Lionel's shoulder, putting it all out in the open. "She trusted me, Lionel! She loved and trusted me, and I got her killed!"

"It's not your fault, Anlace." Lionel soothingly comforted Father.

"She trusted me, and I got her killed!" Father's anguish was on full display. An emotional wound that had festered for eighteen years was now opened, and the blame and shame that had burdened him my whole life was being broken before our very eyes. He wept uncontrollably in the safety of Lionel's arms as the brothers covered him in prayer. I was speechless. I had never seen a man broken and weeping like this before. But in all the misery of the moment, I could feel a peace in the atmosphere as well.

When Father's confession was over, I heard Lionel tell him to forgive himself. A groan escaped from deep within him, from the depth of his inward man—then another, and another. Father was fighting against all the lies he had believed for so many years, exchanging them right now for the truth.

"You are a good man, Anlace," Lionel comforted him. "You are a strong leader and a passionate warrior!" More groans came from within Father. "Let it all go, Anlace. This is a defining moment for you. Surrender all your memories of Iska and the time you had with her to Aleph. He is here to heal your wounds." Several more groans and then an almost incoherent stutter of words emerged from within Father. I could only decipher the word "surrender." He kept saying the words several more times. Then Lionel said, "Now, forgive yourself, and let the burden go!" Then came another stream of words that were hard to understand, but I could decipher the word "forgive".

Father repeated these words aloud to Aleph, in the presence of us all. His posture began to straighten, like strength that had been lost was returning. Lionel stayed with Father and allowed him to continue weeping. As the moments passed, Father grew calmer, and the atmosphere became peaceful. You could feel it everywhere. Then I looked up and saw Father looking at me.

"I'm sorry, my son," Father said softly. I ran up and threw my arms around him and Lionel.

"It's okay, Father. I understand and will not do it," I replied.

"Yes, you will," Father affirmed. "You will go into the enemy camp, and Aleph will be with you."

Lionel and I were given a tent in which to strategize, pack, and discuss the plan. Our cloaks were in the hands of several adept seamstresses from Thorne. They were busy covering all the white with an ugly brown material. After several hours of sewing and patching, our cloaks were done and returned to us. The regal white had been covered with an ugly fabric. Not one bit of white could be seen inside or outside of the cloak. Nobody in Shalistar would recognize that we were really wearing guardian's cloaks.

While the seamstresses were preparing our garments, I packed several bags for us. At first it was just a couple of items, but it grew to a collection of useless stuff, so I dumped out the bags and started over again. I was nervous and didn't have a clear thought in my head. Lionel was still in a meeting with Father. I found myself pacing back and forth until I was staring at the weapons rack. Several long blades rested there. Next to the rack were several scabbards for the swords to rest in. I selected two long blades and sheathed them both.

My thoughts were interrupted as the older man entered and immediately began barking orders. "Not those! We only take daggers, no swords. Peasants do not know how to use swords, and it will be a dead giveaway," he said as he came up next to me. He reached past me and grabbed two daggers resting in a chest next to the rack. "Here. Take this." He handed me a thin, sharp iron dagger no longer than my forearm. "These will work nicely. You remember your training on short blades, correct?"

I began to summarize some of my lessons over the years. "That's correct," Lionel encouraged me. "The most important piece to this mission is stealth. I don't expect you to have to do any of the killing. You will accompany me as a prop or an addition to my disguise. Having a young man with me makes my story even more viable. I will take out the clerics, but I do want you to be prepared, just in case something unexpected happens." He continued laying out our plan. As he did, half of my mind took another direction in thought.

I had never had much of an opportunity to get to know Lionel. Thinking about that now, it seems strange. We had lived together in the sanctuary for sixteen years, but for whatever reason, our dialogue was always on the surface. Maybe it was me. Lionel always seemed to me to be the older member of our order who smelled funny and made authoritative statements. He could definitely wield a blade, though.

The only brother I have seen best Lionel in combat, was Father. And that was only one time! It was when I was twelve years old. I guess Lionel was having an "off" day, but Father beat him, and Lionel found himself on his back in the center of the ring. Everyone in the courtyard that day would remember it forever. Lionel, however, wasn't too happy about the loss and remained distant from the brothers for the rest of the week.

I was able to bring my mind back into the situation and continued tracking with Lionel as he finished laying out the plan. Before long, my best friend Samuel entered the tent and told us it was time to go.

Father and the rest of the camp gathered to see us off. One of Groth and Loretta's carts had been provided, and two large casks of wine had been put in the back, along with a bunch of odds and ends that people had donated. The horses were even loaded up as well. We donned the ugly camouflaged cloaks, received prayer by all who gathered, and were sent on our way.

Father walked with us a short while until we were at a dangerous place where our plan could be foiled, and our identities compromised. I could tell Father was still struggling with letting me go, but he didn't say anything and continued to encourage both of us.

"Once the final cleric is eliminated, set fire to the cask of wine." Father could see the worried look on my face and guessed my thoughts. "Don't worry, clerics are like officers and are held in high esteem. They will have their tent to sleep in and be honored with their own cask of wine to drink. Samuel will be in place on the cliff overlooking the camp, awaiting the signal. Once the fire is lit, we will be on our way to get you out of there. Don't take any unnecessary risks…"

Lionel cut Father off at the remark. "Boy, I was sneaking around in the shadows before you were even born. These clerics won't even know what hit them."

Father smiled at that remark and gave each of us a hug. After Father's embrace, he looked at me. "Don't do anything unless Lionel commands it. Is that understood?"

"Yes, sir."

"Good. Now go, and may Aleph guide your path!"

Lionel and I sat on the bench steering the horses, moving closer to the enemy's camp. The sun was setting in the west, and the colors of red, orange, and gold illuminated the frosty peaks of Shaddyia. We came up over the hill and saw the garrison on the horizon. It was shabby at best, as though a bunch of household goods had been piled up on both sides of the road. Behind the camp in the distance was the North Road Bridge. The wooden structure allowed travelers to cross over the Antioch River and move into the valley below the Ternion Mountains. To the northwest was an outcropping of cliffs that stretched back northeast. That is where Samuel would be posted.

Six soldiers came into view at the front gate to the camp. As we approached, their black golden armor shone as the last rays of sunlight left the world.

The soldiers looked tired and bored until they saw us approaching. With our presence revealed, they straightened up and feigned attentiveness. One of the six left their comrades to inform their commander of our presence. My stomach turned in circles, and sweat droplets formed at my temples. I have never been so nervous in all my life. And then I looked over at Lionel and almost smiled at what I saw.

He had completely gotten into character and was slumped over. In his right hand was a crutch that one of the families had donated to our plan. Lionel was an amazing actor. I knew the plan, and he completely fooled me. He appeared to have aged thirty years before my very eyes. He even grunted with every breath he took, as though he had lived with pain in his joints for years on end. I thought quickly about ways to improve my character and made some quick decisions as well.

We continued the slow approach until one of the soldiers commanded us to halt. "Good evening," he said politely. "What brings you two out this far in the foothills this evening? Let us hear from you," the soldier commanded, pointing to my companion.

Lionel shifted so he could lean on the cart, and after several grunts for the imaginary pain in his legs, he got down slowly until his feet were on solid ground. He then responded to the soldier brilliantly. "We are on our way to Hammerfist and

Northcrest to sell our wares. We decided to cut through the Rift to save some days of travel. It's been a long road, and if you don't mind, we will be on our way."

"Sorry, mate! The road to The Rift is closed by order of the magistrate," the lead soldier replied.

Lionel grunted and looked at me. "Stupid boy! I told you we should have gone around! You are dumb as a post, you know that?"

"Don't blame me!" I responded. "This was your idea!" The pantomime continued, and I got lost in my character. "If you had listened to the vendor in Sommerset, we would probably be there by now!" Lionel suddenly lashed out with the crutch he was holding onto, trying to hit me with it.

"Come here and let me knock you into next week!" Lionel shouted.

"Yah, just try it old man!" I said, shaking my fist. "You're going to be on your back, and there's no amount of wine on our cart that will stave off the pain of that."

"Insolent boy! How dare you treat your elders this way?" Lionel replied.

"ENOUGH!" shouted a new voice. This voice carried great authority. This soldier approached us, leaving the rest of his men at the gate to the garrison. As he came near, I noticed he was tall and muscular, about the same age as Father. The hood of his cloak had been pulled back, and he had long dark hair that he wore in a tight ponytail. Across his face was a black beard, speckled with gray hairs throughout. "You two are causing quite a stir!" the newcomer stated. He was looking at us, studying us closely.

"I do not appreciate my men being distracted, but you can't tame the human spirit. My men are bored and need something to help pass the time."

"I understand. My brothers Tab and Pierce used to bore me all the time." Lionel began to weave a long story, but the commander stopped him.

"I really have no interest in you or your family, old man. In fact, the only reason I have not run you through with my sword is because I am in the middle of a bet. I actually wagered that I would go the entire week without killing anyone! I have two more days to go, and I do not plan on losing now. However, you do have something we greatly want," said the soldier, pointing to the casks in the back. "It's been a long week. Would you and your boy care to take refuge with us this evening, and in return, share some of your wine?" My heart leapt. The enemy had taken the bait!

Lionel looked over at me and groaned. "I think the boy and I could use a bit of rest."

"You have my word: you will be safe and none of my men will harm you." The commander gestured for us to follow him into the garrison. Without a moment of hesitation, I steered our horse toward the entrance, and before I knew it, found myself right in the middle of the enemy camp.

Lionel and the commander came into view shortly after. The commander pointed Lionel to an area by a fire on the right side of the camp, letting him know that we could rest there for the evening. Lionel limped over to me, continuing the deception with great skill. As he came within earshot, he said, "What are you waiting for, lazy bones!? Unload the wine! These thirsty soldiers are waiting!"

I nodded and began unloading the first cask. Before I could move it an inch, I had a line of soldiers at the cart asking if they could assist us, no doubt caring more about the cargo than our wellbeing. I humbly accepted, and they worked the cask off the cart. When the barrel hit the ground, a cheer came up from all around. Several soldiers patted me on the back and thanked me.

The wine barrel moved off to the left side of the camp and was placed in front of a cluster of tents. Several soldiers busily worked to get the lid off the cask, while another fetched some drinking goblets. In less than five minutes, the lid was off, and the soldiers were greedily scooping goblets into the cask, filling their cups to the brim.

The sound of laughter rang forth as they drank, which was pitiful to see. These soldiers only found peace and happiness at the bottom of a wine barrel. Suddenly, I felt a sharp pain on the side of my head and heard Lionel's character voice shouting at me. "That second cask isn't going to get itself off the cart! Move to it, boy!" The pain I felt had been the crutch Lionel was holding. He had whacked me with it on the side of the head. I made a mental note to discuss this character Lionel had created with him later. In the meantime, I got busy unloading the heavy cask. This time I felt a gentle but firm hand on my back, and a steady, polite, voice spoke.

"Do you need some help with this one?" I turned around to see four men dressed in all black from head to toe. Their heads were cowled with the hood of a cloak, and on the chest of the mid-section was the golden dragon. My entire being instantly went cold, and I heard Aleph's voice from the inside of me.

"Stay calm. These are the clerics," He spoke. I looked at each

of them and said nothing. I just nodded my head, and they came up to grab the wine barrel and heave it off the cart. The clerics were tall and muscular but thin of frame. The thought of Roderick murdering Tobin right before Father's eyes came to my mind, and fear started to creep in. I thought to myself how these men had the power to control fire, and it made me start to sweat all over again. *"Relax, my son. They will not see you—not until it is too late,"* Aleph finished.

Again, I felt a sharp pain as Lionel's crutch smacked the side of my head. "What are you doing, boy? Daydreaming!? Get to work!"

I finished unloading the cart of some other supplies the camp might be interested in. I took over some salted pork and several loaves of bread, setting it down next to the thirsty soldiers. I walked along the camp distributing the meat, making a mental count of the number of soldiers in the garrison. Since the wine flowed, nobody paid any attention to me or Lionel. They were too busy in their merriment to notice us. As I moved to the north side of the camp, I looked out to where our scouts were positioned, high on a cliff overlooking the camp. I could barely make out the form of Samuel. I continued walking all around the camp until I had reconned everything. Once I had the information, I headed back to the small campfire.

I returned to see Lionel resting and still in character, slumped over and grunting. He had laid out our sleeping mats and was warming his hands. I sat close to him, and in a hushed voice, I gave a report.

"Forty total. One commander, two officers, four clerics, and thirty-three soldiers. Six are at the front gate, two are on each side of the camp guarding the north and south, and three are on the east side. The rest are here in the middle. Lionel nodded quietly and motioned his head back towards the east side of the camp to a large tent. I could see one of the clerics coming out, kneeling over the second wine barrel, and filling a goblet. Lionel continued to look forward, not turning at all, as if he could see them out the back of his head. In the light of the fire, he appeared to be deep in calculated thought. He was going over the strategy in his mind and what he had to do.

We waited several hours for the camp to get deeper into their barrels before we made our move. Lionel stretched in character and reached back into the inside of the disgusting brown cloak he wore. His fingers felt around for a fissure that no human eye could see. The seamstress who had worked on his cloak had carefully sewed a secret pocket to hold a tiny brown cloth bag. Inside the tiny brown bag was a pinch of powder. The powder contained ingredients unknown to me, but Loretta promised me that just a pinch in a barrel would make any grown man sick for days.

With the tiny bag concealed in his hand, Lionel stood up and walked slowly on his crutch towards the cleric's tent. I looked around the rest of the camp to see who would be watching. Attention within the camp was on the wine and laughter, while all sentries positioned on the edges were focused on what lay outside. The commander and his officers were laughing merrily and drunkenly inside their tent as well.

Lionel continued slowly towards the cleric's tent. As he got within reach of the wine, I saw him trip and begin his descent headlong into the barrel. It was comical. He let out a cry and dropped the crutch as he fell forward. He reached out his hands to grab the sides and missed, which sent his arms and body into the barrel. There was a large splash, and wine went everywhere as Lionel was immersed up to his armpits in a barrel of wine.

There was a cry from within the cleric's tent, and all four of them came out to surround Lionel. They cursed him for falling into their precious wine barrel, telling him he was a fool who should watch where he was going. Another cleric grabbed Lionel, heaving him out of the barrel and onto the ground. Lionel lifted his hands and began groveling in apology. He was telling them he only meant to examine the amount of wine that was left. The cleric picked him up roughly, pushed the crutch into his hands and shoved him away, telling him to "go back and sit by the fire."

Lionel limped over to me and collapsed, drenched in wine. He then slapped me. "Where were you, boy?" he shouted in character. "I could have drowned, you know!" I didn't mind the pain as his palm slapped the side of my face. It was the only thing that kept me in character and stopped me from laughing out loud.

We watched as the four clerics laughed together over how Lionel had fallen into the wine barrel. What they had not seen was how Lionel had expertly opened his fist when he was immersed in the barrel and let the poison loose within. In about fifteen minutes' time, the formula would take effect, and they would wish they were close to a privy. I shuddered at the thought of the bowel movement that was about to be released. In absolute naiveté of the near future, they filled their goblets with the poisoned wine and went back to their debauchery.

◇

It did not take long at all for the poison to run its course. We saw the first cleric run out of the tent, holding his bottom and looking for a secluded place to relieve his bowels. Then another ran out doing the same. After the fourth cleric had run off, I looked to Lionel. He nodded and pulled the cloak's hood over his head.

Leaving his crutch on the ground, he rose. His movements were quick and agile, moving from one shadow to the next through the camp. I could not believe what I was seeing. Never in my life had I expected this older man to have such agility, but here it was on full display. Moving in the direction of the first cleric, he disappeared from my view. Several moments later, he darted toward the second cleric.

I cannot imagine the look on their faces or the thoughts in their minds as their lives were ended suddenly. I felt pity for them but knew this was necessary. It was either them or us.

Lionel appeared out of the shadows from the direction of the fourth cleric and made his way back toward me. He was not limping anymore; his character was broken. He gave me the signal that it was time to finish this. Without hesitation, I reached into the secret pocket of my cloak and searched until I found another small pouch. It contained another one of Loretta's concoctions—granules that were used to stoke a flame and cause a fire to increase in intensity. With the powder in hand, I ran over to the wine barrel.

As I stood beside the barrel, I looked around one last time at the camp. Everyone was completely oblivious to anything except wine. I opened my fist and let the granules fall right next to the barrel. Once a small pile had been positioned correctly, I took the small log that was still aflame and touched the pile of granules.

There was a short, continuous popping sound as the flame contacted the granules. I quickly set the log down and ran in the opposite direction. I heard a soldier shout the words, "Hey you!" But that was as far as he got. What followed was a loud explosion of fire and wine spraying in all directions. The powder had ignited in flame and set the barrel on fire to the point of combustion. The explosion sent flaming wine in all directions. The flames quickly ignited the cleric's tent, setting it ablaze.

Lionel grabbed me, and we ran off toward the back of the camp to hide. The soldiers had all come running towards the fire in alarm. They were shouting and screaming. Then we heard a louder voice in the direction the fourth cleric had gone.

"Over here! It's a dead body!" There were more shouts of outrage. We were hidden under a cart, but didn't have much time left before we were found. I prayed to Aleph that Father would be here soon.

The booming voice of the commander could be heard. "Where are the old man and the boy? Find them! This is their doing!" I could hear soldiers moving all around us. Lionel and I stayed as quiet as we could. I could see the feet of soldiers moving in on our location. I held my breath, waiting for the end. Several soldiers were only a few feet from where we were. We heard a shout from the front gate.

"We're under attack!" The soldiers standing near the cart began to move away from us. Lionel and I got out from under the cart. We saw the backs of the soldiers as they moved towards the front of the camp. "We heard shouts of soldiers yelling, "Where are the clerics? They have archers! They are coming through! It's the order!"

I came out from hiding and watched as my brothers stormed the front gate and entered the camp. In a whirl of steel and white cloaks, they were on the enemy. The four soldiers on the battlements north and south were dispatched by a handful of archers from Thorne. Groth and Loretta had led a charge around the east side, taking the soldiers out who stood guard there. Before anyone could calculate the numbers, my brothers had dispatched over half of the camp. I could see the commander and his officers amid the melee, trying desperately to defend themselves, but it was no use. Our strategy had been carried out perfectly, and they had no chance. After several minutes, the sounds of battle ceased, and all was quiet.

Father and the brothers stood over a group of soldiers with their hands held up in surrender. They had seen their commanding officers fall in battle and decided it would be best to lay down their arms. Father commanded my brothers to stop the attack. The soldiers were quickly tied up and placed on the south side of the camp.

We worked to put out the fires, and when everything was smoldering, we packed up the cart with provisions. Shortly afterward, the rest of the caravan arrived.

We were unloading our packs to set up camp within the garrison when I saw Stewart ride in and run over to Father. After a short discussion, Father called all of us to pack up. We decided not to stick around but move quickly out the east gate to the North Road Bridge.

Stewart's report was not positive and told of an army that was days behind us, with nearly five hundred soldiers and forty or so clerics. After Father made the announcement, everyone was tense and wanted to evacuate as quickly as possible. We continued to move along the road in haste. Not until we had reached the valley, and we knew we were safe, did we rest.

I awoke early the next morning to a surprise. Esgar was sitting across from me, staring. She had a funny look on her face. She was still in a battle with her thoughts; I could tell it was taking its toll on her. She looked weary and tired.

"Good morning," I said groggily.

"Morning," she said blankly. "Do you want some breakfast? I was about to make something different today and thought you might like some."

"What are you making?" I asked, stretching out the last bit of sleep.

"I caught some fish during the watch last night. I thought I would cook them with some of Loretta's special grill spice. Might be good?"

"How can I refuse that?" I asked sarcastically.

"You can't," she said, going over to a bag of supplies. She opened the bag, reached in, and pulled out a small container of spices. Loretta came into view from the other side of camp. Leaning in, she shook her head, signaling to Esgar that she was putting the wrong ingredients together.

"No. You need to use a pinch of this and a bit of that." Loretta instructed, pointing to several other bags of herbs.

"This one here. Groth likes the kick this one provides. It will give the fish a bit of spice, but it's great for flavor without being too strong."

Loretta had become our resident alchemist, providing everything from spices for food to the dangerous flammable powder we used to destroy the wine cask the night before. Esgar was enjoying Loretta's cooking lesson, not only for the female interaction, but because it kept her mind busy on other things and helped her hide her feelings toward me. I liked watching her interact with the woman from Rivertown, and Loretta enjoyed having an apprentice as well, one who appreciated the complexities of herbs and spices.

"There you go. Now you got it," Loretta encouraged Esgar as she watched her prepare the spices. "Just sprinkle a little of that on your meat, and you should be good to go." Esgar reached for another small bag, and before she could remove any of the contents, Loretta corrected her. "I wouldn't add that. It is too strong. Spice should be subtle. Don't overdo it, because a little bit goes a long way."

After several more minutes of mixing, with the newly concocted grill spice ready, Esgar moved over to the makeshift table that held several pieces of delicious looking carp. She had already cleaned the fish and began sprinkling the spice on the fish evenly. With the spice on the fish, she moved over to the frying pan that had been sitting in the fire for a bit, getting nice and hot. The fish hit the pan and immediately began to sizzle. After several seconds of popping, a fragrance lifted into the air—the smell of fish and spice cooking over the fire. An aroma entered my nostrils, and my stomach reacted. The growl was so loud, Esgar heard it and laughed out loud.

"That hungry, huh?" Esgar teased.

"Famished," I replied.

"Don't worry, we are going to take care of those hunger pangs momentarily," Esgar stated, not taking her eyes off the frying pan.

The fish continued to cook, and Loretta was preparing rice balls to serve on the side. Esgar continued to carefully flip the fish in the pan, making sure each side got the same amount of cooking time. The aroma eventually spread throughout the entire camp, and it drew a crowd into the area around the fire.

Before we knew it, the entire caravan was present. Loretta saw that there was not enough food cooked to serve the entire caravan, so she called Groth over to help. Loretta went back to the table and began preparing more spice. Groth looked around at the circumstance and knew where he was needed. He went to the other makeshift table with the freshly caught fish on it and began working the knife, expertly cleaning the fish. They worked in unison until there was enough food prepared for the frying pan. Before long, all the fish were spiced and cooked, ready to serve.

The first ones to be served this morning were me and Lionel. Esgar handed me a plate piled with a large piece of fish and a hearty-sized rice ball. I looked into her eyes, and as she smiled at me, I silently said, "thank you."

Then the caravan erupted in applause as we received our plate, giving us their thanks for our bravery the night before. I looked across the way to Lionel and met his gaze. He smiled and winked at me. I felt warm inside at this acknowledgment from my elder brother. I was connected to him in a way nobody else could be, and I felt like things would be different between us from this moment forward.

After everyone had been served, Esgar made herself a plate and came to sit next to me. She, Loretta, and Groth had been working hard for the past hour to make sure everyone was served, and they finally had a moment to sit down and enjoy their breakfast. I watched each of them take their first bite and give a consensus of approval.

We had one more day of travel before we reached the Rift and the completion of our journey north—at least for some. I had no idea what lay ahead for me. Aleph needed me for a special purpose but had been silent since Lionel and I invaded the enemy camp. That didn't stop me from waking up early and spending time with him. Not hearing His voice didn't mean I couldn't sense His presence. My senses had been awakened in a new way, and I could see Aleph everywhere. He was in the trees as they blew and in the chirp of the birds as they sang. It was such an incredible experience, and it was different every single time.

That day, I was riding next to Samuel, and I decided to ask my best friend a question. "How do you hear from Aleph?" He looked at me with a smile. "I mean do you hear His voice inside you, or do you hear Him in nature?"

"I hear Aleph most clearly when I'm outside, but also when it's quiet and I'm all alone."

"Does he speak to you?" I continued to press.

"Sometimes," he responded. "But it is not an audible voice. It's like a whisper from the inside." My heart rate began to increase as I heard my best friend confirm my thoughts.

"That's how it is for me, too! It's really soft, almost like it is my own voice."

Samuel looked right into my eyes. "Daeric. This is only the beginning for you. Aleph has plans for you that supersede anything any of us have seen or experienced so far. Not even King Rian himself has heard what you will."

"I just wish I knew what I was supposed to do." Samuel reached out and patted my shoulder from the saddle of his horse. "You will, my friend. I don't think you will have to wait much longer."

As he said those words, almost immediately, the atmosphere shifted. The air became colder as we approached the base of Shaddyia. The valley was beginning to open before us. The steep slopes on the sides of us began to creep back into the mountains until all we could see were trees all around us. And then...we were there.

CHAPTER
20

The Rift. I saw the glorious expanse stretched out in every direction before me. An enormous valley had been cut through the rock of the mountains. As Aleph's tears had fallen on that terrible day in the ancient years, the Shelf of the Ternion Mountains had its own battle. The might of the mountain could not hold back the power of the river as it flowed. The mountain was cut in half, and the river coursed right through the center of it. Aleph then took his hand and scraped a valley into the rock about two miles in diameter. Trees and wildlife flourished in abundance.

The valley was an incredible sight to see. The sun began to set in the west, bathing the area in a golden light. The Ternion Mountains towered in the far north, keeping watch over all the land. The Rift sat at the feet of the mountain range, always under the faithful watch of the three peaks, Lissyia, Kyrdia, and Shaddyia. The only way into the Rift was through the valley to the east or west. The foliage wrapped itself around the valley in a bowl of green, all the way to the foot of the mountains and up into the heights.

Esgar came riding up next to Samuel and me, pointing into the distance. I followed her gesture, and my eyes went to the center of the valley. I saw a long wall of stone and behind it, a large stone fortress with a hollow center.

Esgar explained. "The wall is called the Ternion Gate, built by the men of Raithe during the war. The fortress protects the way to Aleph's Steps, the ancient path that will take you to the summit of Shaddyia. The only way into the mountain pass is through the large gate at the north side of the fortress. Following the path will eventually lead you to the summit."

"How do you know this?" I pressed.

Esgar looked at me and continued without answering my question. "Ten years ago, the magistrate sent many expeditions into the cruel heights of Ternion in search of the summit. These expeditions were a failure, and the magistrate abandoned the fortress and any desire to search for the blade or the summit. Nobody on any expedition ever returned."

"What do you mean by the blade?" Samuel and I asked together.

"They were in search of Aleph's sword Alestor, the mythical blade that would enthrone the wielder in Aleph's light. Anyone who carried the sword would be king, with the authority to command anyone. Long ago, after the time of Rian, the great king of old, Aleph decided the sword would be safe at the summit of Shaddyia, away from men. During the War of Ancients many tried to scale the peak in search of Aleph's temple, which according to stories resides at the summit to this day, a holy sanctuary, built by the guardians." Esgar then galloped forward before Samuel and I could ask any more questions.

We looked at each other in shock. Samuel and I were probably sharing the same thoughts. He then voiced what was in my mind aloud. "How does she know all of this? Has she been here before?" After several minutes of debate, we settled into the saddles of our horses and continued our ride towards the Ternion Gate.

Our company walked together over another bridge, to the north side of the Antioch, and into the heart of the beautiful valley. The horses were restless after our confrontation and were ready to stop working for the day. As we made our way into the valley, we saw tents set up on the north side of the river in front of the Ternion Gate. The turrets along the walls were occupied very sparsely with guards. I rode up to Father and Geoffrey as they were speaking about the defenses.

"Not near enough men. There is no way to hold the fortress if Baelor's army crosses the river," Father said.

"What if we had battlements along the shoreline and a contingent at the fortress to protect the women and children?"

"I believe that is probably our best option. We need to make sure they don't cross," Father concluded.

They were talking as if the battle were coming right here to this very spot, and it filled me with a sliver of fear. Before it could take hold, Esgar rode up beside me. She must have sensed what I was thinking and said aloud.

"Numbers don't always win the battle." Father and Geoffrey looked back at Esgar and smiled.

"Well said," Father stated. Geoffrey agreed, and they cantered their horses slightly ahead of us toward the gate. The valley began to slope upward as we approached the massive wall. We could see a large number of tents set up in front of the fortress. People were milling about doing every kind of activity—men, women, and children. I could see horses, pigs, and cattle as well. If I had to guess, there were about a thousand people gathered before us.

We slowly moved our caravan through the center of the encampment. The men and women were of all shapes, sizes, and color. Each one of them was going about their day as if everything were normal. Children were playing, while women were doing laundry, cooking, and preparing meals. I saw men singing and working together. They were in fact building structures out of wood with tools.

We stopped our caravan in the center of the camp, and people immediately came to help us unload. We were met with praises and blessings from Aleph. They all thanked us for being here and blessed the Order of the Elect. I wondered, "How do these people know we are the order?" As we walked towards a clearing in the center of camp, I heard a war cry and the familiar clang of steel. We dropped our belongings and ran together towards the sound.

We turned right and passed a cluster of tents into the open area. What I saw made my heart stop. Familiar training was taking place in three circular pits. Swords clashed; bodies moved through the air like wind through a keyhole. Two against three. Three against one. One against two. I counted twelve men adorned in cloaks that were white with red trim at the bottom and fourteen in cloaks of white with blue trim.

My heart filled with joy and hope at the sight before me. Father had joined us by that time, and we all looked at each other. We were smiling and thanking Aleph silently in our hearts because now we knew we were no longer alone. Aleph in his incredible wisdom and mercy had reunited us with our brothers from Shelbye and Chisenhall.

Father ran up to two older gentlemen, and they embraced, almost weeping tears of joy at the sight of him. They spoke for a while, and then Father led the two men over to me. I stood there awkwardly as they smiled and stared at me.

"Daeric, my son. It is my absolute pleasure to introduce to you Father Seth and Father Marec." My eyes got wider at the announcement of the men before me. I watched as they both bowed grandiosely before me.

"It is an honor to serve Aleph's highly favored one," Father Seth said.

"If there is anything you need from us, please let us know," added Father Marec. My thoughts were out of control. Here were the two leaders of the original sanctuaries in Chisenhall and Shelbye, and they were bowing to me? It was too much to handle. Father must have known, because he straightened the two brothers and led them over to the other side of the fighting pits to continue their conversation. I turned around to go back to my belongings and saw Esgar watching from a distance with that same embattled look on her face as she debated inwardly. She noticed that I had caught her eavesdropping and immediately went back to the unloading of the cart.

That evening was an amazing night of celebration. Everyone brought forth all kinds of food and prepared a large feast. Tables were set up in the center of camp, and everyone dined together in fellowship. Laughter, tears, fun, music, and dancing ensued. During the party, more and more people arrived, and once again, everyone joined together to help the newcomers get settled. It went on throughout the night. Amid the celebration, all the brothers took some time to separate ourselves from the rest of the camp. Together as a group, we spoke at length about the events that had transpired. The story seemed to be the same all over Shalistar. The reaping had occurred in every major city, from east to west. People had been given a choice. Those who chose Baelor were sent to Raithe for processing. If anyone refused, they were swiftly executed.

Just like the refugees that joined us from Thorne, Aleph had led those who were His secretly out of every city and brought them safely to the Rift. All the sanctuaries had been destroyed. Father told the brothers of our battle with the soldiers and the messengers. He relayed to them how we had been saved by the guardians and how the guardians had battled the messengers in the sky. Being the youngest, I did not know these men around me, but Father knew every one of them. He had served beside most in the past eighteen years.

They were soon talking among themselves of Baelor's army and the coming battle to the Rift. Father mentioned his strategies to them for defense. I saw them nod their heads in approval and add their own comments as well. It was just like when we had strategized the taking of the enemy camp only days before. Everyone was heard as they shared their thoughts about the strategy. I could feel the wisdom of Aleph being spoken, and the effect on each brother was miraculous. Courage was being birthed in a new way within each of them as the plan was made. I was excited and expectant to hear what my role was going to be in the strategy, when all of a sudden, Aleph spoke to me.

"Walk away. This is not for you." That word startled me. It was a command, and it was very abrupt. I actually found myself disagreeing with Him about it. I stood there, continuing to listen to my brothers strategize, pretending I didn't hear the voice. He spoke again. *"Walk away, now."* I was now completely off guard and torn in my thoughts. After several minutes and against my will, I dismissed myself and walked away to the outside of camp. When I was alone, I responded to Aleph.

"What do you mean? Am I not going to fight?"

"You are not," Aleph replied.

"Why not?"

"I have another path for you."

"But what about the battle?"

"It will be taken care of." I hesitated and formed many words in my mind, words of excuse and unwillingness. *"Trust me, Daeric. I have already gone ahead of you and prepared the way."* As if on cue, Esgar came into view.

"Here you are. I have been looking all over for you. You need to come to the leader's tent, where everyone is gathering. We have a visitor."

We walked together quickly. The entire camp had gathered, and Esgar and I were towards the back of the group. I stood up on the tips of my toes to see who the visitor was. I only caught a glimpse, but that was all I needed. Standing next to Father, Marec, and Seth was a large man with a bushy black beard.

He was majestic before the people and wore a suit of

shining armor, not forged of this world. His stature had become larger since the last time I had seen him. He was bathed in a radiant light, and around his broad, muscular shoulders was a white cloak with red, blue, and green trim at the bottom. Around his head was a golden band that split his long flowing black hair to either side of his head. The full moon illuminated the sky and made his dark beard appear to sparkle. Everyone looked at him in awe and awaited his announcement. He took several moments to look at the faces in the audience. Then, he spoke.

"I am Jeru. Your guardian. I bid you welcome from Aleph the Most High. He has bestowed his favor on everyone gathered here. You are most fortunate. Aleph has chosen me to oversee the final act of our world's history. As you all know by now, King Remus and his family have been murdered." A groan issued from the crowd, and several people began weeping.

"Aleph understands your pain, and He sympathizes with you in your trial." Jeru encouraged the crowd for several moments and then continued with his briefing. "The order was given by the cruel magistrate, Balafas. This vicious act, however, was the plan of Baelor, our greatest adversary. With the king removed, an army is now being built for domination. This army is being trained in Raithe. This, however, is only the tip of the iceberg. Baelor desires to see a world in opposition to the plans of Aleph and has deceived the people. Over the years, he has manipulated Balafas to create an atmosphere of witchcraft." The crowd expressed dismay as the truth was shared.

"He has sent his messengers, led by Lucien, their General, to assemble and train clerics. Lucien has sent messengers with an offer from Baelor himself. Because you were chosen first by Aleph, no messenger came to you, and your families were able to escape. Those who were not chosen by Aleph were given an offer by Baelor. Each messenger promised these people power, wealth, and protection. Those who have received Baelor's gift are now imprisoned within a world system of sorcery and fear. The fear within them will be their jailer until all has been put to rest." The crowd murmured all around me, giving air to thoughts of unrest.

Jeru, not wanting to lose the crowd, asked them to settle down. After several moments, all was quiet. "I know this is hard to hear, but it is important for you to know what we are dealing with. Those who have surrendered to Baelor are learning to fight; a select few are adept at the forbidden arts of Destruction and Conjuration and will be able to do unnatural things with their power to cause harm to others."

The crowd grew agitated at that moment, with shrieks of fear heard all around. In response to the fear, streams of pure, blinding light exploded from Jeru's body and moved through the crowd. All the murmuring and crying ceased immediately. We were cloaked in the light together, and all attention went back to the guardian standing before us.

"Do not be afraid," Jeru bellowed. "Aleph is greater than all these twisted devices of evil. He has his own plan and has brought all of us here to help fulfill it. The magistrate's army has been sent this way and will be here soon. I am here to testify that they will not succeed in their plan." The crowd began speaking of hope.

Jeru continued, "the Order of the Elect has been brought from Shelbye, Sommerset, and Chisenhall. They are the appointed captains who will lead us in the battle. Aleph has set them apart since birth for service. They are well skilled in combat and are ready to step onto the front lines if needs be to bring us victory. I present to you, your leaders. From Shelbye, Father Seth."

Father Seth stood up and bowed to one knee before the people, lowering his head. By exposing his neck, he was putting his life into their hands. He had given every liberty to the people and submitted himself to them as a servant. Suddenly, out of the crowd came an older woman. She slowly made her way to where Father Seth knelt. She bent herself down low to his head and softly kissed his cheek. Symbolically, she had stepped out on behalf of the people and received his leadership for us all. Father Seth stood back up and moved back into the line of brothers behind Jeru.

"Next I present Father Marec from Chisenhall," Jeru boomed. Father Marec stepped out and moved in front of the crowd. As Father Seth had done shortly before, Father Marec followed suit. As his head lowered, exposing his neck, a young boy of only six years came out of the crowd and kissed him on the forehead. He placed his index finger under Father Marec's chin and lifted it up so he could look into his eyes. Father Marec began to weep.

"I'm not ready, nor am I worthy of this honor," Father Marec pleaded. The boy gently placed his hand upon Father Marec's cheek and consoled him with words. I heard these words as clear as day within my heart. These words were spoken by Aleph, through a young boy, to Father Marec.

"I have made you worthy. I am your strength. I am your shield. I am your exceeding great reward." The boy finished speaking, and Father Marec slowly rose to his feet. He took his place back in line with the rest of the brothers, who hugged and

encouraged him.

"Finally, I present your Elder and High General, Father Anlace of Sommerset." Father stepped out with grace and confidence. He stood before the crowd and knelt without hesitation. His head lowered, and out of the crowd came a large man robed in white, wearing armor like Jeru. As he moved forward, I could see past the brilliance of his robe, and I noticed who was holding his hand.

It was Margaret! She was the widow I had spent time with in Sommerset. As Lady Iska's spy, she had infiltrated the underground society and reported to Father. The guardian walked in step with Margaret and stopped several feet before Father. Margaret covered the rest of the distance and placed her hand on Father's head in blessing. Father's head remained bowed as the guardian with her began to speak.

"It is our honor to bestow upon you this mantle of authority. Watch over these people and be ready to lay down your life for any one of them. Your life has been one of sacrifice to the will of the Great One. Take this gift, and lead these people into a new life." Immediately, there appeared a large gleaming sword. The guardian lifted it high and then brought the sword straight down. As the tip passed into the ground, only inches from Father, there was a sound of a rushing mighty wind. Father, still kneeling, took hold of the hilt and pulled. As the sword was released from the ground, the blade was ignited in flame. He lifted it high above his head and gazed skyward.

The only father I had ever known had been transformed before me in the twinkling of an eye. Standing before me was a mighty warrior and leader of the people. My heart flooded with gratitude for his lifetime of service towards me and the rest of the brothers. The guardian had spoken truly—his life was one of sacrifice. Before I could put together another thought, Jeru continued speaking.

"Another matter needs our attention. One of you has been chosen for a task of utmost importance." Murmurs and whispers swept through the crowd as they looked around, trying to pinpoint the one to whom the assignment had been given.

"Aleph needs volunteers to travel with him into the Ternion Mountains and assist him as he ascends to the summit of Shaddyia. As he stands before the One, Aleph will pour out his blessing upon him. The climb is very dangerous, and many who go with him may not return. Those who are to assist have already heard it in their hearts. Do not be afraid. Aleph will be with you no matter the circumstance. Where many expeditions have failed, this one will succeed." Jeru finished his announcement and turned directly towards me.

"Daeric, please come forward. " The murmuring reached its apex as I stepped out. The crowd around me parted and allowed me to move towards the front. I walked forward, scanning the people's faces on both sides of the aisle. I saw puzzled looks and gestures of thankfulness all at once. I finally made it to the front and found myself standing before Jeru's massive shining body. "You are highly favored by Aleph, and he wishes to meet with you," he spoke to me, smiling. All I could do was look up into the brilliance and nod my head.

Jeru then turned his attention back to the crowd. "Who will go with this brave young man into the mountain pass?" Several horrifying moments of silence followed. Nobody moved or responded to the call of the guardian. I thought to myself how lonely it would be to climb to the top of the mountain, when suddenly I heard the sweetest voice cry out from the back of the crowd. My heart stopped, and I whipped around to confirm the owner of the voice.

"I will go," Esgar said again as she walked forward to stand beside me. I was overwhelmed with the situation and felt as though I were in a dream. When she finally stood beside me, I looked into her eyes, and she smiled. The warmth of her smile spoke of loyalty that would never die. But there was determination in her stance that showed she was ready to march straight into hell and beyond.

"Count me in!" exclaimed Samuel as he came and stood beside me as well.

"As are we," cried Groth. He and Loretta came over hand in hand and stood next to us as well. Then, like a flood, people from all over the crowd begin raising their hands and shouting out their acceptance of the assignment.

My brothers came around me, patting me on the shoulder and praying for me. The guardians stood away from us and looked on with care. I saw Father enter the circle and the brothers move aside so he could stand in front of me. I didn't know what to say. I stood up a little straighter and looked into his eyes. He was crying. He softly took my face in his hands and leaned in within a breath's length.

"I am so proud of you," he whispered. "I have always known in my heart that you were extraordinary. I know Aleph is going to fulfill his promise to you in ways far beyond what any of us have seen. It is difficult for me because I must now let you go, for you are no longer mine to watch over." I began to speak, but Father held my face more tightly and cut me off mid-sentence. "You have always belonged to Him, son. I was blessed to have stewardship over your upbringing, but you have always been His. I knew this day would come, but it doesn't make it any easier."

"But...I am going to see you again...right?" I asked Father hesitantly.

"The path I am to take is separate from yours," Father finished. To my surprise, tears burst from me like a river.

"No. No. I don't want to go without you. What am I supposed to do? You have always been with me."

"Son, you are not alone. The one who travels with you in the unseen is the most powerful force in this world. You will lack for nothing. He will take care of your needs."

"But it's because of you...that I am here. Because of you I can HEAR! You have taught me all I know about him."

"Yes. But now it's time for you to get to know Him."

"What if I don't want to?" I said in the softest whisper.

"Daeric," Father whispered back, "He is good." Father wrapped his arms around me and embraced me with all the love he had in his body. He held me for several minutes. Then he kissed me on the cheek and whispered into my ear, "You must believe, boy. You must believe. He wants to lead you. Let go of me and go to Him." Then I felt his hands lift off my shoulders as he took a step away. He gave me one final smile before he turned away and walked through the ring of brothers.

After the announcements had been made, everyone went back to their tents for a good night's sleep. The next morning, we made ourselves ready for the journey ahead. We were led to a preparation area inside several tents on the edge of camp. As I walked towards them, we passed the fighting pits, where Jeru was overseeing the combat. Father was nowhere to be seen.

I entered the tent and saw all the equipment that had been assembled. Everything had been prepared for us while we slept. I walked along and saw a pile of different equipment with a name tag on top. I spied swords, axes, bows, and quivers. Some piles had shields, armor, and doublets. Then I came to mine.

I looked at the provisions, and my stomach dropped. I could only see three items on the ground. One pack had a small brown bag in it and nothing else. I had been given a coiled rope and a staff. I looked behind me through the front of the tent, up at the peaks and wondered how we would make it all the way to the top. The situation was frustrating, and I found myself storming out of the tent and quickly walking back to Jeru.

"Is this all we have to take?" I asked brazenly.

"It is," Jeru replied, not looking in my direction.

"Is this a joke? How am I supposed to make it to the summit with only a coil of rope and a walking staff?" I explained. "Expeditions ten times this size have been destroyed by the tri-peaks, and they were much better prepared than we are. This is impossible!" Jeru slowly turned toward me, and his eyes looked straight through me.

"Daeric, you seem to think you are still in control." I could feel Jeru's rebuke hit me with the weight of a hammer. "It was Aleph who asked you to climb and meet him at the summit. He has given you everything you need to get to the top. Where does your confusion lie?"

"Everyone else got tools and weapons," I returned.

"Yes, and they will need them. But not you. He will show you a different path."

"You know it's certain death for anyone who goes up there."

"Yes. But not for you. The expeditions before were all for vanity. Aleph would never allow them to reach the summit, and yes, they had every tool imaginable. But you will succeed where they have all failed. Now, go." Jeru finished and turned back to the melee in the fighting pits. I had never heard Jeru speak like that before. I felt as though I had just been whipped. But he never raised his voice, and I didn't hear the slightest tremor of anger. I decided it would be best if I just walked away now. The conversation was obviously at an end.

I walked back into the preparation area, grabbed my small pile of supplies, and left. I saw Groth and Loretta checking their packs and sharpening the blades they had received. I felt a twinge of jealousy towards them. It was silly, but I felt like they were much better prepared than I was. Our group had assembled, and I got a good look at each of them. It was strange being with all these people around me. None of them knew me, yet they had volunteered to go on a quest that would surely end in death. It was hard for me to look anyone in the eyes, so I kept my head down. As I was rifling through my pack on my hands and knees, I saw Samuel coiling a rope around his foot nearby. He smiled and came over to where I was. I continued looking in the almost empty pack with a disgusted look on my face.

"These people follow you because they have hope," I heard my dear friend say as he sat down on a large log next to me.

"They have no idea what they have agreed to."

"And you do?"

"I know my end."

"No, you don't. If you did, you wouldn't be acting this way."

"And what way is that, Samuel!?"

"You are walking around hopeless. You have your head down as if you are carrying the weight of the world. But you are not. Aleph asked you to climb. That's all you have to do."

"With what? A rope and a staff?"

"That's not your concern, Daeric!" Samuel boomed. "I have no doubt in my mind He can get you to the top alive. Daeric, don't you see what is happening here?"

"I guess I don't."

"Aleph is relating to us again… face to face. There has not been a request in Shalistar for hundreds of years to meet him at the top of Shaddyia. He is going to appear and do something."

"What?" I asked.

"I don't know. But he asked for you. You are blessed. These people look at you and have hope renewed within them. They have lost everything too, Daeric—you and I are not the only ones. You have been my friend for a long time. I know you better than most here. But you have changed. Aleph is working fast and needs your help. Your Father and I both knew this day would come. He believes in who you really are. So do I. Everyone here believes in you—believe in yourself."

"But who am I?" I asked desperately.

"Climb and find out," Samuel said as he walked away from me.

CHAPTER
21

I awoke from a restless night, groggy and tired. I had no desire to spend time with Aleph this morning, but I forced myself, regardless of the circumstances. I found a quiet spot away from everyone and sat down in the grass. I closed my eyes, opened my journal, and let my thoughts drift onto the pages. Why was I so angry, and why did I feel so empty? Only hours before I had been filled with joy and peace, knowing that Esgar, Samuel, Groth, and Loretta would be with me. Now, all I felt was uncertainty. I could not help but think about all the people who were walking into a frozen death. I then felt desperate for Father to be near me. I asked questions out loud, but Aleph didn't have any answers to give—either that, or I couldn't hear him. After a few minutes of waiting in silence for a response, I decided to get up and join the rest of the group.

As the caravan began to leave, I looked around for Father, hoping he would show up to see me off, but he could not be found. I was frustrated to the core of my being. Why was he not here? We had spent eighteen years of life together, and now all of a sudden, he was gone? It was too much to bear at the moment. I sat down with my head in my hands, unable to keep the thoughts of Father at bay.

Esgar came up to me and put a hand on my shoulder.

"Are you okay?" she asked in concern.

"I don't really want to talk about it right now," I quickly returned.

"Okay...I think Loretta and Groth were going to make breakfast for us all before we head out." Hearing that breakfast was going to be made by those two made my stomach start to growl.

"Sausage and eggs?" I asked hopefully.

"Yep, and corn cakes too...with cinnamon!" I turned to look up at her. She was looking down at me with a cute smile. "Figured that would get you out of your funk. Come on." She extended a hand for me to grab. I gripped it, and she pulled me up from my sitting position. I lost my balance coming up and fell forward. She grabbed me by both of my arms and steadied me.

"Are you okay?" she asked as I came to a standing position.

"Yah. I just miss Father," I replied.

"It's okay, I understand. We all need help from others sometimes. I cannot tell you how many times in my life all I needed was a father to give me a hug and encouragement. I just needed someone to give me a hand to help me stand. That is why you and I are here, for each other. I'm going to help you stand!" Esgar finished with a loud slap on my back.

Her words helped me a little—at least, enough to join the rest of the group for breakfast. As I entered the area, everyone was laughing and talking about the journey ahead. Groth and Loretta were their jovial selves, smiling from ear to ear and having a good time as they prepared the meal for all thirty of us. She saw me enter and put down all her utensils to applaud my arrival. Everyone else joined in the round of applause, making me blush.

I just smiled and waved my hand, then quietly sat down. I scratched the side of my face where a short stubble of hair had grown the night before. I didn't feel like shaving this morning, so I just let it grow. I had a feeling I would need as much face covering as I could muster before the end of our journey into the cold.

Loretta passed out the food she had been making since before sunrise. "Be sure to enjoy this one," she told everyone as she handed them a full plate. "It might be the last full-sized meal we have for a while." She handed me my plate and looked me in the eyes. "Are you okay?" she asked me with care.

"Why does everyone keep asking me that?" I retorted. "I'm fine!"

"Interesting comment. That's what Groth always says after he hits his finger with a hammer," Loretta said, still smiling at me.

"Sorry. I had a hard night," I apologized.

"I figured. I think you will feel better after you fill your belly."

"You are probably right."

And she was. I took my first bite, and before I knew it, the plate was empty. I felt better and full of strength. We were sitting together, eating and fellowshipping, when Jeru came into our midst with another elderly man next to him. The man was tall and muscled with long gray hair. When Jeru saw me, he came over with the man in tow.

"Good morning, favored one!" Jeru said boldly.

"Good morning, sir," I replied.

"I want to introduce someone very special to you." Jeru gestured for the stranger to come forth. The man stepped forward, slightly bowing his head to me. "Aleph would like for this part of your journey to be recorded and has sent you a fantastic historian. He has been in Aleph's service for a long time. But don't let age fool you. He is well-bodied and able to travel into the depths with you. May I present...Artour." The man stepped forward and bowed even more deeply.

"It is an honor and pleasure to serve you, favored one!" Artour spoke in a deep and resonant voice, as though he had been speaking in front of crowds for his whole life. Every word was perfectly enunciated.

"Thank you, sir, for being here," I stated slowly. "Father has spoken about you and how you served Father Marec for many years. Your work is renowned, and I'm honored to have your service."

"Yes, Aleph has woven many stories in the past and used me to write them down, but I feel like the greatest story is ahead of us. My pen is ready, and I look forward to the adventure." I made a mental note to spend more time with Artour and then dismissed myself politely.

I took one last walk around the camp looking for Father but could not find him. I decided to walk towards the fortress in my search. Maybe he was walking the battlements, giving out orders to his men. I went into the fortress through the

Ternion Gate and found myself in the middle of a stone courtyard. There were steps on both sides going up into the battlements on the east and west. The walls on both sides connected to the south wall, forming a solid defense. To the north was the last gate that opened into the cold of the mountains beyond. The entry was a heavy portcullis made of wrought iron from many years ago.

I was about to give up my search when I looked to the north. There upon the battlements was Father! He was in an intense conversation with some men, showing them the correct way to thrust with a sword. I put my hands on both sides of my mouth and was about to shout when Aleph spoke.

"No, Daeric. Please leave him alone. His path is separate from yours."

I was having a hard time understanding why Aleph would not want me to say goodbye to my father. I thought a moment about disobeying Him and was about to shout when Aleph gently spoke again.

"He is having a hard time with this, Daeric. Please leave him alone."

"What about me?? I am having a hard time, too! I can't even say goodbye to the man who raised and nurtured me my whole life?"

"I would not suggest it. He has a battle to prepare for, and the world will need him focused." As Aleph said that, I saw thousands upon thousands of people. They were men, women, and children by the hundreds, and they invaded my mind in a split second. *"The faces you are seeing are the faces of my people, Daeric, and your father has been called to protect them. This is bigger than you alone. I have called you for a different purpose."*

The weight of the vision nearly knocked me over. My mental battle had reached its climax as I looked up one last time to the battlements. Father was standing there, but now he was focused on another group of men, instructing them as well.

"Walk away, Daeric. You can do it. Leave him to me." I did not understand any of it, but forcing my body to move, with one last groan, I surrendered to the will of Aleph. Turning away from my father, I walked out the south gate of the fortress.

Unlike the caravan we had acquired by the time we made it to the Rift, the expedition into the heights of Shaddyia comprised of a group of thirty. We were all on foot, taking only what we could carry. Very little food was in our possession. That was the biggest question we had put to Jeru before leaving, but he only smiled and said, "Be anxious for nothing! Aleph has already made provision. You will be well taken care of."

A flurry of questions came from my companions all at once, and Jeru lifted a hand to quiet them. "Your focus is not what happens down here. You must escort Daeric as far as you can. Then, make your way back down another way. That path will be shown to you in the proper time. You have been given weapons not only for the wilds of Shaddyia, but also the enemy. Secret paths to the summit may exist that the enemy may know about, and it is best to be ready." Jeru then gave us some practical advice for climbing. "During your ascent, it is best to go slow. Some of you are not acclimatized to the altitude and may be adversely affected. The air is thin in the heights, and it is best to take your time. Stay together, protect one another, and your mission will be a success.

I bless you all in Aleph's holy name!"

◇

With those final words, we were off and moving through the fortress courtyard towards the north gate. Only a few men and women remained on the battlements; everyone else was back at the camp, preparing for battle. I was hoping that maybe Father would be at the gate to say goodbye, but he was not. None of the brothers were. The only white cloaks in the area were my own, Samuel's and Jeru's, behind me.

The iron workings of the gate screeched loudly as the portcullis slowly lifted. "How long has it been since this gate was opened?" I thought to myself. As we passed under the heavy steel spikes, the ground beneath us went from stone to dirt and rock. The confined space of the fortress opened and large trees were on all sides of us. I looked ahead and saw the path continue upwards until it was lost from sight in the distant fog.

We made sure everyone was present and walked together as a group, beginning our ascent. Esgar and I were side by side. Loretta, Groth, and Samuel went ahead of us, and Artour was behind. Even though our steps were quick and full of energy, I felt hollow and empty without Father. I was uncertain of my purpose and kept to myself, saying very little to anyone. Jeru's words brought me no kind of comfort either. I looked behind me from time to time, wondering when or if I was going to hear the cries of battle.

We took a break in the early afternoon. The path was beginning to grow steep, and the air was becoming thin. I could tell we were all breathing much more deeply than we had before. The chill in the air was noticeable as well. We had all donned cloaks and heavy, warm doublets to keep the cold air from biting our skin. We sat together, passing the provisions bag around. Each one of us took a share of the food. I was the last to receive it, and when it had gotten to me, I noticed there was only enough left for dinner that evening. "This is madness!" I thought to myself. We are all going to starve to death!"

Esgar leaned in close to me and whispered in my ear. "Don't worry. Aleph will provide." I looked up and saw that cute smile again.

"You think you know me?" I asked.

"I know what you are thinking," she responded. I didn't answer, merely chewing the food that had been rationed for me.

We hiked the rest of the day until we could not see the path in front of us anymore, due to the cold and darkness around us. The large oak trees had turned to evergreens, and the ground had a distinctive crunching sound as we walked upon it, throwing up wafts of snow. Looking down behind us as the sun was setting, what little ground I could see was miles away. Looking up from this viewpoint, it seemed we were already halfway up. The air was much thinner, and every breath was harder to take.

That evening we all huddled closely around the fire together, using our bodies to keep each other warm. We passed the provision bag from one to the next. It came to me last, once again. I reached in and pulled out the final ration. The bag was completely empty. Our provisions had run out.

No one else seemed to notice. They laughed and joked with each other as they shared stories about their previous lives. Loretta was in the middle of telling a great story when she was suddenly taken by a spasm of coughing. Groth gently patted her on the back with his hand, asking her if she was okay. Loretta nodded and cleared her throat. She apologized and went right back to her story.

After a night of enjoying each other's company, we opened our sleeping mats and stretched out for the night. I was so exhausted from the restless night before last that the second I laid my head on my arm, I was fast asleep.

I awoke to the cold air on my face and the warmth of the sunlight through the leaves of the trees. It was going to be a lovely morning for hiking up the mountain, but I found myself unable to put a smile on my face. I looked at the rest of my companions as they opened their bags, looking for some source of provision, but finding none. We were probably about four thousand meters from the ground, about to begin our climb, and I noticed the people gathered around me kept looking at me for a speech or word of encouragement.

Since none of them would be making it to the top, I had nothing to say. My thoughts were to tell them to run away and not follow me, but I knew they would not listen to me. If Father were here, he would be able to comfort and pray for the people. But alas, Father had another path to follow. The thought filled me with loneliness.

Esgar sat next to me on the ground and gestured to my pack. "Got anything to eat?" she asked in her dry sense of humor. I watched as everyone opened their bags, hoping there would be some miraculous provision in there that had not been before. Just to put the issue to rest, I pulled open my backpack and looked in. The contents were the same as before. All I saw was the small brown bag for herbs and ingredients. It was large enough to put my hand in and pull out a handful of whatever I had decided to put in there. Then a thought came to me. I reached in and pulled out the small bag. Something was inside of it. Everyone was watching as I opened the bag and reached in. My hand gripped the contents and slowly pulled them out, careful not to spill any.

I opened my palm to see a handful of dried fruit and nuts. I was baffled at the contents of the bag but hungry as well, so I took some and put them in my mouth. The fruit was deliciously sweet, and the nuts were crunchy. Esgar reached out her hand, and I placed the bag in it. She also brought out a handful of fruit and nuts. She smiled, thanked Aleph, and began eating from the pile of food in her palm.

"What were we going to do when the food ran out? How could everyone be smiling and full of energy? Did they know that to go forward was to embrace death?" I wondered. The bag was passed from Esgar to Samuel, who portioned out a meager amount and passed the sack to the person sitting next to him. They did the same. I watched as the bag made its way through the camp. "Surely we must be running out of food," I thought. But as I continued to watch, people kept on reaching in and pulling out generous amounts. The bag made its way around. It landed in the hands of Groth, and he shared it with Loretta, who was still coughing from the night before.

Esgar leaned over and whispered into my ear, "What is wrong?"

"I don't know," I whispered back.

"You haven't been yourself since the announcement was made."

"I'm sorry, Esgar. These people are looking for a leader and I am afraid I am not it. How can I minister hope to them when I can't see any myself?"

"You are overthinking this whole thing," she replied pointing her finger to her head.

"Am I? I'm curious. What did Aleph tell you?" I returned.

"To go and climb with you."

"That's it?" I asked in shock.

"That's it."

"And you are willing to just go out on that?"

"Yes," she replied with confidence.

"But why?"

"Because He requested it."

"What's that supposed to mean?"

"If you knew Him, you wouldn't ask why."

"Wait a second…you think I don't know him? Have you forgotten that I am a brother of the Order of the Elect?" I asked with my chest puffed out.

"That's who you were."

"So now I'm to go and scale an unclimbable mountain and learn who I am?"

"Yes."

"That doesn't make any sense, you know?"

"It never does. Not to us." She then reached over and grabbed the bag and dropped it in my lap. She had a clever grin on her face as she sat it down. The weight of the bag was surprising and took my breath away. It was heavier than before! "He knows exactly what He is doing," she finished.

She was right, and I knew it. I grunted and lifted the bag off my lap, placing it on the ground. I opened it up and saw all the food was still in there. I immediately looked around me and saw that everyone was happily eating and laughing together.

I looked again in the sack and noticed several food items that had not been there before. I couldn't help but feel foolish at the moment. A tremor of hope rose from within me. Aleph had provided more than enough food for our group to eat and had also performed an outstanding miracle that I could see with my own eyes and embrace with my heart. I looked down and silently apologized to Aleph for having doubted his provision. As if in response, Samuel sat down next to me and patted me on the knee.

"Aren't you going to have seconds?"

We set off shortly after breakfast. The morning was blessed with sunshine, and all around us the animals were singing as we passed by. We followed the path under the leaves of the trees. As noon came, the valley began to close in around us. The path was much narrower as we made our way further into the Ternion Pass, up Aleph's Steps, into the high altitudes. Our company traveled slowly and cheerfully the entire day. Many people took time to walk beside me, and I heard all about their lives before the "night of shadows," as we came to call it.

That afternoon, I was blessed to walk beside Artour, the historian, and learned more about his abundant life. He had spent his years researching and recording the events that have shaped our world. I was especially intrigued about the War of Ancients and asked many questions. He asked if he could share his knowledge with the entire company tonight after dinner. I told him it would be an honor. Artour and I continued our conversation until the entire group suddenly stopped.

Loretta's coughing had become intense, and she was keeled over in a spasm. Groth had his hand on her back, patting her and offering soothing words of comfort. Esgar helped her to sit on the ground and instructed her to put her head between her knees, breathing deeply. After several moments of this, Loretta was able to catch her breath.

We decided to make camp on the snowy ground and began to set fires. The company worked together with cooperation, and everything was set up in no time at all.

I was concerned for my friend. Esgar and I discussed her health in hushed voices that nobody could hear.

"She is not doing well," Esgar stated in concern,

"I agree, but she is not going to go back. The woman is as stubborn as a mule," I replied as I watched Groth spooning water into Loretta's mouth.

"She needs to be at a lower altitude," Esgar suggested.

I thought it would be best to assess the situation and walked around the camp. I could see all our breath leaving our body in a cloud of warm air. Here we were, thirty of us, probably at six thousand meters from the ground. The trees were sparse as we found ourselves in the thickness of the snow-line. I looked behind and could barely see the Rift from where we were. To the west, nestled into a crevice of rock, I could hear and see a majestic waterfall crashing into the rocks. The water that cascaded down the wall filled the atmosphere with a calm, soothing sound.

I cared about my friend and decided that in the morning I would call a meeting to ask for volunteers to take Loretta back to a safer altitude. But this evening would be spent enjoying Aleph's provision and the fellowship of company.

The evening was a pleasant surprise. As we all sat down for dinner, we expected more fruit and nuts; however, when Esgar reached in to take a handful of food, we were blessed with a bountiful supply of ham and peas. Esgar prepared a pot of snow she had gathered and set it over the fire. She told us this was a soup she made when she lived in Sommerset for that brief period of time. She boiled both the ham hock and peas into a soup. Loretta donated a wonderful spice to the meal as well. Esgar tried to stop her from getting up but realized it was a fruitless pursuit and let her have her way.

With difficulty and coughing, Loretta leaned over the pot and garnished the stew with several spices, and before we knew it, dinner was served. The pot never needed to be filled again. Aleph made sure the soup was never empty. Every person in camp bent down over the fire and filled their cup with the steaming fare. We all filled our bellies and sat back in peace.

The evening continued with songs and laughter. Stories were told all-around of how Aleph had led people and their families to the Rift. Each story needed to be recorded for all to read, and in that moment, I thought about what it would be like to author a book like that. It brought a smile to my face and a warmth in my heart.

In the final hour of the day, Artour, the historian, stood before all of us in the firelight. His posture was straight, his movements fluid. When he spoke, he looked into all our eyes. His voice reverberated off the rocks, yet was soft and gentle. As he spoke, I thought of Jeru and how he sounded a whole lot like him. Artour was graceful as he moved around the fire, capturing everyone's attention. Every now and again, he would be speaking to someone directly in front of him and in the middle of a sentence, whip around, catch the audience behind him unaware and project his voice while hammering a point home. His long gray hair would be in his eyes from the movement, and he would part the strands with his fingers to the side of his chiseled head before continuing his speech. He was a master orator and captured everyone's attention. Although he was well over 70 years of age, he moved and spoke with ageless beauty. He had finished his introduction and began to tell us about the world as it was in the Ancient Days.

"In the beginning," Artour continued, "Aleph began to write. In fact, the name Aleph means "the Beginning." That is not his only name. He has many. Another name I like is "Tav," which means "the End." He is both the beginning and the end, and that is the way he began to write his story. He has knowledge of the future and can therefore write out every possibility for all of our lives. It is important that you know this because it will help you understand why things happened the way they did in the Ancient Years.

"In the beginning, Aleph was there alone, writing a story. First, he created a setting: Shalistar, our world. But...there are other worlds than this one. Then He created His characters: humans. We are His creation, His imagination. But...we are not the only ones. He wrote the end for us in the beginning, and it is a beautiful ending indeed."

As he continued, we all sat around the campfire that night, listening to Artour create a beautiful history in our minds. We held on to every word spoken. He weaved images of the false one, Baelor, and his servants as they declared war on Aleph. He showed us the kingdoms of not only this world but all the others that were affected by this tragic day, when being a servant of Aleph was not enough for Baelor. He had to have it all and deceived many guardians to rally to his cause. We saw the battles across Shalistar and the people who were caught in the middle of this war. Buildings of all shapes and sizes burned to the ground as the eternals fought. Great kings and their armies rose and fell during that time. Many were deceived by Baelor in a quest for power. As puppets on a string, Baelor used every one of them to play out his drama. It went on for many years. Then one day, amid all the chaos, Rian, the young king, climbed to the top of the mountain and sat before Aleph. After they had fellowshipped, Aleph himself descended with him and met Baelor and his armies.

"The Battle of Ancients." Artour continued. "This was the apex and pivotal point in our history which shaped the future we are living in today. It took place in the valley we just left, the Rift. The armies stood on both sides of the Antioch.

Baelor himself had manifested and was in the enemy camp, awaiting this fateful day. He had until now driven Rian's army all the way to the foot of the mountains where they had nowhere to run. Morale was low, and Rian's army had lost all hope, even with the presence of the guardians in their camp. When they woke up to find their king gone without a trace, hope was diminished. In the darkest hour, Baelor's army attacked. Swords clashed; shields clanged. The voice of agony left countless bodies as lives were sacrificed on the battlefield. On the third day, as Baelor's army began to move once again upon the king's army, Rian returned."

Artour became animated as the story reached its climax. He moved quickly back and forth between us, his voice growing louder as the tale reached its conclusion.

"As he walked through the camp, all eyes had to turn away. Aleph's presence was upon him, and Rian's body glowed like embers in a stove. Emitting from the man on fire was an incandescent light that shot out in all directions with brilliance. Every step he took was illuminated with radiance. Morale was instantly ignited, and hope returned to the army as they watched their glowing king walk out of the camp and into the battlefield. Several soldiers ran in haste to stop him but soon fell back, covering their eyes from the brilliant light that surrounded their majesty. Rian continued to walk fearlessly up to the lines of the enemy until the river was all that separated them. Groans and cries escaped from the army across the river as they looked upon the countenance of their adversary.

"Altogether, Baelor's soldiers pulled back the drawstrings of their bows and sent a rainstorm of arrows upon Rian. None of them found its mark. As the projectiles came down, they ignited in a wisp of flame and gave a whispered cough as they vanished into the thin air in a cloud of ash. It was no different when they launched heavy boulders from trebuchets. The stones exploded in all directions as they plummeted towards Rian and his unseen deity. After the final attempt, the air was quiet. The flowing waters of Antioch stood still and became serene. Baelor's army looked on in awe at this solo warrior who had defied all-natural understanding and showed tremendous feats of cosmic power.

"Suddenly, there was a rush of wind across the river. In seven different places came large splashes that sent water spraying into the air, and then once again, everything was silent. The amazement of all was further heightened when, six feet above the splashing, there appeared out of nowhere seven immense gleaming swords. The hilt of each sword was facing downward toward the water. The swords were nearly four feet long, with their blades reaching toward the heavens.

"The light from around Rian vanished, and the glow with it. He stood on the bank before Baelor's army with seven floating swords before him. Rian took hold of his sword and drew it mightily from its scabbard. Instantly the swords' blade caught fire and was infused with Aleph's holy touch. At once, the seven blades before him ignited into flame, and the guardians who held the swords were revealed to the enemy.

"The rest was ordered chaos. Aleph himself made his presence known with an innumerable guardian army. Enrobed in light, He stepped onto the surface of Shalistar. As his feet touched the dirt, the ground trembled and quaked. Fissures appeared throughout the entire valley and a groan of exhaustion echoed from mountains around. Baelor, wrapped in a cloak of darkness, emerged from within the ranks of his army and stood before the guardians. With the black trumpet, he called his messengers from the deep darkness. Just as the guardians had, they appeared from within eternity and surrounded their Dark Lord. In a symbol of honor, Aleph bowed and gestured with his hand for Baelor to join him in the circle of flames. It was then that Baelor, after so many years of resistance, finally met his creator on the battlefield in hand-to-hand combat. There before the eyes of the mortals who were gathered, the Eternals of Shalistar fought.

"Guardians flew skyward, and the messengers met them high above the river. Swords clashed, as the battle cries were heard all the way from Raithe. Baelor turned and drew himself up in a battle stance, preparing to attack. Aleph, without any hesitation, held out his hand with his palm facing Baelor. He opened his mouth and shouted one word."

"Enough!" As he spoke, a mighty wind came from his mouth. The skies thundered and rained. The ground opened and swallowed one third of Baelor's army. The river was transformed into a massive tidal wave that crashed into those remaining. The messengers above met the winds of chaos that came from Aleph's breath and fell back to the ground with a crash.

"At the sound of Aleph's voice, Baelor was knocked completely off his feet onto his back. He lay in a fetal position, screaming in agony, with his hands grasping the sides of his head. His cloak had come off from the top of his head and a golden crown was revealed that sparkled with electric fire. Baelor was on his knees, trying to grasp his crown. His fingers never found it. Suddenly, in a final scream, the crown that was on his head began to lift off. He jumped up, grasping desperately for it as it traveled through the air. He made one final attempt to ascend and pin it to his skull, but he was met by two guardians who flew into his sides. They held his arms out wide, flew skyward fifty meters, and then sharply shifted direction toward the ground. Baelor was crushed into the dirt under the mighty weight of two guardians who held his arms outstretched as far as they would go. They held him down and grabbed his head. They pulled roughly, making him watch the scene that was occurring. Baelor screamed in protest, but the guardians would not relent.

"The crown was floating through the air to the other side of the river, where Rian still stood, transfixed on the scene before him. The crown stopped briefly over Rian and then settled gently onto his head. Aleph, from the other side of the river, called out to him."

"*Come.*" At that command, Rian stepped into the river and found himself walking safely over the now shallow waters. He crossed and stood next to the presence of Aleph.

Baelor, still screaming, looked up as Aleph stood over him. His shrill voice was silenced.

Aleph gently kneeled, looking his broken servant in the face. "*Say it,*" He whispered.

"Never!" spat Baelor. His face and body were then shoved into the ground by the strength of the two guardians.

"Say it now!" the guardians bellowed. From their hands came electric fire, which entered Baelor's body. He screamed again. The guardians pulled him back up and held his head tightly as Aleph's gaze pierced into his blackened soul.

"*Say it,*" Aleph calmly whispered once more.

With great reluctance and intense hatred, Baelor spoke the

words of his damnation. "I surrender."

The guardians released Baelor, and he collapsed into a pathetic heap on the ground. Once again, the air was still, and all was calm. Aleph gently leaned down to where Baelor lay defeated.

"Is my time up?" He asked Aleph calmly.

"No."

"Then why do you torment me?"

"The torment will always be with you. You will never escape it. Your time of rule over this world is coming to an end. The crown has been passed to my king. You will now await your judgment for treason."

"Can I stay here?"

"Yes, I still have use for you. But you have no authority over my people. Whatever they say is the same as if I were speaking to you. That goes for your messengers as well. It has been spoken."

"Yes, my Lord." Baelor whispered under his breath.

"Now...go!" Baelor and all his messengers vanished before Rian's eyes. "Aleph stood and turned to Rian. With his hand outstretched, Rian bowed before Aleph and received his kingdom. The War of Ancients had ended."

Artour was on his knees before us, with his head bowed and his hands clutched tightly together at his chest. A peace had settled over the entire camp. Loretta had stopped coughing. We sat in blessed silence for quite some time before quietly laying down for sleep. Snowflakes began to fall lightly on our camp as my eyes closed. Although the cold snow fluttered the entire night, not one member of our company felt it. We were all wrapped in the warmth of Aleph's touch and slept peacefully under his watchful eyes.

CHAPTER
22

Every member of our company experienced supernatural energy as we made ready for the climb into the heights of the Ternion Mountains. Even Loretta's labored breathing had been steady that morning. It was as if Aleph's breath had blown through our camp in the night and created new strength and life in every one of us. All effects of altitude were gone! We all awoke feeling comfortable, even this high up, so close to the peak of Shaddyia. A supernatural warmth enveloped us. We even found ourselves removing pieces of clothing, getting everything just right before sitting down to breakfast.

Aleph's sack of provision was miraculous this morning. We removed eggs and sausage, Loretta's specialty. After all the provisions were cooked and everyone ate their fill, we were off. The snow crunched under our feet as our boots treaded over the ground. The cadence of our march was hypnotizing. We climbed another thousand meters that day. The company made the climb enjoyable. I traveled beside many people and discussed various topics of interest. Everyone was getting along, and morale was high. It was amazing. People from all over Shalistar walked beside me at different intervals all throughout the day. Of course, my favorite traveling companion was Esgar. We spent the afternoon walking side by side, talking about interests, dreams, and desires. The talk made the day pass in the wink of an eye. Before we knew it, all the trees around us were gone, and we found ourselves in the heights of Shaddyia.

That evening, Groth shared with us how he and Loretta met. It was a silly story. They both had come from wealth and were on holiday with their families in Marthyla. They had gone to the vineyard to have dinner and were one table away from each other, sampling delicate red wines and tender meats, when suddenly there was a stampede right through the center of the restaurant. The cattle destroyed everything except the bottle of wine that was in Loretta's right hand and the glass that Groth had gripped in his left. They were in shock at what had happened. Groth asked Loretta to fill his glass, and he took a long drink from it. Afterwards, Loretta asked him to share the glass with her so she could have some. They both sat there together drinking from the same glass and ended up spending the entire night talking.

They learned that they were both from Chisenhall but did not know each other yet. They made it a point to spend more time together after they both got home, and they did. Eventually, they got married. During the war, Tark had destroyed all that they had and as a result, it led them on a journey to Raithe, but they never made it. They stopped in a quiet village by the river and opened a little store.

We all slept well that evening and continued our march the next day. The path began to get narrower and started to wind around the knees of Shaddyia. A bitter wind blew in, seemingly from all directions. The frigid weather bit all the way down to our bones. I had never felt anything so cold in all my life. It took my breath away and made it hard to even think. As we moved together, the way got steeper and more difficult. Several members of our company decided not to go any further and ended up turning back. I could not blame them; it was as if Aleph's wrath were being poured out upon us and He was setting his will against us reaching the top alive. It was a complete opposite from the day before when the sun was shining and the birds were singing. But up in the heights at around sixty-five hundred meters, not much survived, and all that allowed anyone passage upward was the will of Aleph, himself.

Just when we thought it could not get any worse, Aleph put another obstacle in our way. Our travel was suddenly halted, as we came upon an ice crevasse. The expanse split the path completely in two, barring the way for all but the most dedicated of travelers. The chasm was quite large at nearly ten meters and would take a large leap to cover the distance. Because our feet were frozen and numb, this was a difficult task.

We all decided we needed to discuss the rest of the journey and came together closely, using each other for warmth. We decided as a group who would continue and who would stay behind. Once everything had been worked out, the larger men took the smaller framed individuals and "sling-shotted" them across the chasm.

It was quite a flight as I flew over the vertical cavern. Soon enough, Esgar and I stood on the other side, panting in the cold air, talking about where we were planning to set up the base camp. We looked over to the other side as the two slingshot volunteers, Groth and a larger man named Torrin, were about to throw another individual.

They each stood slightly in front and to the side of the smaller person. The smaller ran forward, and the larger men pulled an arm with both of their hands, hurling them forward with the momentum of the run. The next volunteer was in place, breathing heavily and awaiting his helpers. Groth gave the nod, and the volunteer ran as fast as he could, without slipping, towards the two men. I watched in amazement as Groth and Torrin expertly grabbed the arms of the volunteer and with a loud grunt, launched him across the chasm. As the body flew through the air, I saw Groth lose his step and slip. As if in slow motion, I saw his giant mass fall face down and land with a loud crack. We all heard him grunt as the wind was knocked out of him.

Loretta cried out from behind, "Are you all right?" He laid there motionless for several seconds before he began to stir. Suddenly, a snapping sound reverberated through the whole pass. We all stood still and silent. The first snap was followed by several more, which turned into a gut-wrenching crack! Groth looked in horror at the surface underneath him, right where his head had landed. The ice under was breaking away from the rest of the path and upturned into an incline. In a desperate panic, his arms flailed out to both sides trying to grab onto something to keep him from going into the deadly abyss.

Finding nothing to hold onto, his body continued to slide down the ice into the crevasse. The air was filled with his scream as he went over the edge. In a final act of desperation, he flung his arms out one last time. His left arm wrapped itself neatly around a lone branch jutting out of the ice. I looked on in disbelief from the other side of the crevasse. What was a branch doing this high up in the mountains? How had it survived? How could it even hold the weight of this heavily built man?

Loretta was screaming and begging those around her to help him. Without another thought, Samuel and Artour dove face first down the incline towards the rim of the ice that opened into an abysmal, narrow expanse. They both grunted when their breath left them as they felt the ice under them break their descent. Shrill voices exclaimed in panic all around me. On the other side of the fissure, we watched Samuel and Artour plunge headlong towards the rim. I watched as two more men positioned themselves instantly behind them, kneeling in the safety of the snow and grabbing hold of Samuel and Artour's ankles as they dangled over the edge of the crevasse. Loretta was giving orders, trying to keep it together. The rope Aleph had given us was thrown around the chests of these two kneeling men and two more men from behind, held it in place.

Groth was holding on for dear life to the strong branch, his legs dangling over the frozen oblivion. Their hands were only inches from his helpless mass.

"Let go of the branch with one of your hands," Samuel said calmly. Panicked voices were still creating a good bit of noise.

Artour shouted from his position. "Quiet everyone!"

After all the voices had stilled, Samuel spoke again. "Groth, let go of the branch."

"I can't. If I do, I won't be able to hold on," Groth shouted back, almost deliriously.

"We will not let you go, my friend. Reach up and take my hand. Then take Artour's," Samuel explained. Groth lowered his head and glanced into the awaiting death below. "If you do not grab my hand, you are going to fall. Trust me! I will not let you go," Samuel said more urgently. Groth continued to look down into the icy depths. "Look at me!" Samuel urged. Groth slowly turned his head upward. His gaze was fixed on Samuel, who was hung over the side of the icy wall with his hands outstretched. "I promise you, I will not let you go. If you pull me over with you, then so be it. I WILL NOT LET YOU GO!" Samuel cried out.

Groth took another look down and began to silently cry in desperation. With one final groan of resolve, he let go with his right. Groth now hung over the crevasse with one hand. In a surge of adrenaline, he swung his body towards the ice wall and reached up to Samuel. With his left hand held tightly around the branch, he pulled his entire mass upward. As his chin came up over the branch, he reached out with all that was within him. His right hand closed with a clap around Samuel's. My brother then took his other hand and wrapped it around his forearm. The tension was felt by all who were supporting Samuel's weight. They groaned and repositioned themselves for a better grip.

Artour, hanging over the edge, reached out his hands. Groth, now in Samuel's grip, let go of the branch. Samuel groaned under the weight of the body that was now hanging on by his hands. With all the strength he could muster, Groth reached up with his left hand and clapped it safely around Artour's. Artour took his other hand and placed it around Groth's forearm like Samuel had done earlier. As one, they pulled the rope tight, and the two men behind Samuel and Artour pulled on their ankles. Soon, Samuel, Artour, and Groth were all safely heaving for breath, crying tears of joy on the snow-covered path.

Even though I had been part of the meeting earlier, it took me several minutes of looking at the large expanse of the crevasse to realize our company had been split. There was no way for those on the other side to come over. Even more frightening was the fact that nobody on our side could go back. Samuel, Artour, Loretta, Groth, and the rest of the company were not to go any further up the mountain. I didn't know what to say. It had all happened so quickly. I just sat there and stared at my brother and the others lying in the snow gasping for air. I took a deep breath of the thin, cold air and closed my eyes. The next emotion I felt rising from within was the all too familiar searing hot anger. I couldn't take it anymore. The emotion swirling inside me boiled to the surface. I clenched my fists and pounded them into the ground. From my mouth came a deafening scream of frustration. Esgar knelt quickly and put a hand on my shoulder to calm me. I jerked away from her touch and continued screaming my angst at Aleph. Then I heard from across the crevasse the authoritative voice of my friend.

"That's enough, Daeric! Do you want to bring an avalanche down on us?"

"I can't do this, Samuel!" I shouted back.

"STOP COMPLAINING, DAERIC!" Samuel's voice silenced me. "Obviously, Aleph wanted me here, on this side. No matter what happens to me and the others, you are to continue with the one thing he asked you to do," Samuel countered as he pointed towards the summit far above our heads. "Climb."

"Will you be alright?" I asked nervously.

"Have we been without a single need yet? He's brought us this far, hasn't he?" Samuel asked pointedly.

"You make it sound so simple," I said as I laughed. That was when I felt again the sweet precious touch of my faithful female companion.

"It is, Daeric. We climb. Together," Esgar said as she looked into my eyes.

"His light shines upon you!" Samuel shouted from across the chasm. "Take comfort in that! Let go of everything you know! He is about to show you who you really are! Now go!" Those final words reverberated with echoes in my heart. I carried them with me as we continued along the winding narrow path towards the summit of Shaddyia.

Within minutes, we were once again alone in the cold snow. We marched at a miserably slow pace as the gusts of frigid wind pummeled us from all around. It was even colder than before. I could not feel the warmth of Aleph around me anymore. My mind could not process anything except the pain of the stinging, bitter wind. The more I tried to fight against the feeling, the more the cold wrapped its jagged, icy fingers around our entire being. Esgar and I put our arms around each other and supported the other as the climb got steeper and more treacherous. The volunteers behind us followed our example and did the same.

One step at a time, we moved forward. The winds howled at a deafening volume. We could not hear anything in the vicinity around us, and the snow flurries made it almost impossible to see anything further than ten meters in front of us. Every time I looked behind me, I saw fewer and fewer numbers of people than what we had started with from the crevasse. The report was that many had gone back down or looked for another way off the mountain. The consensus, in general, was that the people could not take it anymore and had given up.

The path was too steep to walk in several places, and we had to scramble on our hands and knees to progress. I lowered my body close to the freezing rock and moved upward, one step after another. Esgar was several feet behind me, struggling even more than myself. Beyond her, the number in our group had reduced itself to only a handful. I couldn't blame them one bit for wanting to get off this mountain. I was battling unseen forces in my mind that were screaming at me to quit. It was nearly impossible to think of anything else but the cold.

I climbed upward for what seemed an eternity, knowing that if I stopped, I would not continue. Esgar was right there with me at my heels, climbing behind me. One rock, then another, then another, and then another. Our rhythm was in sync as we slowly ascended. Our bodies were numb, and it was hard to feel anything. Even the rocks under us seemed to disappear. It went on and on for hours. Just when I thought we were climbing endlessly into a vertical void of cold nothingness, we reached level, snowy ground. We collapsed together into the snow, shivering miserably. I quickly looked over the edge of the steep wall of rocks for the company who was traveling with us. They were gone, and we were alone. Once again, the anger rose within me.

"Why?" I silently asked Aleph. Before I could get an answer, Esgar's hand closed around mine, and then her body pressed against me. She was shivering from head to toe.

"Daeric, I'm cold. I'm so cold," she said miserably.

"I'm cold, too," I responded. "I don't know what to do." Fear took hold of us like a thief. Despair penetrated our very being. We were absolutely terrified of going any further. Then, my head was filled with a very simple thought.

"Maybe death won't be as horrible as you think. You won't be cold anymore." I began to entertain these thoughts and felt myself start to drift away from the cold, away from the wind, away from the despair, away from everything.

"Daeric," I heard a voice whisper.

"What?" I responded in a whimper.

"You are not done yet," Aleph replied.

"I can't do it," I spoke.

"You were never meant to. I am."

"Then do it. You don't need me."

"Yes, I do."

"I'm not the one. I can't go on." My eyelids were caked in frost. They were heavy, and it was hard to even keep them open.

"I know."

"Then how can I if I can't do it?"

"Trust me," Aleph said sternly.

"Can you tell me please?" The world all around me began to dim.

"Climb."

"Why?"

"Climb," Aleph stated more firmly.

"WHY!" I screamed at the top of my lungs, and then all was dark and quiet.

"Climb." The final word of Aleph's whispering voice brought me back to consciousness. I have no recollection of how long I had drifted off. Esgar was still shivering next to me. I noticed the sky was dark. The sun, which seemed worlds away, had set some time ago. I struggled to pull myself into a sitting position and felt a soft, warm light shining on the left side of my face. I turned towards that direction, and my heart was instantly filled with strength and overwhelmed with emotion.

To my right, I saw carved into the rock of the mountain a small alcove. The cave was sheltered above and on three sides with solid rock. In the center of the niche was a blazing fire and a spit. On the spit, a rather delicious looking animal was skewered. Its flesh had a glow of golden brown, and the aroma it produced filled the air. My stomach, which had been ignored all day, began to grumble. On the ground of the cave were two furs spread out around the sides of the fire. In the corner was a small table, and on it sat a carafe of water, two goblets, plates, and silverware.

A soft wind blew by, and I heard His voice whisper to me from within the breeze.

"Trust me."

I quickly bent down and shook my companion.

"Esgar, Esgar. Wake up." I saw her begin to stir from the cold darkness she had drifted into. Her eyes opened, breaking the frosty seal over her lids, and she stared at me from the depths. After several moments, I could see she had come back to reality and recollected in her mind all that had surpassed. I then took her hand and gently helped her into a sitting position. She was trying to steady herself, and I had to catch her before she fell back into the snow. Once she had gained her equilibrium, I took her head and turned it towards Aleph's provision. She stared into the warm light of the fire that sat in the center of the alcove and smiled. Then emotion overwhelmed her, and she began to cry tears of joy.

CHAPTER
23

Esgar and I sat huddled closely together under the cover of the mountain rock, next to the fire. Thinking we were in a dream, we ate and drank our fill of Aleph's provision, waiting to wake up at any moment. The animal was thick and tasty, rich with flavor and satisfyingly delicious. The water from the carafe was cold and refreshing. Energy returned to our drained bodies as we leaned back against the cave wall and looked into the flames of the fire.

The brutal winds blew outside of the cave but miraculously, they did not quench our fire. Allowing the warmth of the flames to comfort me, I closed my eyes and thought of Father. Where was Aleph leading him to, and what army would he meet when he got there? I thought of Samuel and Artour with the rest of the company. Had they gone back down, or were they still at the edge of the crevasse? Had Aleph provided another similar cave for them as well? My thoughts were interrupted as I felt Esgar lie down and put her head on my chest. She put her arm around my back and squeezed tightly. I felt my whole body go numb as her touch sent warm shivers through me.

"Sorry…you are warm," she said as she snuggled closer. I

felt her body move as well. I slowly reached out my hand and began moving it softly and slowly through her long dark hair. She closed her eyes and exhaled softly.

"Aleph, take me now," I thought.

Esgar opened her eyes again and continued to stare into the flames.

"They never go out," she said dreamily.

"What's that?" I replied.

"The flames in the fire. They are not going to go out. It will keep on burning as long as we are here."

"I think you are right." Then I decided to change the subject. "What was it like to be a princess?"

Continuing to stare trance-like into the flames, Esgar responded. "I was in prison. There was no freedom to choose who I wanted to be. There were schedules that had to be followed without an argument. I was forced to…" She stopped, holding her breath. The inward battle was playing itself out again. She took a deep breath and decided to change her choice of words. "Everything I said in public was given to me on a piece of paper." I watched as she moved her gaze from the flames out into the clear night sky. "The part I hated most was the fear that controlled us. We had to watch everything we said and look around every corner. It was such a nightmare. It is incredibly morbid to think this, but I am thankful, because the death of my family released them from the bondage they had suffered under for so many years."

Esgar began to cry, and I held her even closer. She wrapped her other arm around me and stayed there for several minutes, weeping in my arms. As I held her, I felt a surge of adrenaline that filled me up. Curled up with me was a precious and amazingly strong-spirited woman. All I wanted to do was stay beside her and protect her. After the tears had dried up, I asked her a question boldly.

"What were you forced to do?"

As I asked that question, I saw another wave of fear and shadow come over her. She closed her eyes and shook her head.

"No…I can't. I don't want to remember," she said almost in tears once again.

"It's okay…you can tell me."

"No, Daeric, please don't make me go back there." She was now crying again.

"What was it?" I asked carefully.

Through tear-soaked eyes she looked up at me, searching me, desperate for a way out of saying the words she was about to speak. But finding none, she whispered.

"I was forced to learn magic." The words hung in the air, like a dead body from the end of a noose. I could feel the atmosphere change almost immediately. There was a foreboding heaviness that was not there before.

"I'm sorry." It was all I could say.

"Please, don't make me talk about it," Esgar pleaded.

"Okay." I consoled her. "We don't need to talk about it now."

"Thank you, Daeric. Thank you for understanding," she said, smiling as she wiped the last of her tears away. "It was a long road, but when Aleph freed me and led me away from my captors, it took me several years to even be able to open my bedroom door without holding my breath, wondering if they were coming for me. But Aleph, in His patience, showed me that freedom is a choice. I decided to choose to be free. I was not going to be held down by the bondage of fear anymore. Then my family and I went on vacation to Shelbye, and you know the rest of the story."

I looked down at Esgar and felt a longing in my heart that I had never felt in my life. I understood in that split second why Father would have to sacrifice everything for Lady Iska. Esgar stayed there, snuggled in my arms, for the rest of the evening, until we both felt Aleph's presence move over the entire camp. The day was at an end, and our eyelids were heavy. We each went to our own bed and snuggled into the warmth of the soft fur, falling into a peaceful slumber.

The sky was clear and bright in all directions the next morning. We were in great spirits because the blistering cold from the day before had disappeared. As we made ourselves ready for the climb, we noticed a sack in the corner of the cave that we had not noticed the night before. We opened it up to find a wonderful collection of nuts and dried fruit. Aleph once again had provided a nice breakfast for us before we continued the ascent.

Esgar and I stood on the ledge of the mountain and looked up to the summit of Shaddyia. The sky was bright blue, speckled with a handful of clouds. It was cold, but nothing like the day before. Our bodies were completely rested. Aleph had taken away every bit of soreness and fatigue in our bones, and we felt ourselves completely ready for whatever lay ahead, or so we thought.

"You think we can reach the top, Daeric?" Esgar asked excitedly. "It doesn't look far at all."

"If the weather holds up...I think it might be possible," I returned.

"I think the worst is behind us." Esgar came up behind me and hugged me tightly. "I think He wants us to make it all the way, today."

"I think you're right." Then a thought hit me like a fiery dart. "Esgar..." I began. "Look at the rock from here. It's really steep and icy, and Samuel has the rope." Despair flooded in as quick as lightning.

"You are right, he did have the rope."

"How can we scale this rock without a rope?" I began to raise my voice.

"I'm going to climb," I vaguely heard Esgar say behind me as my back was turned toward the vast openness of the Ternion Mountains. I continued my rant for several minutes. I heard Esgar excitedly talking to me from the recesses of my mind, but I didn't pay any attention to her. I was letting Aleph have every bit of my anger. After I was empty of harsh words, I turned around to see my companion had vanished from the space in front of me. I felt a tremor of fear within me. "Esgar?" There were several seconds of silence. "Esgar? Where are you?" I looked around the cave and finally up the sheer icy rock of the mountain face.

Staring down at me fifty yards up the rock was the beaming face of my companion. She was standing on the edge of a sheer rock looking down at me. Her smile was spread from ear to ear.

"Esgar?" I asked unbelievingly. "How did you get up there?"

"I climbed," she responded.

"You climbed?" I quickly returned.

"Yes."

"You climbed up there? Without a rope?"

"Yes, Daeric. You can do it too."

"What do I do?" I heard myself asking with courage and hope.

"Put your foot right there." She pointed several feet in front of where I was standing.

"Right here?" I asked as I placed my boot in the spot on the rock wall.

"Yes. Now Aleph is going to show you the path. Follow it," she calmly stated. Suddenly, I saw it. The rock in front of me was highlighted with a brilliant illumination, and I could see the hidden path of foot-stones.

"You see them, don't you?" Esgar shouted from the ledge.

"Yes. Were they here all along?" I asked excitedly.

"I don't know," she replied. "Now just step on the illuminated stones. Go one at a time. The path is there for you to follow. Just take it slow and easy," Esgar instructed.

I did exactly as she said, pressing my body close to the rock face. I used my hands and feet, placing them on the hidden stones, and slowly climbed upward from one rock to the next. I took a moment and looked straight up and saw the sky. It took my breath away.

"How is this possible?" I heard myself asking. Then I heard

Aleph speak one word to my heart.

"Climb."

Courage filled my entire being, and I continued working my arms and feet together. Strength filled me as the adrenaline pumped through my body, and I moved steadily upward. One stone after another, right and left and then right and then left. I was infused with warmth from the top of my head down to the soles of my feet. The climb became easier and easier as I climbed higher and higher. I looked up at the edge where Esgar stood.

"I'm doing it!" I cried out.

"You're doing great. Just keep climbing," Esgar encouraged me.

I reached for another step and then another. Then I found myself taking larger steps up the rock. I could not feel the ice, nor were my steps hindered by the slippery rock. I looked down behind me and saw the ground distancing itself further and further away from me. Each step I made up the mountain was easier than the last until the unseen winds at the top of Shaddyia were not resisting me anymore but helping carry me higher and higher.

Then before I knew it, I was on the ledge next to my companion. She wrapped her arms around me. My heart fluttered, and I held her back, receiving her affection. We stayed in our embrace for several more moments.

"Congratulations for making it up here," Esgar said. "I knew you could make it."

"It's amazing! Feels great!" We stayed there for a short moment sitting on the ledge, holding each other's hands and looking out into the vastness of the world around us. Once I had caught my breath, we continued our ascent up the mountain.

The hidden stones were once again illuminated by Aleph, and we began our climb. I went first this time, with Esgar slightly below me. We enjoyed the climb up the impossible face of Shaddyia. Aleph's presence was all around us, keeping us tightly against the rock and helping to carry us upward. We decided to take our time and enjoy the beauty of the glorious day around us. We stopped when the rock leveled out and sat down looking at the breathtaking expanse of Shalistar beneath us, admiring the artistry of the creator.

Thinking about Aleph's skill and imagination, which created such a vast and beautiful world, made our heads spin, and we were in total awe of the scenery. We could see the snow capped peaks of Lyssia and Kyrdia to the east and west and the lands that stretched out beyond them. In that moment, I could not help but wonder if this was the only world Aleph had created. Artour had alluded to the fact that this was one of many created worlds only days before. At that moment, I could only agree with the elderly historian.

I felt a tinge of guilt in that moment as well. I had doubted Aleph the entire journey long, and yet he was still patient with me. He never shouted or got angry. He simply let me be wrong. That thought brought more laughter forth. I was absolutely amazed at his goodness in that moment. Here I was with the woman I loved, climbing safely up the highest mountain in the world. We were on our way to a place nobody has walked in thousands of years. Father had always told me Aleph was good. It was not until that moment that I truly realized just how far his goodness extended.

We continued climbing upward, I looked down at Esgar and noticed she was crying and smiling. I could only guess that she was thinking the same thing I was. We were doing it. We were doing what nobody could do. The foot-stones continued to be illuminated as we used our hands and feet to scale the unscalable mountain.

In a flash, the rock wall vanished, and we were on solid ground. The incredible expanse of the world was all around us, in every direction. We had made it to the top of the sheer rock face! We stood on the snow-covered edge looking northeast, standing at the bottom of the final rise to the summit of Shaddyia. We looked upward and could see the faint outline of some architecture resting at the top of the mountain. "That must be Aleph's temple," I thought to myself.

The winds blew mightily on the shelf, and we once again held our arms around each other. With a perfect balance, we walked slowly up the rise. Snow was up to our waists, and the going was slow, but we took steady strides upward, continuing our ascent. The summit loomed closer and closer with every step, and the textures of the massive stone structure could be clearly seen. We pushed harder and harder through the resistant snow until we were finally standing in front of a large set of marble steps leading up to the front of the massive temple.

"This is it," Esgar said, smiling at me. "Are you ready to meet him?"

"I don't know. How can anybody be ready to meet Aleph?" I asked strangely. "What am I supposed to say?"

"I can't answer that. I'm trying to figure it out on my own,"

Esgar added blankly.

"Well...I guess we can go figure this out together," I concluded.

We began our ascent up the large staircase to the base of the temple. With every step we took up the steep case, the temple revealed itself more and more. As we stood at the top, the entirety of the sanctuary was before us.

It was a massive stone structure with multiple levels, held into place by a line of marble columns. The stone was not of this world and seemed to glow with a soft shimmer of light. The temple rested at the precipice of Shaddyia and looked out on all sides of the open world.

The pillars on the bottom floor of the south-facing side met in the middle of the structure, where there was a large wooden door. The door was peculiar, to say the least. We came closer to it and saw the intricate carvings in the wood that showed guardians around a throne with beams of light coming out in all directions. Upon the wood were deep red splatters all over the door which appeared to be blood that had dried so long ago. Aleph was always very good at remaining mysterious, but this was completely out of the ordinary, and other-worldly. We looked beside the door on both sides and could see none. The blood was deeply stained into this door, for whatever reason.

The roof of the temple was laid with small tiles of some sort that were the same tint as the setting sun. The tiles of the roof were laid in a pattern that moved inward from all directions to the center of the temple and then met with another stone tower that rose high into the sky. We followed the structure up and up to the peak of the tower, where we could see a flicker of flame. It was as though the peak of the roof were on fire. We looked closer and could see the outline within the flames of a sword.

"Do you see that?" I asked Esgar pointing to the peak of the roof.

Esgar met my gaze and followed it upward. I saw her eyes flutter as she investigated the deep blue sky and then rested firmly on the flame.

"Aleph's mercy!" she exclaimed. "I think that is..."

"Alestor! The blade of Aleph." I heard a darkly familiar voice speak from behind us and was instantly filled with fear. In unison, we whirled around and looked in horror at a figure perched on top of the nearest guardian statue, like a raptor waiting to dive upon its prey. He was dressed in black, with a glowing red band around his forehead, parting his long dark hair to the sides of his face. I stared, open mouthed at the man who was not a man, the murderer of Agus Tull and thousands of others. Staring back at us was none other than Lucien, the chief messenger of Baelor.

CHAPTER
24

Lucien relished the silence in the air. He took a deep breath and hopped down from the statue, never taking his eyes off us. Our fear was tangible, and he was savoring every drop of it, feeding off it. He looked directly into my eyes. As he did so, there was a flash of brilliant light, and once again, I could see him in his true hideous form, a grotesque creature with red eyes and a beak like a raptor. His black wings stretched out, and the fires of hell blazed around him.

Then the vision ceased, and I was back on the mountain top at the door to Aleph's temple. Lucien was there, standing only feet from us back in his human form. My lip trembled as I opened my mouth and asked a question aloud.

"What do you want?" I asked. Lucien turned his eyes skyward towards the peak of the tower.

"I want what every messenger wants," he said smoothly.

"I don't understand," I responded.

"You wouldn't. You humans have no clue about eternity. You live one lifetime and then move on. I have been here in this disgusting world for a thousand lifetimes, and I still find myself a prisoner."

Esgar was shaking next to me and I could see the fear in her eyes as I asked my next question. "Who are you? What is your name?"

Lucien chuckled at that. "You humans have such a limited vision. You think in such a temporal mind and truly believe this life is worth living, that you must have the answers to everything, or your mind will not be satisfied.

"Who I am does not matter, but just to put your mind at rest, I will answer. My name is Lucien. I am a messenger of Baelor." Lucien pointed his finger right at me. "You are Daeric, son of Michael and Abigail, Aleph's favored one." He then pointed to Esgar. "You are Princess Kristina, the daughter of the late King Remus and granddaughter of the late King Tark." Esgar looked at me with knowing eyes. This was not the first time she had seen this Dark Man. "Are you satisfied now?"

"No!" I shouted. "Why are you really here?"

Lucien paced back and forth, rubbing his palms together and looking bored. "Look behind you." We hesitated to do so. "It's okay. If I wanted you dead, you would be." What he said made sense to both of us, and we turned looking up the final small staircase at the front door to the temple. "I will do my best to explain spiritual principles to you decrepit humans, so be sure to pay attention.

"Before you is a door. Aleph has allowed that door to be here in Shalistar. If you were to go up to the door and turn the knob, it would open. This has only happened one time in this world's history. King Rian came to the top of this mountain and turned the knob, opening the door. When he did that, I was loosed upon the world as your adversary.

So, you see, simple ones, when a door is opened, there will always be an adversary, for this is a spiritual principle, written by Aleph himself at the start of this world. Ever since I came into this world, I have been assigned to torment Rian and his family line. From generation to generation, I have destroyed the minds of kings and imprisoned them in fear. Kristina, you are no different. I have tormented you for your entire life, and only now do you see the truth!"

Esgar took a step towards Lucien, and I reached out my hand to keep her back. "How did you get here?" she shouted.

"Young one. I am Baelor's chief messenger. I can be where I choose!" Lucien coldly stated. Now, please don't interrupt me again or you will confront the nasty side of me." I placed a hand on Esgar and gently pulled her back a couple steps until she was standing next to me. "Good. Now that I have your attention, I will continue." Lucien continued to pace back and forth, stealing glances at us from time to time as he continued his monologue.

"I did not come here to engage you in combat, but rather to offer you a deal. You are Aleph's chosen and highly favored one, the one who is to prepare the world for its final act, bringing a message of hope to those who are lost. This will begin when you walk through that door behind you. What I have to offer you is power beyond imagination. What if you could control fire?" Suddenly a burst of flame erupted from his fingertips and shot into the sky. Esgar huddled closer within the folds of my white cloak. Seeing the sorcery erupt from Lucien's fingertips made me wrap the cloak completely around Esgar.

"What if the power of frost and chill was yours to command?" There was a loud cracking noise that split the silence, and a large spear of ice flew from his hands, shattering as it hit a nearby rock. "Or better yet, what if you could call lightning to you in the field of battle?" Again, there erupted from Lucien a string of electric energy that struck the statue behind him where he had been perched only moments ago. The lightning wrapped itself completely around the statue until the entire structure was smoking. "I can give you the power to levitate." As he was saying this, his body rose into the air. "I can give you the authority to summon help to your side in battle." Lucien spoke several guttural words of magic, and out of nowhere appeared two ethereal creatures from out of the air. One was covered in flames with glowing red eyes, and one was covered in stone with huge arms and legs that could crush any human quickly. Lucien spoke another word and the ethereal beings vanished.

"This is the power I offer you, and so much more. Look upon the world, Daeric." Lucien turned around and stretched his arms out as far as they could go. "This world is Baelor's. Aleph has given it to him, and it is his to give to whom he chooses. He has sent me to you today, to make you this offer. If you will only abandon your quest and leave this mountain top, then all the world will be given to you along with all the power I possess. You and I will return to Raithe and remove Balafas from his seat of power. You and your lady can then rule the world as you see fit. All you have to do is give up this fruitless quest, and all of this will be yours." Lucien turned back towards Esgar and me, smiling a crooked grin. "What do you say?"

The air was silent on the top of the mountain. No wind blew at all. I whispered quietly under my breath for Aleph to help us and expected any moment for him to show up in some way, but alas, all remained still. There was no voice inside of me, speaking any words of comfort. I was all alone, with Esgar cowering inside my cloak. As I held her protectively in my arms, I began to tremble in fear. If I refused, Lucien would unleash every bit of magical power he possessed upon us. My cloak would not protect us for long. I looked down at Esgar and asked her quietly, "What do we do?" She only shook her head, trembling herself.

I looked back up, and Lucien was still staring right into me, smiling. He was not in a hurry. He knew he had me. His words were burned in my soul at that moment. I could see no other way but to surrender. This was the only way to keep Esgar safe. I reached out my hand to take Lucien's, signifying that I accepted the deal.

Then suddenly my thoughts, as if captured, were taken back to the campfire, where Loretta was drawing on the ground the diagram of time and how Aleph resided outside of it. Then I was taken to another moment by the campfire in which Artour was dramatically retelling the Battle of Ancients. I saw clearly in my mind the guardians swooping down and grabbing Baelor, carrying him skyward, then reversing direction and smashing him into the ground. I could see King Rian standing there as Baelor was held by two guardians. The crown that was upon Baelor's head began to lift off, and he screamed and grasped for it desperately. It was too late. The crown was moving through the air, and instead of it landing safely upon King Rian's head, I saw myself standing there and the crown came to rest upon my own head.

There was a shaking and mighty earthquake all around me. I heard Aleph's voice from within say the words. *"Lucien is lying to you. He has no authority to give you anything. Everything he had was taken from him. I have given you the crown, and all that I have is already yours. The words from your mouth are the same as the words from my mouth. This has been written, and it has been spoken. We are one my son. We are co-creators in this world. I create through you and reveal myself to all through you. Have no more fear. He cannot hurt you."*

I came back to the mountain top, holding Esgar closely with one arm and reaching out with the other to Lucien. He was coming near, still smiling. He reached his black gloved hand out and was only centimeters from my own. I returned his smile and retracted my hand quickly away. Instantly the smooth grin upon Lucien's face vanished and was replaced by a look of understanding and hatred.

"So, you have refused the offer of Baelor? You are a foolish boy."

"No, Lucien! It is you who is foolish! I solemnly rebuke you in the name of Aleph the creator!" Suddenly Lucien grasped both sides of his head and screamed as though he were on fire and trying to put out the flames. "You cannot keep me from the will of Aleph!" I continued to decree. "It has been spoken! Aleph has commanded me to be with Him, and His will shall be done!" Lucien continued to stagger backwards, screaming and holding his head, trying to keep the words from being heard.

"You have damned us all, boy! You have no idea what you have done!" Lucien screamed as he fell to his knees. He was a miserable pile at our feet, screaming for us to leave him alone and let him go. I almost took pity on him. "You will open the depths of hell! The Nephilim are coming! There is no stopping it now, boy. You have damned us all!"

An explosion of light came from above us and a guardian appeared at the peak of the tower. I followed the stream of light as it came closer and landed beside us. A larger guardian than I had ever seen appeared before us, wrapped entirely in light from head to toe. Esgar and I covered our eyes from the brilliance. All we could hear was the loud shrill screech of Lucien. I forced my eyes open and watched as the light from the guardian wrapped itself completely around the figure of Lucien. As the light penetrated his being, the true form of my adversary was revealed before me.

No longer was he a human in front of us, but in our waking sight we could see the hideous demonic form of a large black raptor-like bird with a long beak full of razor-sharp teeth. Its massive wings were stretched as wide as they could go. They had no feathers but only flesh and bone. It was a hideous creature to look at. Taloned claws at the end of bony arms were held up to the glowing red eyes, trying to keep the light from entering its being. The shrill cries continued as the brilliance passed through until the light was gone. The foul creature was in a fetal position whimpering in defeat. The guardian was now approaching to my left. The light that had shone so brilliantly before was beginning to wane, and I could clearly see the face of my rescuer.

"Blessings to you, highly favored one!" It was the familiar booming voice of my friend, Jeru.

"It's you!" I cried out to the large guardian.

"It is. I have come here to lend some assistance against the adversary," replied Jeru, pointing to the demonic form of Lucien. "This foe has been here before. He used to reside here with Aleph a long time ago, until deceit was found in him, and he was banished from Aleph's holy presence." Jeru then removed from within his white cloak a gleaming sword that burned with a never-ending fire. I immediately looked up at the peak of the tower and saw the flame was no longer there. Jeru now held Alestor in his hands and was holding it out to me. "The sword is now yours. Aleph wants you to have it, and in time you will wield it like Aleph himself."

I reached out my hand and it wrapped around the hilt of the sword. The flames of the sword tickled my hands and arm as I held it firmly before me. I raised it above my head, and the blade ignited into a larger flame. I swung it around a couple times and then brought the blade down like I had been trained to do for so many years. After several swings, I looked back over at Jeru.

"What do we do about him?" I asked, pointing to Lucien's pitiful form.

"You do nothing. He is unfortunately necessary, for now. This is a defeat he will never forget. But his time has not yet come."

"What did he mean when he said the Nephilim are coming?" Jeru turned me around and led Esgar and me back towards the temple.

"These are matters that do not concern you for now. Leave Lucien to me and my companion. Jeru gestured, and there appeared another guardian who was standing beside Lucien. The guardian lifted the form off the ground. Lucien continued to whimper.

"Please don't make me go back to Baelor. My time has not yet come," he pleaded with the guardian.

"What will happen to him?" I asked Jeru with concern.

"His wings will be clipped, and he will be thrown once again from this mountain top, never to return ever again. All he wanted was to be set free from the bondage he chose. That can never happen. He will continue to be the adversary, fulfilling his part in the story until the very end."

"What's happened to Father?"

"Your father and your brothers are in the capable hands of Aleph. He has a path for each of them to walk in. Your companions up the mountain are also being cared for. Aleph will lead them safely. Remember Daeric, this is much bigger than just you alone. We all have our part to play in Aleph's story."

"What will happen to Esgar and me?"

"You two will walk through the door behind you and finish your quest. What happens on the other side of it is unknown to me."

"Will we ever see you again?"

"That too is unknown. I sure do hope so," replied Jeru, with a large smile spread across his face.

"I do, too. You have been a good friend to me. To all of us."

"It has been my absolute pleasure to serve you, favored one." I ran and buried myself in his arms. His entire mass filled my small stature.

"Take care of Father. Don't let him go on without hope. Continue to give him strength and let him know we are safe."

"I will do as you command, my Lord," Jeru replied. Our embrace ended, and I looked once again into his bushy bearded face. He had tears in his eyes but was continuing to smile. "I'm very proud of you. You finally understand."

"Yes, I do." I stated in confidence. "I now know who I am." Jeru held my gaze for several more seconds, then stepped backwards towards the form of Lucien.

He commanded his companion to move the form to the edge of the mountain. I watched as they held Lucien over the expanse of nothing. The shrill screams escaped from him as Jeru pulled out a sword and cut the wings off the creature. In one last act of desperation, Lucien tried to lash out at Jeru, and the guardian kicked out his foot, which landed directly into the chest of the demon. I saw the wingless creature's body shoot out over the side into the expanse, screaming curses as he fell.

Then, in a shimmer of light, the guardians launched themselves into the air and flew off. Esgar and I were once again alone on the top of the mountain. We turned and faced the door to the temple, and without any further hesitation, took each other's hands and walked to the top of the stairs. I reached out my hand and moved it across the smooth wood of the door and over the deep crimson stains.

"Are you ready?" she asked expectantly.

"Yes." I replied.

It was quiet on the summit—so very quiet. I could hear my heart pounding out of my chest in excitement and curiosity as I reached out and touched my hand to the knob of the door. Esgar sidled up close to me, put her hands on my shoulders, and peaked over me to see what I was doing. We both held our breath as I turned the rusted knob. It gave a slight squeak as it turned to the right. Then we heard a mechanical click as the latch separated itself from the plate. I took another deep breath and held it for a second.

"Open it," Esgar whispered sweetly into my ear.

Without further ado, I slowly opened the door. The hinges whined as the wood began to swing outward. A brilliant light escaped from the door as it opened. The light penetrated not only our eyes but our bodies. It carried with it warmth and strength. The light seeped through the crack and got larger and fuller as the door extended itself. I could not take the suspense anymore and pulled until what lay beyond was completely accessible.

Radiance escaped and filled the entire mountain top around us. We were wrapped in a shimmering golden light. Esgar and I looked through the door to see where the light had come from and could not see past the brilliance.

"It's now or never," Esgar stated boldly. I looked over at her and abandoned myself to the adventure.

"Why not? We've come this far." Without another thought, we walked hand in hand through the threshold, into the great beyond.

The End of Book I

To be continued in Book II titled…

THE SCOURGE OF BAELOR

EXCERPT

BOOK II
THE SCOURGE OF BAELOR

I sat on the edge of the cliff facing east as the sun rose before me. The rays from its brilliance begin to form along the wasteland and scorch the surface of dry rock. I had just finished writing everything down as best I could remember it. Aleph made sure I was up at sunrise before the rest of my companions had awakened. We had a lot to discuss about everything that had happened earlier.

We had made it out of the Desolate Plains of Virym, barely hanging on to the thread of life. A pack of clerics had tried to take us out, but we had successfully outsmarted them. Our goal lay only miles away, with nothing left between us and Hammerfist except for a large stretch of thirsty, lifeless ground. I spent a good amount of time this morning studying the outside walls of the hard stone fortress before me.

The city lay on the top of a large rock peninsula overlooking the barren wasteland to the southwest. You could see the sharp and uneven skyline of the buildings from miles away. They were carved out of the hardest stone and matched the desolate, dull brown color of the rock all around it. Hammerfist was a brutal joke for travelers from Northcrest. Once they reached the desert plains, the skyline would appear and hope would rise; however, as you traveled into the dunes, the exhaustion of countless rises and crests in the sand would overcome you and the city would seem further away, never getting closer and always out of reach, taunting you. Once you finally made it to the last valley, you were treated with another impossible obstacle.

The sheer rock face seemed to mold itself into the foundation of the city and provided no footholds, making it impregnable from three directions. The only way into the city was from the east, allowing the defenses to reign fury on any approaching army. As I took in the scenery, I chuckled to myself. Aleph never made it easy.

"Have I humored you, Anlace?" I heard Aleph softly whisper from within me.

"I thought we were supposed to be hidden? Wasn't this supposed to be an infiltration?

"It is."

"How do you figure that?" I replied. "The city is fortified on three sides. There is only one way in."

"That would seem to be case... from your point of view."

"What do you mean?" I asked my creator.

"There are hidden roads, older than the city. Look past the surface of this problem, Anlace. All you can see is the precipice, but what I need you to start looking at is beneath the surface," Aleph rebuked me.

"I don't understand."

"It's okay. I am here to help you. What you do not see is hidden from you because you have your eyes on the massive fortress looming in front of you. It's a stronghold for sure, and one that

must come down. The only way to infiltrate these types of enemy encampments is to soften your viewing perspective and allow yourself to take in all that is around you, just as when you fight an enemy with the sword. Close your eyes."

I followed Aleph's instruction. *"Now, I am going to breathe on you, and when you feel the soft wind blow across your face, I want you to open your eyes and look out again. This time, take your eyes off of the stronghold and observe the whole picture in front of you. I have already provided the answer for you, and it is now time for you to see it."*

It was now quiet. All I could hear was my steady breathing. The cool of the morning air was still and silent. Then suddenly, I felt a soft wisp of air blow right past the tip of my nose. If I had not been still, I would never have even been able to feel it, but it was there. In obedience, I opened my eyes and looked out once more into the horizon. My eyes immediately wanted to go to the massive hulking structures sitting on top of the rocky peninsula, but I willed myself to divert my attention from the stone city.

I looked to the north and saw nothing but dry wasteland as far as the eye could see. I stretched my focus as far as I could and drew it slowly back to the walls of the city, looking for the answer Aleph had given me. There was nothing. I tried again, this time looking out as far south as I could until my eyes began to water. Then once again, I slowly came back until my gaze was at the southern walls. Again, nothing stood out. I was getting frustrated, but decided to continue.

I stood up from my sitting position and leaned over the side of the cliff I had been sitting on. I looked as far down as I could without losing balance and falling over the side. Then, I held my gaze steady for several seconds. Again, I felt the wisp of Aleph's breath on the tip of my nose. I slowly moved my eyes along the floor of the valley. As I scanned the horizon below me, I could see streams of wind moving through the sand and blowing up clouds of dust into the air. I reached into my bag and pulled out the magnification device given to me by Merwin before the Battle of the Rift. I brought it up to my eye and magnified my gaze. I continued moving it towards the base of the sheer western cliff—and then I saw it.

There was a small sliver in the wall of rock. The fissure was camouflaged in the morning by shadow and would be cooked by the brilliance of the sun in the afternoon. Travelers, or any person for that matter, would easily miss it, but it was there, hidden from all. I observed as the dusty streams of wind blew past the crack in the rock. Suddenly, I noticed the stream split, and dust was carried into the fissure. Upon further investigation, I guessed that the crack might be able to fit a human body through it, but only one at a time. Excitement rippled through me as I lowered and stowed the magnification device. Aleph had shown me the way! A hidden path within the foundation of rock led to the city from underneath. It was now time to awake the others.

As I entered camp I could smell the tantalizing aroma of sausage and eggs over the fire. I smiled as I saw the familiar shape of our resident herbalist hunched over a pan, adding just a pinch of grill spice. According to her it was the extra kick of flavor that all delicious food deserved. She then moved quickly from the pan to another pot, checking the temperature of its contents, moving with purpose and not wasting a beat.

Loretta looked up and greeted me with a dramatic wave

of her hand and began speaking at the same speed as her movements. "Morning, sir! You look as fine as fiddlesticks! Did you figure out a way into the city?" I looked curiously over at Loretta. "Oh don't worry, after a long road trip with you and climbing a mountain with your son, I pretty much figured out both your mannerisms. He takes after you in many ways. Always needing to get away and solve problems out in his mind. Always early in the morning, I might add. Then when he comes back, he's right as rain."

"I am truly impressed with your observance."

"Groth has always said it's my best attribute."

"Only beside your cooking!" Groth boomed as he came out of his tent. "Good morning, Anlace. What's on the agenda for today? Are we going to infiltrate a heavily defended enemy city?"

"That seems to be the plan, yes."

"Please tell me we are going to do it after breakfast. I'm starving! My stomach is gnawing on my backbone!" Suddenly, a groan erupted from the tent to the right.

"You three just couldn't let an old man sleep in a bit now could you!?" growled Lionel as he threw open the flap to his tent. "You pups could definitely do with some manners. The elderly have brittle bones and need an hour or two more of sleep if we are going to be productive."

"Maybe we would if you were not snoring all night!" Merwin exclaimed as he came into view with several bundles of dry sticks in his hands.

"Where in Aleph's keep did you find kindle in this forsaken place?" asked Lionel.

"You don't want to know," Merwin replied with a grin.

Lionel decided the answer was sufficient and huffed himself over by the fire, where he sat down, continuing to grumble under his breath. Loretta skipped over with a cup of morning drink and placed it in Lionel's hand, giving him a pat on the shoulder.

"Breakfast will be ready soon," she stated and skipped away.

Lionel could only stare at the cup that so quickly appeared in his hand. He took a quick sniff of the contents and was overcome with the aroma. It made him smile, and he softly replied with a thank you before he went back to sipping the drink.

"Where's Samuel?" I asked Merwin as he came to stand beside me, handing me a crisp red apple.

"He was up as early as you. I think he went to find a water source. Not much out here, and I can't imagine finding one. He is persistent, I'll give him that."

"Somebody has to be!" Samuel exclaimed, as he came into view, carrying a large water sack.

"Where did you find that?" I asked him.

"Aleph," he replied shortly. We all looked around and shrugged in agreement.

With everyone gathered, we shared the bountiful breakfast that Loretta had prepared, and when the meal had been finished and the dishes cleared, we sat together in a circle to begin our discussion of the infiltration that was about to happen. I looked around me at this small group of warriors and smiled. Aleph had really gone above and beyond this time. Only months before, we had been in the midst of thousands, and now we were a group of six—hand selected by Aleph to infiltrate an enemy city to bring about change. I could not begin to imagine how He was going to do this.

ABOUT THE AUTHOR

Stephen Early is an enthusiastic entertainer who has spent a lifetime honing his creative skills in writing, voice acting, presentations and theater arts. He has been a lifelong fan of the science fiction/fantasy genre and grew up reading the classics like The Lord of the Rings, The Chronicles of Narnia, Treasure Island, The Adventures of Tom Sawyer and many more. As a humble servant, Stephen's deepest passion is showing youth and children alike how to dream in a world full of adventure. He lives in Texas with his beautiful wife Esther and their four lovely daughters. For more information on this book series, go to eternalsofshalistar. com. You can also follow us on Facebook or on Instagram at #eternalsofshalistar.

Made in the USA
Columbia, SC
02 July 2022